Troubled Midnight

Troubled Midnight

JOHN GARDNER

Thomas Dunne Books
St. Martin's Minotaur ⚔ New York

THOMAS DUNNE BOOKS.
An imprint of St. Martin's Press.

www.minotaurbooks.com

Library of Congress Cataloging-in-Publication Data

Gardner, John E.
    Troubled midnight / John Gardner.—1st ed.
        p. cm.
    ISBN 0-312-33721-3
    EAN 978-0-312-33721-6
    1. World War, 1939–1945—England—Fiction. 2. Detectives—England—Berkshire (England)—Fiction. I. Title.

PR6057.A63T76 2006
823'.914—dc22   2005054757

First published in Great Britain by Allison & Busby Limited

10 9 8 7 6 5 4 3 2

Also by this author

James Bond Novels
Licence Renewed
For Special Services
Icebreaker
Role of Honor
Nobody Lives For Ever
No Deals, Mr. Bond
Scorpius
Win, Lose or Die
Brokenclaw
The Man from Barbarossa
Death is For Ever
Never Send Flowers
SeaFire
Cold
License to Kill (From the Screenplay)
Goldeneye (From the Screenplay)

The Boysie Oakes Books
The Liquidator
Understrike
Amber Nine
Madrigal
Founder Member
Traitor's Exit
Air Apparent
A Killer for a Song

Derek Torry Novels
A Complete State of Death
The Cornermen

The Moriarty Journals
The Return of Moriarty
The Revenge of Moriarty

The Kruger Novels
The Nostradamus Traitor
The Garden of Weapons
The Quiet Dogs
Maestro
Confessor

Novels
Golgotha
Flamingo
The Dancing Dodo
The Werewolf Trace
To Run a Little Faster
Every Night's a Bullfight
The Censor
Day of Absolution
Blood of the Fathers (Published under name of Edmund
McCoy and republished 2004 as Unknown Fears)

The Generations Trilogy
The Secret Generations
The Secret Houses
The Secret Families

Suzie Mountford Books
Bottled Spider
The Streets of Town
Angels Dining at The Ritz

Autobiography
Spin The Bottle

Collections of Short Stories
The Assassination File
Hideaway

www. John-Gardner.com

For Trish
Who lent me her name
And twice gave me her love.

THIS IS THE fourth book in a series concerning a young Woman Detective Sergeant – Suzie Mountford – middle class, bright but inexperienced and, in the first instance, naive and vulnerable. The previous books are, at the time of writing, available through Amazon.co.uk and the titles are *Bottled Spider, The Streets of Town* and *Angels Dining at The Ritz*. Each is self-contained and all the reader has to know is that young Suzie Mountford has been attached to Detective Chief Superintendent Tommy Livermore's Reserve Squad, at New Scotland Yard since 1940. She has also been Tommy's lover, but has become somewhat disenchanted with him as the relationship develops.

I make no apology for the fact that the premise of this book has already been used by at least four – possibly many more – novelists. It is a good premise and it's a starting point for the ingredients, the characters.

Also there never was a CO of the Glider Pilot Regiment stationed at RAF Brize Norton called Tim Weaving. Indeed I doubt if any of the Glider Pilot Regiment staff at Brize Norton in the final months of 1943 were named after the characters I have placed there.

I lived in the beautiful market town of Wantage from 1936 until I was married in 1952; I was more or less educated there; went off to serve my country from there in 1944 and spent vacations there during the three years I was up at Cambridge between 1947-1950. I still regard myself as Wantage born and bred, even though I wasn't born there. In those days it was in Berkshire and I cannot think why Oxfordshire has now embraced it.

Most of my descriptions of Wantage at that time are accurate, but I have built an extra house. There never was a Portway House standing in Portway looking out across King

Alfred's School playing fields. Because there was no such house, there was, of course, never a murder there. There was never a Captain Bunny Bascombe VC, so there was never an Emily Bascombe.

If some old Wantage folk imagine they can see themselves in the odd character woven into this book they must be wrong because it is a work of fiction. The same applies to some of the names. There may well have been some people with names like Wilson Sharp, Christopher Long, Pete Alexander, Peter Mulford etc. etc. but they are not the people who appear in this book. How could they be?

John Gardner
Hampshire 2004

The difficulty of controlling the operation once launched, lack of elasticity in the handling of reserves, *danger of leakage of information with consequent loss of that essential secrecy.*

Field Marshal Lord Alanbrooke: *Diary* reflections on Operation *Overlord*. June 1944

Sometimes these cogitations still amaze
The troubled midnight and the noon's repose.

La Figlia che Piange
T.S.Eliot

RITTER CAME ALL the way from Hamburg, what was left of it, to see him: Nicholaus Ritter of the Abwehr whom he'd last seen in 1938 when he'd stayed in Hamburg and offered his services to the Nazis in the belief that Hitler was the strong man of Europe. It had been difficult in '38 because you had to be a loyal Nazi to work for the Abwehr; you also had to be a German and the Abwehr were twitchy about an Englishman making such an offer. His first meeting with Ritter had been a preposterously clandestine affair at the railway station in the first class dining room. Of course they didn't think they'd even be enemies of the English then. Nick Ritter worked in the Military District X Headquarters where he was really in charge of Air Espionage, but he had employed Sadler who now felt pleased that Ritter himself had come all this way, to central France, to see him.

"We have new offices," Ritter told him. "Very smart and still standing. They used to be a Jewish Old People's Home. No need for Jewish old people any more." And he laughed.

On the Sunday morning Ritter was gone and he spent the day with the other two men. The sunshine was warm and he sat close to a stand of pine trees on the edge of a great lawn with a water garden in the distance. So Sadler, as he was now known, smiled his secret smile: the one that hinted of evil known only to him. Who would believe it: him, Sadler, sitting here, miles out in the occupied French countryside in the fourth year of the war?

"*Sattler*," the one with the buckteeth said. "In German, *Sattler*."

"Ah. Yes," he nodded. "*Sattler*. Sadler."

He didn't know exactly where he was: couldn't pinpoint it or give a map reference because they had brought him by night. But he reasoned that he had to be between twenty-five and fifty miles south of Amiens because the train had stopped at Amiens on the way from the coast. The blinds of his carriage were down and he was locked in but he'd cheated and pulled back one side of the blind, squinted out and saw they were in Amiens station. After that they travelled for around fifty minutes, at steady speed, so he reckoned between twenty-five and fifty miles before they pulled into the siding and the one-platform halt. He thought in miles because England was his home; he couldn't think in kilometres, and when they got to the house Ritter was already there and they had dinner.

"I wanted you to know how specially pleased we are with your work," Ritter told him. "The Führer doesn't know your name but he is impressed and has asked that you be presented with this." This was the Iron Cross First Class with Oak Leaf Cluster. After he had pinned it on Sadler's breast, Ritter unpinned it and said he'd hang on to it, for safekeeping. "Rommel says we will destroy them on the beaches," still holding the medal cupped in his hands, the box on the table. "That will be the end, when they are finished. Or, if not the end then the beginning of the end, or perhaps the end of the beginning as someone has already said." He laughed. "I could never work out what Churchill meant by that." He lifted an eyebrow and laughed again.

Later he told Sadler that he might not be in charge of things for much longer. "Our friends in the RSHA are making inroads. By the time it comes for you to do your duty for the Fatherland I think they will be in command and you'll answer to them alone: to Schellenberg and his like."

The RSHA was the Reich Security Administration, the Party intelligence service, the SD and its domestic partner the Gestapo. The thought did not make for easy sleeping.

In the morning Sadler had woken in a comfortable bed with a uniformed servant pulling back the curtains, letting sunlight into the room, bringing coffee and fresh rolls – real coffee and newly baked rolls with apricot preserve. These people did themselves well, which gave the lie to the stories doing the rounds in England. As far as England was concerned Germans fought for a loaf of black bread: rations in the Third Reich were meagre, but, Sadler told himself, not everyone would be as well fed as the officers here. Nothing in his world was ever really what it seemed.

They had changed his name to Sadler just after he arrived on the previous night; told him, in English, that they had to ring the changes. For operational purposes he would now be known as Sadler. One of them muttered a colloquial expression, 'Wir brauchen ein Tapetenwechsel.' Literally, 'We need a change of wallpaper,' and for a moment he didn't understand. Then they laughed, the two majors from the Abwehr: German Military Intelligence, really funny men.

The jolly pair asking their questions: one calling himself Clauswitz and the other, a slight short man with protruding teeth reminding Sadler of a rabbit, called himself Hindenburg. Much laughter at that. Hindenburg indeed. That well-known double-act Clauswitz and Hindenburg, for one week only here at the Adolph Hitler Palace of Varieties.

He already knew their real names: Major Klampt and Major Osterlind, knew them well from when they were lieutenants back in the thirties when he had first made himself available to the Abwehr. Dietrich Klampt and Frederricht Osterlind: Dieter and Freddie, old amusing friends who had trained him in the house on the outskirts of Hamburg.

In the space of two weeks they had taught him rudimentary coding, using simple ciphers; they also set him on the way to learning the Morse Code; taught him the rules of surveillance, aircraft recognition, calculating the layout of military camps and airfields and from that deduce how many people were stationed there. He learned how to sift through local newspapers and find nuggets of information; ask leading questions from strangers. They played Kim's Game to hone his memory and taught him how to throw someone who was shadowing him in a built-up area. From a tough nut-brown gnome of a *Fallschirmjäger* sergeant he learned the art of silent killing, a skill he was later to put to good use.

Now, on this summer Sunday afternoon they told Sadler of their appreciation for what he had done, and said they understood about him not being able to give them the facts concerning Siegfried, Jack and Josefine – where they were, how they were operating. Well they knew about Josefine they told him, but did he hear anything?

All three were reporting in regularly, they said, and the product was not complete rubbish. Some of their information was good. All the same, Sadler told them what he'd heard about Camp 20, just in case. One couldn't be too careful. Sometimes it was just called The Twenty Committee.

In Roman numerals though Camp 20 was Camp XX.

Camp Double-Cross: where they turned captured spies, playing them back against their former masters.

He was trying to get more information, he told them, but it was difficult. If people were being held in Camp XX nobody was talking.

As for Sadler, originally known as Sparrowhawk, it was easier for him to evade the security services because he was a ghost, invisible, a born and bred Englishman. During that morning he started to wonder if he was the only agent they had in England: the only one sending them substantial information.

They got to the point quite quickly: there was *real* work for him now, and they spent most of the time going through what was necessary, suggesting ways he could go about the job, telling him what he knew already, that it wouldn't be an easy job to get the minutiae of the Allied plans to invade occupied Europe. They talked inside the house, oppressive he thought, with old furniture, the kind of thing you expected in a house like this, heavy and unrelenting, highly polished with the scent of wax everywhere. The tables were particularly weighty with thick barley sugar twisted legs, sideboards that were so sturdy they would never groan under the weight of food. In the bedrooms there were headboards a mile high and wonderfully carved, making you think that possibly there would be grips on the footboards, shaped like male feet, just to give you purchase during the serious business of making babies for the Fatherland. There were solid dressing tables in the bedrooms as well, so functional you'd have second thoughts about letting the triple looking glasses glimpse a naked thigh, a breast or a man's exposed genitals.

In the morning the air raid warnings warbled and they actually heard some American Flying Fortresses very high and droning south. In the early evening the warnings sounded again.

"It's how it goes these days," said Clauswitz. "The Yanks in the mornings and the Tommies at night."

"No rest for the wicked," Hindenburg chuckled. "We never get even a stray bomb here. Not nowadays."

They had lunch in the cool house and it reminded Sadler of being at home for the holidays, coming in from the garden after being in his tree house eating plums and watching people go by on the main road that skirted the copse at the bottom of the neatly striped lawn. He had begun early in his life, watching people without their knowledge, spying on friends, following people.

"They're coming, you know," he said, and the two men nodded gravely. Clauswitz told him they knew that well enough, "But with your help we'll possibly be ahead of the game."

Hindenburg smiled knowingly and said that General Rommel – "I beg his pardon, Field Marshal Rommel" – was confident that the beaches would be denied to the attacking armies. "I personally heard him say that the beaches will be slaughter yards for the Tommies and Yanks. Heard him say that in Berlin. He will be put in charge here very soon I think."

Sadler said he was glad to hear it and Clauswitz repeated, "We know they are coming, and we know it will be a substantial attack. All we need now are your reports." A bleak smile with a coldness behind the eyes. Uncertainty? Sadler wondered.

"When d'you think?" he asked.

"Not this year for sure." Osterlind shook his head. "They've yet to appoint the Supreme Allied Commander. That's why you're to do the job. They'll probably come in the spring. Maybe early summer. It's far from easy. There are limited times. They can't pick and chose." The smile again, then, "It's up to you, Sadler," which made him feel terrific, worry pouring in on him.

Then there was the other, almost suicidal, instruction.

"Before it happens, should the opportunity present itself, you should dispose of the Supreme Allied Commander."

"Kill him," Osterlind added as though they hadn't made themselves clear.

Sadler said he hadn't been appointed yet, and they chorused that it was only a matter of time.

"Before the New Year," Klampt said.

"Around Christmas."

The enormity of what they were asking ballooned in Sadler's mind like some terrible explosion.

"Most of our intelligence comes from Lisbon these days," Klampt said, almost casually, sealing his deduction that most of their agents had already been swallowed up.

"Who is likely...?" He began and Osterlind jumped in.

"If the British have their way it will be their Chief of General Staff, Sir Alan Brooke, failing him, then Montgomery of course."

"But this is not certain," Klampt grinning as though he had a special source. "My informer thinks they will have to let the Americans take the lead and in that case it will, of course, be Marshall. General Marshall."

His job, after supplying them with details of the invasion, would be to remove the Supreme Allied Commander, but only if he had a straightforward chance. *A clean shot, you might say," Osterlind told him.* Sadler's hands were sweating and he could have sworn that he smelled cordite in his nostrils. The very nature of this command consumed him, making his hands tremble. Not that the killing worried him, he had killed before, it was the terrible clarity, the visibility, of the target that concerned him. Would he ever have a clean shot at the SAC?

That evening, about eight o'clock, they put him in a car after giving him a cold meal, salad, tomatoes, cucumber and a wonderful potato salad, with thick slices of ham and crisp crusty bread. Before he went they drank a toast, "To the Russian riders." Laughed because it was such a good code word, though Sadler frowned because it wouldn't take a mathematician to work it out. An obvious code word, he considered. Too obvious.

A sergeant accompanied him to the little wayside halt that had no name; and the express stopped specially for him, the sergeant boarding with him, showing him to an empty compartment which had *Reserviert* stickers on the windows and a lock on the corridor side, the blinds pulled down like the one on the previous evening.

The sergeant brought him coffee and checked if there was anything he needed and he remained in the compartment for just over two-and-a-half hours. It was dark when they arrived and the sergeant waited until everyone else had left the station, most of them army stationed at the defences. Then a pair of sailors came up, sent to accompany him to the quayside where a U-Boat from La Rochelle was tied up, a skeleton crew on board: tired men with dead eyes who had just completed two months out in the Atlantic, men from the Grey Wolves.

Sadler said goodbye to the sergeant who remained stiff and formal, surprised that his special package was relaxed and friendly.

The U-Boat captain shook hands but did not speak and Sadler went below where he changed back into his uniform, then stretched out on a bunk and waited – twelve hours, then more time with the U-Boat submerged, waiting for nightfall again. A petty officer rowed him ashore in a rubber dingy. An hour later he was on a London train, crowded, dirty, filled with smoke and uniforms. In the corridor a woman crouched down saying she was searching for cleaner air, and a drunken soldier fell over as the train swayed on a bend.

He had been away for four days. Nobody missed him. That was the kind of man he was. The kind who was never missed and had difficulty summoning a waiter.

On the August Sunday when Sadler was briefed by the Abwehr in France, so Detective Chief Superintendent Tommy Livermore and Woman Detective Sergeant Suzie Mountford spent the day in the market town of Wantage which lay under the Berkshire Downs, where the Roman Ridgeway once echoed to the tramp of marching legions.

Chapter Two

"YOU EVER WANT to be me?" Tommy asked.

"Be you?" the question puzzled Suzie, lifting her voice just short of a screech.

"Yes. Ever feel you'd like to be me?"

"I don't understand."

"Read it in a book."

"In a book?"

"Yes – lovers often want to be the other person. Love's known for it, heart."

"I'd never want to be you. God, no. I wouldn't want to have to shave every day, and I wouldn't want your body either, not with..."

"Not with what?"

"Never mind."

"You've never complained about my body before."

"No, but I wouldn't want to *wear* your body."

"Oh." Tommy sounded disgruntled, turning down the corners of his mouth.

"Poor darling." Suzie reached over and kissed him on the cheek, realising that she hadn't done that – shown that kind of spontaneous affection – for quite a long time.

They had been in the Coffee Room of the Bear Hotel having tea because it was almost four o'clock, beautiful view, looking down on the cobbled courtyard at the back of the hotel shimmering in flat sunlight as they drank their tea and ate the little triangular cucumber sandwiches.

"Let's go have a nose round, eh?" Tommy said and she smiled at him, took his hand and let him lead her down the narrow stairs and onto the cobble stones that went right to the gates at the back and out in front of the building, all the way to the pavement, what the American GIs called the sidewalk, along the east side of the Market Place.

"Oh, a bear," she said, still a shade high-pitched, looking up at the black bear, chained and with a bunch of grapes in its mouth, high on a plinth on top of a pole that made up the extraordinary inn sign.

"Name of the hotel, heart. Bear Hotel."

Suzie Mountford felt extraordinarily happy because they were on what Tommy called 'a frivol'.

When they had first become lovers, on her posting, in 1940, to the Reserve Squad – Tommy's elite unit inside the Metropolitan Police Force – he was forever surprising her with trips here and there at a moment's notice. Recently all that seemed to have come to an end: after she'd refused to agree a date for their planned marriage.

Until now.

They had been working hard – the pier murder last month, 26th July. Pier Murder was what the papers called it, at one of East Anglia's best-known watering places: a girl, Angela Williams, who sometimes looked after two roundabouts for small children, the little merry-go-rounds squeezed in between the full-sized carousel and the Pier Theatre where a scratch company was playing to good business, Rookery Nook one week followed by Noel Coward's Hay Fever the next, the theatre right out at the end of the pier. In fact this year, 1943, was the first year the pier had been back in business since the start of the war in the autumn of 1939. The girl, Williams, turned a big wheel that made one of the roundabouts work, the little kids sitting in small cars, miniature London taxis and racing cars. Grinning fit to bust. Pleased as Punch.

It was Angela Williams looking after the small children's roundabouts who was found dead between the two machines, neck broken, clothing disturbed – police jargon for knickers removed so you'd know what else had happened. Unsavoury. July 26th 1943.

The combined wisdom of Scotland Yard had it that: first, murders were usually perpetrated by members of the victim's family or very close friends; and, second, that if you didn't nab the killer in the first forty-eight hours you were in for a long, and possibly fruitless, haul.

This one had taken Tommy over three weeks of intensive sleuthing, and even then the unmasking of the murderer had been almost an accident: a young lad working among the stage staff at the Pier Theatre, a lad called Pearse who was almost the invisible man as far as Tommy and his squad were concerned. Suddenly they spotted him and Tommy did the algebra and geometry, fixed him in their sights and they got him – blubbering and confessing in some terror once accused.

"Poor boy," Tommy said, "not a real killer but a stupid mistake he'll regret for the rest of his life."

Nobody said he probably didn't have much of a life left and they all went back to London to see what would be thrown up next, but on the Saturday morning Tommy suggested that they drive up to see Suzie's mum and stepfather – the Galloping Major.

They were welcomed with huge excitement and plenty of food. Suzie's mum, Helen, had a deal going with a butcher in nearby Wantage so they had a nice piece of beef on the Saturday night. "I was saving it for Sunday lunch," Helen told Suzie, "but Tommy says you can't stay to Sunday lunch."

Tommy hadn't told Suzie, so she got quite shirty with him, over in the Coach House. "Why can't we stay to lunch, tomorrow?" she asked, face twisted up in her not so convincing impression of anger.

"Because we can't," Tommy smooth but firm. "We can not." Three words equally spaced.

"Bugger it, Tommy, why the blazes not?"

"I have other plans."

And that was that. When Tommy had his mind made up

there was no gainsaying him, so they slept pleasantly in the Coach House that was the last thing Suzie's father had accomplished with their property before his fatal accident: did the old place up, two bedrooms and a wide open room with a kitchen off on the ground floor: very smart, a lot of exposed pine and nice carpets. Her mum put them in there, of course, because she didn't really want them sleeping together in the main house: didn't like to think of her daughter having a bit of nookie with Tommy under her roof, without the benefit of a priest as she would probably say.

In the end it was a lovely surprise when instead of taking the London Road, Tommy drove them to the little market town of Wantage that seemed, from The Bear Hotel, to be a nice and interesting place – nestling in the Vale of the White Horse, as all the guidebooks said, with the ancient Roman roads nearby, the Portway running through the town and the Ridgeway just above them on the Berkshire Downs; and the great King Alfred's birthplace, Alfred King of Wessex, the one who burned the cakes.

Now they were standing, looking across the square, outside Arbery's haberdasher, big windows and white paint, barley-sugar twists at the corner of the windows, when there was a snarl from above and they glanced up to see a North American Harvard aircraft in the all-yellow livery of RAF Training Command turn on its back about fifteen hundred feet above them, its big Wasp engine grumbling as it completed the roll and disappeared over the rooftops. For Suzie the noise seemed to score a tangible trail against the great bowl of deep blue sky.

"Silly bugger," Tommy still looked up, craning his neck. "Don't think they're supposed to do that. The engine can cut out inverted. Not supposed to do it over built-up areas."

"Showing off?"

"'Course."

"And that's King Alfred over there?" nodding towards the grey-white statue that stood on a rough stone plinth in the centre of the Square.

They danced around a red Oxford bus just leaving from outside Gibbs – printer & stationer – then threaded their way over to take a closer look.

"Like his frock," Tommy chuckled.

"And the hat," Suzie agreed.

Alfred wore a belted robe that ended just above his knees, and a long enveloping cloak, an elongated pudding basin helmet perched on his head, a scroll in the left hand, while the right rested on the haft of a long-handled fighting axe, single-bladed with the curved head by the king's right cross-gartered boot.

"How do they know he was born here?" Suzie asked.

"Biographer says so. Geezer by the name of Asser. Born here in the ninth century."

She thought bloody Tommy's a know-all. "When the years had only three numbers, right?"

"Absolutely: measured in the hundreds. Axe signifies his warlike reputation, scourge of the Vikings, and the scroll has to do with his dedication to learning and education."

"So he's a Saxon king?"

"Known for it, heart. That and the legend of the burned cakes."

"Fleeing from the Vikings; took shelter in a cottage. Lady of the house told him to look after the cakes she was baking. He didn't, cakes burned and the woman boxed his ears. Right?"

"That's how it goes."

Suzie craned up, gazing at King Alfred the Great's face. "Doesn't look very Saxon to me."

"No, more your Saxe-Coberg-Gotha than your Saxon."

The statue's face certainly had the features more moulded

to Edward VII than a Saxon.

"Fact is," Tommy continued, "the fellow who sculpted him was a relative of Queen Victoria, had a studio in the grounds of St. James's Palace so it's not really surprising.

They diced with death again, returning to the east side of the square and walking up to the silent and closed fish shop on the corner, The Regent Cinema across the way looking oddly out of place: *Suspicion* on Monday to Wednesday and *How Green was my Valley* Thursday to Saturday. B Picture, Gaumont British News and shorts – Full Supporting Programme.

They turned right into Newbury Street, the Post Office across the road, then Clegg the Chemist, The Blue Boar to their right.

They strolled on up Newbury Street and Suzie took his arm.

Old married couple, she thought.

"All this is a very posh girl's school, run by the Wantage Sisters," he said.

Not on your life, she thought referring to the old married couple thought.

"Very, very posh school. Posh and spikey." Tommy grinned.

"What's spikey?" she asked.

"High Church, heart. Bells and smells, genuflecting, plain-song, vestments of gold thread, more Roman than the Pope himself."

"I'm High Church," Suzie gave him a tight little smile and remembered Father Harris, making her confession to Father Gibbs and being caught up in the wonders of the Mass.

They came abreast of The Royal Oak public house on the corner of Portway, across the road stood a little sweet shop – *Readhead* it said above the window.

"Up here we'll find King Alfred's School," Tommy continued.

Like a bloody travelogue, she thought.

"Bit pretentious, King Alfred's School," he said. "Like to think it's a public school, but it ain't."

"I wonder if you can get violent creams under the counter at Mr Readhead's," she dreamed. "What we used to call them, our favourites, violent creams."

"I think he's more your sherbet dabs and gobstoppers. Violent creams are middle class nutty."

In the Mountford family the joke had been that Suzie adored violet creams that she always spoke of as violent creams. She was surprised that Tommy even recalled the tale because he seemed quite immune to childhood humour.

There was a short row of houses on the same side of the road as Readhead's shop, then a wide expanse of school playing fields, a gap from the houses, then one house on its own: three stories high, steps up to the front door and a little black and white sign, Portway House.

They came to a pile of grey stone buildings that made up the school on the right and a small stretch of prefabs, temporary classrooms across the road next to a solid grey building that said *King Alfred's School, OTC* carved in stone above the heavy door.

They crossed the road, Tommy still chuntering on about schools and the like, pausing at a memorial gate for those fallen in 1914-18.

"Going to have to add-in the current squabble," he grimaced and hurried Suzie along, loitering again outside Portway House where a slim attractive woman was closing the door and coming down the steps, hurrying as though late for church.

"Funny place to build a house, unless it's got something to do with the school," Tommy said quietly as the hurrying woman moved out of earshot. She had given them a hard look, as though they were potential troublemakers, as she came into the street and crossed over near The Royal Oak.

They came abreast of Redhead's shop, headed right, crossed the road and walked on past neat rows of houses, then a black wooden building set back from the road, identified by a sign that told them it was a British Legion Old Comrades Club close to a wide expanse of grass, dotted with swings, a chained maypole and a small round shelter – a recreation ground where young children could play on the swings and older kids could make their own fun in the long grass that ran up to the skyline.

As they approached the entrance, the gates already removed like every other piece of ornamental metal in the town, leaving only two somewhat new looking red brick stanchions, a couple were walking out, the boy no more than sixteen years old, the girl around the same in a thin summer dress, yellow with little blue flowers. They held hands as though trying to save one another from some unseen fate, occasionally glancing at one another with adoring eyes.

After they passed, Suzie glanced back to see that the rear view showed a fine display of grass cuttings and burrs across the youngsters' backs.

Up to no good in the long grass she thought as she tried to match Tommy's step head down starting to toil up the long hill.

Half way up they passed a man on his way down – a countryman dressed in tattered trousers a shirt with no collar and a waistcoat.

"This hill got a name at all?" Tommy hailed him with a slightly superior wave and one eyebrow up.

The fellow hardly paused, "Workhouse 'ill, though some'll call it Red 'ouse 'ill on account of the Workhouse being made of red brick."

"The Workhouse is still working then?"

"People round 'ere live in fear on it. Segregated it is. Don't get to stay with your wife if they take you in there. Good day to 'e."

The spike, the workhouse, the poorhouse, whatever, stood almost at the crest of the hill. They stopped just short of it, standing on the grass verge looking down on the town, Tommy a couple of paces behind Suzie.

"Nowhere like England on a summer afternoon," Suzie muttered.

"Beautiful." But he was looking at Suzie as she turned her head, the burning sun catching the highlights in her hair, the natural lighter gold streaks, the handsomeness of her face, sleekness of figure visible under the summer skirt trembling on her hips and buttocks. She was all Tommy wanted, yet, and yet.

"Tommy, you've enslaved me," she said when he took her the first time in her mother's *pied-à-terre* in Upper St Martin's Lane where they now lived in secret bliss – Scotland Yard wouldn't really have held with a marriage though Dandy Tom now said he'd got over that hurdle. No, she corrected in her head, no, it's not all bliss these days.

Standing almost on the brow of Workhouse Hill, Tommy thought back to that time, three years ago, during the Blitz, when he had tried to shape her, mould her from the inexperienced, naïve young plainclothes girl into a woman with confidence and comprehension. He had so badly wanted her as his wife but recently she seemed to have shied away from him, like an untested colt. He had been unable to capture the great clamp of feelings they had experienced, one for the other and this made him sad.

"Wonderful," she said now. "Look at that," as three Wellington bombers flew in a Vic straight over their heads. She turned to look back at him, her light grey-green luminous eyes alight, one small, but workmanlike hand touching her hair, lips parted and creased into a smile. "What a view," she said, and Tommy followed her gaze towards the grey tower of the church of SS Peter and Paul, rising from among the red brick and grey slate roofs of the houses far below.

On that first night together in '40s London she had pushed him away, held him at arm's length and said she now knew why the newspapers called him Dandy Tom, giving his manhood a playful tweak. Suzie Mountford was a quick learner he'd thought at the time.

"Tommy, look. What the heck are they doing...?"

In the distance two Armstrong Whitworth Whitley bombers, twin-engined, slab-sided, twin-tailplanes – flying suitcases as they called them – circled to the south each towing a large snub nosed glider. The aircraft were approaching the airfield almost out of sight, about a mile to the north of Wantage.

"Gliders," Tommy said watching the first aircraft line up and release the big sailpane – a Horsa, all wood and canvas – that seemed to hesitate for a moment as though it had no forward momentum, then it slewed around and dropped its nose, heading towards the airfield at an angle of forty-five degrees, sushing in, flaps extended, sliding down the unseen wires, straight across Wallingford Street, down, down, down until it slowly pulled up, grazing its way on to the runway.

The other Whitley released its glider, the aircraft, the big cumbersome Whitley bombers turned then came down after each other to overfly the airfield and drop the towing cables.

"Gliders?" Suzie repeated. "What's that all about?"

"Guess they're going to give Hitler a taste of his own medicine." Tommy gave his side-on smile: turning up the corner of his mouth so his teeth showed – what he called his terrible smile.

In 1940, May, when the German army was blitzkrieging its way across the continent, they had used their airborne forces to great effect, taking airfields, catching the Dutch with their clogs off and using glider borne troops to neutralise Belgian strongpoints. Again, in 1941, the battle for Crete, their paratroops – *das fallschirmjaeger* – came out of the skies, by way of hundreds of Ju52s and DSM gliders. Tommy now watched the

Airspeed Horsa gliders with their huge wingspan, almost 90 feet, angling down and he thought of the same craft multiplied by hundreds and filled with armed men bumping down in the early morning in occupied France: surprise package for the Nazis one day soon.

As early as June 1940 Churchill sent a memo to the Chiefs of Staff calling for the training of airborne forces. Within the year there were soldiers wearing red berets with parachute wings high on the right arm, while large numbers of Royal Marines Commandos also sported the parachute badge.

As they stood, Tommy and Suzie, looking across the miles of open country lying behind the town of Wantage, a crocodile of sad elderly men and women crossed the road into the Workhouse, the men and women separating and being led to their various segregated quarters. They looked browbeaten, silent with ragged clothes and sullen manners. 1943 and this brutal Victorian social assistance still persisted.

Tommy gave a small sigh. "I don't know, but I think that's a Spike that should be blunted."

LIEUTENANT COLONEL TIM Weaving sat in the right hand seat of the second glider: Colonel Weaving, CO of the Glider Pilot Regiment at the Heavy Glider Conversion Unit, Brize Norton, seeing his pupil, Sergeant Peter Day through another landing and at the same time getting a lift to Grove Aerodrome, a mile out of Wantage, two birds with one stone. As their tug aircraft peeled away from them after the trainee pilot had pulled the handle releasing them from the cables attached inboard on the leading edges of the wings, Colonel Weaving experienced that odd, stomach-rolling, heart-stopping moment as they seemed to be poised, unmoving, still in the air. It was always the same, the sense of being suspended, hanging in the silence, until the pilot put the nose down and turned to the right, lining up with the runway around two miles distant.

The flight deck of the Horsa glider took up almost the entire nose of the aircraft: two sets of controls, basic instruments and the sense of really being in a greenhouse balanced at the sharp end of the glider.

Weaving always felt exhilaration at the start of the descent and now he glanced to his left, checking that Sergeant Day had the lever right down to fully extend the flaps, the big slatted oblongs dropped out from the trailing edges of the wings. "Keep the nose down," he muttered feeling the aircraft press upwards, reacting to the drag of the flaps.

When it came to the landing technique, the big Horsa had none of the sophistication of powered flight. In simple terms you pointed the nose towards the runway, at an angle of almost 45 degrees, making a dive towards touchdown, using the flaps and elevators to slow the aircraft, lifting the nose into a stall as you got really close to the ground. Around them the air hissed, building in volume so that it sounded like heavy breakers on a shingle beach.

Tim Weaving knew Wantage well: glancing to the left to see that they were crossing Wallingford Street, glimpsing the elegant Queen Anne house that Emily told him had once been a brewery, seeing the road winding up into the Market Square and, for a second, over the roofs just getting a flash of Emily's house on Portway. She knew he was coming and he wondered if she had managed to get some ham for tonight. They'd have ham and salad, tomatoes and lettuce from her own garden. He felt the saliva turn acidic in his mouth as he thought of the malt vinegar she'd sprinkle on the lettuce and possibly the brown sauce she'd put on the table to bring out a taste of the ham.

"Start your pullback now," he cautioned the sergeant as they slid over the last houses and into the open country that ran up to the threshold of the runway. The nose rose, for a moment like a fairground ride, the speed bleeding off as they crossed the boundary fence, lifting and stabilizing, sinking in the stall to the runway, then the bump and rumble as they touched down, Sergeant Day braking as they ran on, rumbling and bumping.

"Keep her level Sarn't Day. Level. Brake. Come on. Harder." And they slowed to a stop using about two thirds of the landing area, waiting for the team of erks coming out onto the runway and manhandling the machine off and onto the taxi track, beside the other Horsa that had come in from Brize Norton.

Sergeant Long, the instructor who had been sitting in the rear of the machine, now came and stood behind the Colonel, muttering something about it being a shade fast, but an above average landing.

As they climbed out, Tim Weaving walking towards the jeep standing ready for him, so one of the Whitley tugs came roaring down the runway at around fifty minus feet to drop a tow rope onto the concrete for the handling party to drag back and reattach to one of the gliders.

"You'll be okay now, Sarn't Long?" Weaving smiled.

"I'll get him back to Brize in one piece, sir. Yes. See you tomorrow, sir."

"Bright and early," said Tim Weaving.

They all knew. The Colonel has his bit on the side waiting in Wantage, lucky bugger. His driver – bodyguard really – from Brize would pick him up in the morning early, bring him back to work.

AS SUZIE MOUNTFORD and Tommy Livermore walked back down Workhouse Hill, two half tracks, Bren Gun Carriers, came rattling behind them, overtaking and chewing up the Macadam and tarmac. There were good-natured catcalls and jeers from the men sitting in the rear of the vehicles, and Suzie lifted a hand to wave.

"Don't encourage them," Tommy said, pouting a bit.

"Why not? Who knows how long they've got."

A big four-engined Stirling crossed directly in front of them, left to right, low, probably heading to Harwell which was an OTU, mainly Wellingtons. In the distance a pair of training aircraft, Tiger Moths, looped and rolled.

"Everywhere," Suzie said. "They're everywhere, aren't they?" She continued with a long and somewhat passionate soliloquy about the thousands of men and women at this moment assembling and being readied for the assault on Hitler's Fortress Europe.

Tommy mused that she should have had an orchestra in the background playing 'Land of Hope and Glory', then 'There'll Always Be An England'. "Love it when you talk dirty, heart." He grinned.

That night he made love to her in the quilted bedroom in The Bear Hotel and while it was all happening he muttered, "Do the poor people do this, heart?"

"'Course," Suzie breathed back. First time she'd not found an excuse in months.

"Well they shouldn't, it's much too good for them."

It was neither new nor original but Tommy liked his little jokes.

They had no idea that they would be back in Wantage before Christmas. 15th December, 1943. A Wednesday. A double murder. Scotland Yard called in.

Chapter Three

TOMMY TOOK TWO cars. Suzie Mountford with Cathy
Wimereux, the WDS who had taken over from Molly Abelard
and was given full privileges, carried a weapon and had done all
the tough-guy courses. Cathy – a tall girl, five ten, five eleven,
old gold hair helped a shade, and a good figure from all the
exercise – was all set to become a legend in her own lunchtime,
just like Molly had been. We're a Norman family, she admitted.
"Nobs at one time, we bear the name of the resort which, family legend maintains we once owned. Wimereux. Sounds good,
but I was brought up in an oversized flat in Bayswater. A long
way from Normandy watering holes."

Shirley Cox came as well, pleased as punch because she was
seldom allowed in the field, a WDS now, bit full of herself.
'The Field' was anywhere north of Watford and south of
Walthamstow.

As for specialists there were Ron Worrall and Laura Cotter,
with Dennis Free, 'Smiler' as they called him because he
always looked happy. Could have called him 'Happy' but they
preferred 'Smiler.' 'Smiler' was there to take the snaps and do
lots of other clever forensic things like measuring for the tra-
jectory of missiles, or doing the chalk marks around bodies.
Asset to the Squad, Tommy called him: liked Dennis Free,
thought a lot of his talents.

Wednesday, 15th December 1943. Winter already in the air,
tripping coldly up the nostrils and slapping people around the
face, burning the cheeks. Christmas only ten days off now and
lucky if you could get a chicken, let alone a turkey; as for
Christmas puddings, forget it: dried fruit was like gold dust.

The Reserve Squad had been given a second car after all the
run-around they'd had on the Ascoli case in '42. Another
Wolseley, but not another driver so 'Smiler' had to drive Ron
and Laura, while as ever Brian drove Tommy. Cathy, Shirley

and Suzie in the back, cramped but putting brave faces on it. It was said that Brian had been a chauffer at Kingscote Grange where Tommy had grown up, heir to the Earl of Kingscote: the honourable Tommy Livermore who had lived on the huge Kingscote Estate. Billy Mulligan, executive sergeant to the Reserve Squad, had some sort of connection with Kingscote from way back in the thirties, maintained that Brian was more than a chauffer, said he was a minder as well. Certainly Brian had that extra something about him, carried himself well, never told tales out of school, kept his trap buttoned about the long relationship Suzie had conducted with Tommy.

"What's the guff, Chief?" Cathy must have known Molly, they all deduced, because she had the same way about her, always calling the DCS 'Chief.'

"You know as much as I do." Tommy was all zipped up, silent, nursing the facts in his head, not releasing them for general consumption. "Two dead. A man and a woman. The man appears to be military and is not the woman's husband. Both dead in a cellar. House in Wantage, Berkshire. Up the road from your stamping ground in Newbury, Sarn't Mountford." Looked like butter wouldn't melt in his mouth.

"Yes, sir. Know it, sir." For the benefit of Cathy Wimereux who may *not* know about her and Tommy; and a squadron of pigs had just taken-off from the aerodrome at Abingdon, she thought.

It took them four hours, nearly five, London to Wantage by a circumlocutious route, London to Oxford then over to Wantage via Boar's Hill, past Frilford Golf Club, on through a dozen villages showing the first signs of winter. Not a direct route by any stretch of the imagination and to add to the frustration they were held up all over the place by convoys of lorries, British and American Army convoys, one heavy load on a special RAF transporter, even a long and cocky trail of three ton trucks and command cars belonging to the US 8th Air

Force, off we go into the wide blue yonder, keep the wings level and true!

When they finally arrived – up the narrow Grove Street – into the Market Place, "We want Mill Street," Tommy sounded short, snappy, not willing to give anyone the benefit of the doubt. Brian, in the lead car, swept round the square twice before realising that Mill Street forked off from where Grove Street joined the Square, hard against the Town Hall, new in the 1870s, Victorian mock-Tudor and fussy, part of the 'new' bit now taken over by The Cosy Tea Rooms. "Have to see how cosy that gets," Tommy muttered darkly as they turned into Mill Street, purring down the hill, past the big mill building at the bottom, on the left just beyond The Shears' public house. "I'd like to know how many pubs they've got here," Tommy again grunting, playing the eccentric for the sake of the girls. "Looks like two for every man, woman and child living here."

And they pulled up in front of the Police Station.

A uniformed inspector was down the dancers and at the car's door, reaching for the rear door, just as the second Wolseley pulled up behind them. But Tommy, being Tommy, was at the front next to Brian, unfolding himself and beaming over the car roof, noting well enough that the inspector was out so fast he must have been keeping *cave* peering out of a handy window.

"Turnbull," said the uniformed inspector. "Michael Turnbull. Honour to have you here, Chief Super. Honour indeed."

He would have continued to pour his verbal homage at the visiting DCS who pulled a sour face and quickly plugged the gap with, "Just want to get on with the job, Inspector. Need to talk to your CID: get briefed and start work." He even ignored the proffered hand, brushing past the uniformed senior officer in charge of Wantage Police Station as if he didn't exist. Suzie thought he was getting close to his high-handed manner, not his best side in a strange place, and it didn't do much good for the actual building either, because Tommy's team tended to look away from the wretched inspector who was by now building up a florid colour on his cheeks. Unhealthy.

Tommy disliked fawning; hated drawing attention to his supposedly aristocratic background. He saw it as often as not as a creeping, bum-licking, unnecessary bit of braggadocio, usually an attempt to ingratiate the culprit with the Livermore family. So Tommy put a stop to it whenever it appeared: as it always did when they were called out to provincial murders, which were after all, like love, their reason for living.

"Turnbull," Inspector Turnbull introduced himself again as he hurried up the steps behind the Detective Chief Superintendent. "Michael Turnbull."

"Heard you the first time, Inspector. Sorry to rush you but I'd like to get on. Take a look at what's happened. Time is of the essence, careless talk all that kind of thing, eh?"

Oh, Lord, Suzie thought, he's giving the man his run-around-the-garden treatment. She hated Tommy when he was in this mood. Indeed, Tommy was adept at confusing the issues, leading others down blind alleys or losing them in the long grass. Suzie ought to know: one of his least endearing habits. She'd been in the long grass with him, metaphorically speaking of course.

Inside the station it was all grey and functional; no sign of the female touch, dust on the dark furniture, dull bluish linoleum under foot. A uniformed officer stood beside the front counter waiting for customers, old ladies who'd lost their cats, old soldiers who weren't fading away, or old lags who were giving themselves up for a more peaceful life, away from the wife.

"Need an office," Tommy lunged towards the nearest door handle. "This'll do, Turnbull. We have this one, yes? Murder Room."

Inspector Turnbull was going to fat, a shade short of the height requirement of five foot eight inches and pushing retirement age, but who counted these days? They needed inspectors and chief inspectors to take charge of country patches like Wantage – not exactly the front line trenches when it came to crime-fighting these days, so Turnbull would fit neatly into the market town. He looked a quiet, nonconfrontational kind of man, apart from the ludicrous greying toothbrush moustache that seemed to have a life independent of its owner. Yet even this, Suzie had to admit to herself, broke up the hatchet line of his face, thus obeying the first rule of camouflage.

Tommy waited in the doorway to the right of the front counter, still staring at Turnbull, questioning him with his terrible smile.

"Mine actually," the inspector grimaced, "But you're welcome to it, sir. Too big for me really. There's a nice cosy one at the back I can move into." He even looked pleased about it. Perhaps, Suzie wondered, he would rather be away from the customers now murder had reared its ugly head.

The rest of the team were pushing in on Inspector Turnbull, filling the little lobby that formed the Police Station's entrance hall.

"Bit small," Suzie spoke low, referring to the office.

"Good," Tommy glared round the room. "'Nother couple of desks. Two more phones, four chairs. It'll do us well. What about diggings, Inspector?"

"I've had *you* booked into The Bear, sir. Our best hotel." He pronounced it 'otel after the manner of the middle classes. "The rest we've spread around. Blue Boar, King Alfred's Head..."

"I have to be close to the Chief!" Snapped Cathy.

"As do I," muttered Suzie.

Shirley Cox rolled her eyes and Laura Cotter's eyebrows

tried to attack her hairline.

"Yes," Tommy agreed. "Could you do that, Inspector?" Giving the impression that he would prefer the whole team to be billeted in one place. "Easier for us, eh? Understand?"

"Of course, Chief Superintendent. Of course." Nodding, with vacant eyes.

"And now your CID people?" As if he expected Turnbull to produce them here, in the middle of the office.

"All three of them, yes, sir. They're all up at the house. Murder site."

"Your entire CID's up there?"

"I only have one detective sergeant and two detective constables, Mr Livermore; and one of those constables was only brought in this morning from Oxford."

Tommy had walked away from him, into the room, a hand patting one of the two desks, sliding along the woodwork like the hand of a dragon wife testing for dust, catching out the maidservant. "The murder site?" he queried.

"There are two bodies, sir. One is the commanding officer of the Glider Pilot Regiment at the Heavy Glider Conversion Unit, Brize Norton. A Colonel Weaving. Tim Weaving. The other is the wife of Wantage's greatest war hero, Captain Bobby Bascombe VC: Emily 'Bunny' Bascombe. It appears that Mrs Bascombe was, shall we say, keeping company with the Colonel. Now they're both dead."

"And where is the gallant captain?"

"Last seen at the Primo Solo bridge in Sicily. July. He's a POW. They put him in the bag and actually spirited him back to Germany when they realised they'd struck gold. He was with the Eighth Army, got his VC at Tobruk. Wantage has a kind of history with VCs. Next to The Bear you'll see the VC Gallery, stuffed full of grisly portraits of men winning their Victoria Crosses."

"And your entire CID is at the murder site?" as though he

hadn't even heard the bit about the Victoria Cross.

Turnbull nodded.

"And where would that be?"

"Portway House. Portway. Stands on its own overlooking the College playing fields."

"The College?"

"Locals call King Alfred's School, the College."

"How terribly affected!" Tommy muttered. In her mind, Suzie saw that lone house on the hot Sunday afternoon back in August, the woman leaving it, coming down the steps, slim attractive, hurrying as though late for church, glancing back from the corner by The Royal Oak giving them a suspicious look.

"Witnesses?" Tommy raised his eyebrows.

"One who found the bodies. The Colonel's sergeant. Came to pick him up this morning."

Tommy nodded, "And where is *he*?"

"Here, sir. I've brought him back here. He seemed shaken up."

"A soldier shaken up?"

"Yes, Mr Livermore."

"Only the one witness?"

"Only the one, yes."

"We'll go straight out to the house then," Tommy already moving, purposeful. "You deal with everything else then, Turnbull...? Keep the witness safe. Feed him strong tea. I'll talk to him later."

"Of course, sir."

Tommy took one step closer to the door, changed his mind about something. Stopped, turned round, "Sarn't Cox?"

"Yes, Chief?" From Shirley, ready for anything and head stretched forward to better attend what her boss had to say.

"Want you to stay here, Sarn't Cox."

"Sir."

"Stay here and get this office sorted, draw stores, look to Mr Turnbull for me. This'll be our Murder Room. Open a Murder Book. Got it?"

"Right Chief." Knowing that he meant her to keep an eye on things.

"Help Mr Turnbull with getting our billets organised as well."

"Sir."

Turnbull had been trying to get an edge in, "Oh, there is one other thing..."

Tommy almost at the door to the street, signalling Dennis Free to follow him, hand out towards Brian, pausing, looking back, and an elderly lady hurrying in, making small 'oh' noises. Confused.

"...There's a bit of an oddity looking for you. Came here. Sent him on to Portway House."

"Oddity?"

"Hush-hush. Probably because of the Colonel."

"Yes. Of course, yes." His voice rising, "Brian, come on man."

Behind them the elderly lady, bent from the waist, a slow mover, was at the front counter. "It's about my 'Pooh-Pooh,'" she said. "My Siamese."

TOMMY GAVE BRIAN the instructions in clean, brittle orders – "You're clear left so into the Market Square, keep right...keep right...exit left...straight on...what're those bloody cars doing, playing at Giddy Goat?...straight on....turn right up here by The Royal Oak...slow down Brian...it's only about forty yards up here on the left....Yes....Behind the ambulance..."

And they arrived, a bit fast but sliding in neatly behind the slab-sided ambulance with Dennis bringing the other Wolseley to stop almost touching their rear bumper.

Tommy was out of the car almost before it stopped and Suzie had her door open, just behind him, and Cathy out before either of them. There was a uniformed constable on the door – Portway House in black on the little plaque – who hadn't had the practise of recognising police vehicles.

"You can't come in here, sir. Sir, if you could…" Tommy flashed his warrant card and the constable looked very puzzled, so Suzie calmed the man and went in after Tommy leaving Cathy to sort things out. The others were slower getting out of the second car and Tommy had to shout from the top of the cellar steps, behind the stairs, "Dennis. I want Dennis down here. Everyone else wait upstairs."

The scent of death mingled with that chill, cold brick smell you get in cellars, wonderful on a hot summer's day, not so pleasant in early winter. The walls were of rough stone, whitewashed showing up the blood splatters all the more clearly when they finally got to them.

"Livermore, DCS Reserve Squad," Tommy intoned extending his hand towards a large man, tall and strapping, with a lively open face and amused very intelligent eyes.

A younger man stepped forward, "This is the doctor, sir. I'm DS Stimpson. Blinder, they call me. Blinder Stimpson." He didn't introduce the other young man standing near the cellar steps.

"The senior CID man," Tommy said, almost absentmindedly, to himself.

The curved ceilings had to be over six feet high in the tallest places because the doctor's head almost touched the brickwork, under foot there were grey paving stones, big and laid without care so they produced an uneven patchwork. The whole place was built in an L-shape, about twenty feet long and some twelve feet wide, spacious, ending in a reinforced archway leading to the ninety degree angled cross-piece. Naked light bulbs were set in the wall, low-wattage and clouded, diffusing the light and putting up shadows that added to the eeriness of the place.

Tommy, turned down the corners of his mouth and began to walk forward, towards the arch, sensing the doctor and Suzie behind him and pretty certain that the bottom of the L was where the bodies lay.

They were both there, very dead. The male, in uniform except for his boots and socks and his trousers that had been pulled off. You could see round his genitals where the lighted cigarettes had burned holes into the flesh, horrible, black and red you could almost hear the screams. He was tied to a wooden stand chair, the kind of thing you might have kept in your kitchen, and his body was slumped forward against restraints so you couldn't see the agony written on his face. Suzie thought the back of his head looked like a loofah that had been dipped in blood. She remembered the family story that had her Auntie Nan – her dad's sister – going into a chemist and asking in her often confused way, 'I want a foolah, please'.

Then she saw the man's hands and feet, unnaturally bent and marked, oozing blood with a shard of bone sticking from the middle of his right foot.

The woman had not been in a chair: she had probably been kneeling in an odd and awkward position, bound with what could have been a clothesline that passed tightly around her neck, pinioning her arms. Finally the ropes were anchored hard to her ankles, biting into the flesh, and bending her legs up so that the feet were drawn up behind, almost to her buttocks. She had probably knelt in this uncomfortable position but now she was tipped forward, the upper half of her body lying on the floor, inclined onto her right side, her face pulled back as if in a retch of agony, the rope digging hard into her flesh and the skin around her lips and cheeks now bluish, mouth half open as if in a terrible last cry, tongue lolling, the eyes still open, glazed, gazing into eternity.

Tommy made a dismissive sound. Then, "If she relaxed she'd put intolerable pressure on her own throat, on the windpipe. That's what finally happened?"

"Not all by herself," the doctor said from behind him. "She had a little help from someone."

Tommy walked between the bodies, moving carefully, watching where he put his feet, making certain he didn't disturb anything: bending, peering.

Snooping, Suzie thought. Doing his job, intruding on the two deaths.

"You know who she was?"

"Yes. She was a patient of mine. Emily Bascombe. *Mrs* Emily Bascombe."

"You can formally identify her?"

"I can. Mrs Bascombe."

"You've examined the bodies?"

"Haven't moved them, but yes, as far as I could."

"Come to any conclusions?"

"Neither had what you'd call an easy death. Badly treated."

"Ever seen the man before?"

"Colonel Tim Weaving. I'd met him several times. Glider Pilot Regiment. He was the CO over at Brize Norton."

"Cause of death?"

"Someone bashed the back of his head in. Unless when I do the PM I find he's been shot, stabbed or poisoned, I think the bash on the back of his head'll have done the business. Nasty."

Tommy sniffed the air, turned and began to walk towards the stone steps leading back into the small hall but stopped when he saw DC Free coming down.

"Got your box of tricks Dennis? Good, then take some snaps for me. It's unpleasant but I suppose you're used to it now."

"I don't think you ever get used to it, Chief."

"Maybe not. Doctor?"

"Yes Mr Livermore."

"Was that just plain sadism back there? Or have I missed something?"

"It looked as though someone – maybe two – was like a child doing horrible things just because he could: pulling the wings off flies."

Tommy nodded, turned round and walked back to watch Dennis taking pictures of the bodies. It was as though he couldn't bear to leave them, standing waiting as though they'd suddenly give him a clue to how they died. Suzie stood apart, not even peeping into the section of the cellar where the bodies were.

After a couple of minutes watching Dennis Free, Tommy gave a big shrug, sighed and turned back into the long narrow room, with its whitewashed walls and uneven floor. He motioned for Suzie to go ahead of him and as she reached the slabby stone stairs she saw, with surprise that Cathy Wimereux had been standing at the top and realised she shouldn't be surprised because she had seen her move out of the way to let Dennis down.

"It's all a bit nasty, Cathy," Suzie said, out of the corner of her mouth.

"So I gather." Cathy Wimereux didn't even look at her.

The door at the top of the stairs had been left unpainted or treated on the inside but nicely cleaned off and fresh with cream paint in the hall, like the rest of the woodwork. Was there some kind of analogy here? she wondered, giving a wan smile to Ron Worrall and Laura Cotter who both stood close to the cellar door. God, she thought, what horrors have gone on under this roof: fears, night-shriek, dread? What awful things happened? She shuddered.

Ron carried the big leather case that held all the gubbins for latent prints, evidence bags, a small tool kit and some lenses.

They called it the Murder Bag but it was often used for more mundane crimes. Laura carried a small electric sweeper. Before the day was out they would have removed every tiny piece of what they called 'foreign matter,' which meant everything that couldn't be tied to the two bodies.

Tommy, coming up the stairs behind Suzie, thought; Lord, how that girl's body moves inside her clothes. Never have I known a girl who can so set me up by just being herself.

Tommy was concerned. When he had first taken her as a lover she had no other desire but to learn from him and please him. She appeared to believe that she would only be happy if she was married to him, but of late the desire seemed to have slackened off, lost its urgency. No telling with women, Tommy thought as he emerged into the hall. Women? Mysteries. You never knew with any of them.

He told Ron and Laura to go down and do whatever they did around the bodies of people who were dead from murder: collect the minutiae. Someone's done some dreadful things to that pair. So what was the purpose? What the motive? Just for the fun of hurting someone, hearing another human cry out? He shook his head, not saying any of this out loud. Then he walked towards the door. "See everybody back at the station," he said as a uniform moved to open the door for him.

Then he seemed to change his mind again, stopping and leaning back towards Suzie. "The way that woman was tied up, heart. The Bascombe woman, Emily Bascombe."

"Yes, Chief."

"The way she was tied, I think Molly told me about that tie. They teach it up at Achnacarry. Use it on prisoners, deprives them of sleep. Relax and you strangle yourself." Achnacarry was where the Commando Training Centre was located. Anyone said he'd been to Achnacarry you knew he was a tough bugger.

"Not very Agatha Christie is it, Chief?" Suzie tried to

lighten the load.

"Neither Christie nor Dorothy L Sayers, heart. They don't really describe battered bodies much, do they?"

"Don't describe them at all." She stood back to let him precede her to the front door, but he changed his mind again, turned around strode across the hall and started to go up the stairs. Suzie followed him: like a little poodle, she thought. Follow him everywhere like a little snuffling bloody poodle.

Tommy went from bedroom to bedroom, standing in the doorways and taking in each room. The master bedroom had been slept in. Double bed, pillows dinged both sides, curtains still drawn. The other rooms showed no sign of having been occupied and they ended up to the far left of the big landing, the large bathroom, floor covered in grey and black lino, all nicely set out. Victorian fitments, a big bath with claw feet, set high from the ground. A lavatory with a heavy polished seat and a good-sized hand basin. On the inner wall there was a fireplace with glazed tiles, Dutch scenes in blue, man and a woman in costume, a couple showing a barge and another with a windmill. Delft? Suzie wondered. Glazed tiles round the fireplace with the hearth blackened and cleaned: a mantelpiece above with a small alarm clock in the centre.

"You could swim in that," Tommy said, nodding towards the bath. Then Suzie followed him out onto the landing again where he loitered, looking down from the balustrade into the hall with its black and beige tiles, and smaller tiles making an ornamental edging: a long oak table pushed under the stairs with a sit-up-and-beg telephone just visible, a notepad sitting beside it.

Tommy paused for a moment as though wondering about something as he looked down, then Suzie found herself following him downstairs and, this time, out through the front door.

A little knot of people had gathered across the road, against the red brick wall marking the boundary to one of the large houses on the other side. They just stood there, these people, not talking but whey-faced, shocked, looking at a house where murder had been done as if the bricks and wood were crying out, giving a sign.

He started down the steps with Cathy in the bodyguard position, just behind the left shoulder, as poor Molly always said, Suzie close behind Cathy.

As they reached the pavement, so a figure detached itself from the group across the road: navy blue double-breasted blazer, brass buttons, well-pressed grey flannels, highly polished shoes, the tanned face of what Suzie always thought an adult male angel should look like (until Sister Margaret Mary spoiled it all by saying they were neither masculine nor feminine angels; all angels were genderless). His walk was so languid that Suzie had the distinct impression he had been forced to push himself off the wall in order to assume a standing position: not so much a walk as a stroll, and hair the colour of light gold, smooth, silky and of that infuriating consistency that allowed it to be hit by a gale force wind, but then returned to its normal, smooth, unruffled state without recourse to hand or comb: every single hair back in its place.

She was aware now of Tommy, suddenly stock still and a shade pale by her side.

"My God," he muttered. "A spectre from my past."

The young man sauntered across the road, approaching slowly, a thin smile flicking over his lips, lifting and twinkling around his cool grey eyes.

"Curry?" said Tommy. "Curry Shepherd?"

"Hello Tommy." The voice was not Tommy's Eton drawl, but it was as languid as the man's walk.

"I was told that you'd been killed. Belgium, May 1940." Tommy looking and sounding puzzled, frowning, deep furrows and eyes partly closed.

"Yes," said Curry Shepherd.

"In fact there was a memorial service for you."

"I know. I heard about that." A smile and a raise of the hand. "Seems they got it wrong didn't they? Very much alive, Tommy. Come back to haunt you."

Chapter Four

TOMMY SAID IN his world-weary drawl, "Gave me quite a turn, Curry. Thought I was seeing things for a moment: the dead walking and all that."

Curry Shepherd's mouth curved into a smile, and the smile turned into a grin. He didn't look straight at Tommy but stared at Suzie, like a man delighted with an unexpectedly wonderful view.

"Rude to stare, Curry!" Tommy barked, and Suzie noticed the younger man start as though a lightning bolt had struck nearby.

"WDS Mountford. Curry Shepherd." Tommy waving a hand between them, meticulous about introductions.

"How d'you do?" said Curry, looking her straight in the eye. He had, she noticed, lovely grey eyes.

Suzie smiled and gave a little nod, and went on feeling uncomfortable.

They shook hands. He really is beautiful, she thought, felt a distinct frisson coming through his fingers, like an electric current.

Tommy was speaking again. "Curry was with me at m'tutor's."

"A shade after you, Tommy." Curry corrected. "You were head of house when I was at m'tutor's."

Suzie knew the language because she had met a couple of other people who had been at Eton with Tommy Livermore. M'Tutor's was the la-di-da Etonian way of saying they were in the same house at school. But she felt even more uncomfortable. Couldn't explain it. Didn't know why. Young Curry Shepherd made her feel strange, was all she knew. Edgy. Gave her a little tingle. You know.

"Your people here wouldn't let me have a shufti at the bodies, Tommy. Really should see them y'know." Curry talked in the same quirky shorthand all these upper class Harry Poshers spoke, but Curry was not quite as straight-faced as most of them: didn't take himself too seriously, which made a change, and there was melody in his voice: what her mum would've called a 'brown velvet voice'.

"Why on earth should I let you peep at the corpses, Curry? You working for one of those comics down the Street? Or d'you just like looking at dead people? Necrophiliac are we? Aren't you in HM Forces at all, old son?"

"Oh, I'm in HM Forces all right, Tom; and, yes, I was posted missing presumed dead. Near Ypres of all places." He gave one of those now-you-see-it-now-you-don't smiles, his face going back to normal. "Got to talk to you privately, Tommy. Save embarrassment, eh?"

Tommy looked at him hard and suspicious for a good twenty seconds. "WDS Mountford shares all secrets in this outfit, Curry, but we'll get as private as we can." He raised his voice, calling for Brian who trotted round the car, holding open the rear door. Tommy ushered Curry into the back seat. Then Suzie. Finally he climbed in and sank down in the seat, closing the door as he did so.

Suzie felt the padding move as Tommy's weight dinged it, she also felt Curry's left thigh against her and wondered why she was once more starting to feel uncomfortable; but she didn't move, covering whatever confusion she felt, putting her mind as far away from lust or discomfort as she could. Which wasn't really all that far.

"Right, James Morrison Shepherd. Let's hear your story." Tommy seemed to physically relax, putting his head against the leather seatback.

"End of May '40." Curry spoke as though delivering evidence in court.

"I was with General Brooke: that is General Sir Alan Brooke. On his staff. Intelligence Officer – trained, done a dozen postings to get experience. Now I had ended up in a shooting war. We all had. Went up to look at the 5th Division near Ypres: the General gave us a short lecture on the unpleasant connotations the place had for those who served in the '14-'18 show. Round about 26th, maybe 27th May. The 5th Division were getting into position along the canal. The old man wanted to see what the Belgians were doing about defending the place, but they'd buggered off, excuse my polemics, Suzie. I can call you Suzie, yes?"

"Of course," she told him with a sly little smile.

"Nothing going on except some Frogs from the Postal Service of 1st Frog Motorized. I got out to take a look-see along some of the side streets and Jerry started shelling us. By the time I got back, the General and his three vehicles had gone. Finally I was trapped when Jerry blew the bridges."

"So?" Tommy seemed unimpressed.

"So I went to ground and stayed there for the best part of six months. But that's another, and rather long, story." He took a deep breath and swallowed. "When I finally got back I found I was missing believed killed, and the fella at the War House said use it, make it an advantage." He shifted, his left hand going into the breast pocket of his blazer, pulling out a small piece of pasteboard, size of a visiting card. "Military Intelligence, Tommy. It's all there." He gave a fast, attractive grin; almost knowing what Tommy Livermore was about to say.

"Bit of an oxymoron, Curry, eh? Military Intelligence, what?" Tommy took the card and studied it, closing one eye and giving young Shepherd the occasional droll look, lifting an eyebrow, squinting at him sideways on. Finally he grunted, sat up straight and muttered, "Better make the phone call then, eh? Better get you sorted, young Shepherd. Right?" He flung the door open and slid out, shutting it again. Rather angrily Suzie thought.

She felt the seat blossom as Tommy removed his weight, but Curry didn't shift, still thigh to thigh, rather enjoying it. She said, "What's this all about?" Joined at the hip, she thought. Fancy.

"Oh, Tommy being pedantic. Checking up on me. Doesn't change much does he?"

"I wouldn't know. I've only known him since 1940 and he's stayed roughly the same since then."

"Still brutal is he?"

"Oh, I wouldn't say bru..."

"I would. He used to beat people for dumb insolence in the ranks on Corps parades. Corps. OTC parades. Officers Training Corps. School."

"M'Tutor's," she said with a sly-boots smirk. "How horrid."

"I used to think it was like being in Wellington's army. Chaps being flogged for minor infringements on parade. Dumb insolence and the like."

"He called you James Morrison..."

"Right in one. James Morrison Shepherd. James, James Morrison Morrison, said to his mother, said he..."

"Then why the spicy nickname?"

"Curry?" A little laugh. "Oh, nothing to do with spice. We're an Anglo-Irish family. Boat builders. Up near Galway. I'm the eldest son of the present generation and the eldest son traditionally takes over the making of small boats: currach; so Currach Shepherd; hence Curry Shepherd."

"A currach is...?"

"A small boat; a coracle..."

"Oh, yes. And now you're doing..?"

"I didn't say, but your boss, Tommy, is checking up on my credentials e'en as we speak, as they say," this last drawled out exaggeratingly. "Actually, I'm on a little roving commission that I don't think our Ginger Tom's going to like."

She giggled at the Ginger Tom. In some ways it was apt. She didn't think Tommy had ever been unfaithful to her, but he certainly eyed up the ladies: very blatant about it. Mind you she had been unfaithful to Tommy – one night with the Wing Commander: room 504. But that was different. Of course.

"So what d'you do for our Tom?"

She thought for a moment, then said, "Actually Tommy rescued me." In her head she saw Tommy as he was when she first met him. She had been following a lead with, of all people, Shirley Cox.

In the autumn of 1940 Suzie was out of her depth. The Blitz on London was at its most horrible, she was untrained as a detective and her senior officer, Detective Chief Inspector 'Big Toe' Harvey, had been injured by a passing bomb, leaving her unsuitably in charge when a headline murder case landed on her patch.

Fleet Street had a field day, and the papers were quickly awash with stories about this young, inexperienced woman in charge of an atrocious killing. In those days women coppers investigating 'orrible murders raised the hackles in a certain type of 'Concerned of Camberwell' correspondent in the editorial columns. The Yard was angry, thought she'd been professionally putting herself about a bit.

Eventually she was told to keep her head down and, if she needed help, to ring Detective Chief Superintendent Tommy Livermore. She did just that and found a pleasant, if avuncular, voice at the distant end, giving her sensible advice and telling her to just get on with it. He would step in and assist if push came to shove.

Push did come to shove and her cry for help was answered in the reception hall of a tasteless block of service apartments in Marylebone: Derbyshire Mansions where she first came face to face with Tommy.

She was later to discover that his entrances were usually

made with some dramatic bravura, and on this occasion he swished in with his team around him, making Suzie comment, "Orchestra, dancing girls, the lot."

Shirley added, "And a male voice choir."

They both agreed that Tommy himself arrived in great style, the impeccable suit, handmade shoes, greatcoat across the shoulders, the energy, physical presence, and the all-consuming smile. It just about knocked her off her feet. (Just as you could Mr James Morrison Shepherd, she considered now. If you put your mind to it. Same mould as Tommy but much younger.)

The following night – back in 1940 – Dandy Tom Livermore had taken Suzie to dinner at the Ritz where he told her that she was one of a number of hand-picked women detectives who were to be groomed for stardom against the day when women coppers would be *de rigueur* (there were only about three people in the Met who could clearly see that female police were really here to stay. Tommy was one of them: though you'd rarely know it these days). That night she left the Ritz as one of the Reserve Squad, and during the remainder of that horrendous year, Tommy was there for her, and soon after he became her first ever lover.

Now, here he was again outside the car and talking ten to the dozen to Brian.

"Going to the nick," he said once he'd returned to his seat – next to Brian in the front this time, his rightful place. "We've got a lot to talk about, young Curry, haven't we? At least you've got a lot to tell me. You're a Major I gather." Not even a pause for breath. "Substantive rank of Major they tell me. Quite gone up in the world."

"What about me seeing the bodies?" Curry's voice seemed to be saying that Tommy really didn't cut any ice with him because he had his orders to follow, his own agenda and his own most important end game to play out.

"They're pretty terrible and I want the doc to do his business before anyone else sees them. Your bosses say I can show you the happy snapshots when we have them. They also say that what you have to tell me is urgent. So we'll do it down the nick. Okay?"

"As our American allies say, 'aw my aching back.'" Curry didn't even smile and this was a long way from dumb insolence. Suzie could feel Tommy's fury from where she sat in the back of the Wolesley. Indeed, she feared for his spleen. "Ask you a question, Tommy. What's so terrible about the bodies?"

Tommy took half a minute to make up his mind. "Because they're a mess, Curry."

"You know who they are? Identified them?"

"Oh yes. The doc knew both of them. Colonel Tim Weaving, Glider Pilot Regiment and Mrs Bascombe, wife of Bunny Bascombe VC."

"And what kind of mess are they in?"

"Some sod's really roughed them up: some sadistic bugger. Or, and this sounds daft, it looks like someone put 'em to the question."

"Really?" Curry said, as though this fact was the last possible thing in the world to interest him.

Back at Wantage Police Station Shirley Cox had the new office up, running and almost organized, with the exception of the extra telephones that, she assured Tommy, would be installed by noon tomorrow. In his current mood a grunt was high praise.

"You mind if I check up with the Station Master, Chief?" she asked.

"Just see what he's got in the way of digs for us? Doss house? Bed and Breakfast, or palatial hotel suite?"

"Yes. Right. Do your worst Shirley, and if it's a palatial suite it's mine."

As Shirley made her way out, Suzie thought to herself that she had been right when she first saw her in 1940. Shirley was very like Hedy Lamarr: the hair, a quick glimpse of her face and certainly her figure brought to mind that film star who caused such a stir in Hollywood when it was revealed she had – long ago (1932) – done a nude scene in a Czech film titled Ecstasy. Old Shirl could have done a lot of nude scenes and got applause all round from the boys in the Reserve Squad. Some standing ovations an' all.

Suzie looked back towards Tommy who was staring at Curry Shepherd. "So, you're a funny, young Shepherd. Major Curry Shepherd of the oddities. They told me I should ask you for the details."

Curry looked hard at Tommy Livermore. He nodded and, in spite of what he had already been told, asked if someone could definitely confirm one of the bodies in Portway House was Colonel Tim Weaving of the Glider Pilot Regiment. Tommy said yes, the local doctor had confirmed it, and the woman's ID as well.

"Then I'll have to use your telephone." He spoke to the operator about making a trunk call to London, and a minute later had someone on the line. "Firefly for Dormouse," he said, briskly and Suzie thought, 'Gosh, they really do use that gobbledegook with code words, just like in the moving pictures. Gobbledegook was a word she'd learned from one of the American officers when they were in East Anglia: meant to sound like turkeys gobbling all over the place and meant language made into nonsense by elaborate words and technical terms.

"Yes," Curry confirmed to someone at the other end of the telephone. "Of course, sir...Yes, absolutely. Detective Chief Superintendent Livermore... sir, yes I was...Restricted...Totally, sir...Definitely Weaving...Yes, very good. I think they should be exceptionally careful regarding promotions to that spot, sir. Yes,

I'll put him in the picture. That'll be okay, no worry." And more along those line. "I'll see to it, sir...Right..." and he closed the line, hung up the handset and smiled, first at Suzie, then Tommy. "It would seem that, because you're working the murder of Lieutenant Colonel Weaving I can give you the gen. Strictly need-to-know of course."

"Oh, strictly, of course." Tommy was being persistently difficult.

Curry lit a cigarette, didn't offer them to anyone else and blew a long stream of smoke towards the ceiling before starting his tale. "I got back to England in a fishing boat from somewhere close to Ostend. Very cold, January 1941 and the man I saw at the War House had what he thought was a great idea. I was put on to training men who were going to work at Camp XX – Camp 20. They were faced with me, a man who claimed to be Anglo-Irish but could not prove he wasn't missing believed killed in Belgium in '40. Most of them thought I was a real Nazi infiltrator. My old boss, General Brooke wasn't told and he was approached several times, said he doubted that I was alive." Taking another lungful of smoke and bringing it down his nose this time – brandished his smoking tricks did our Curry. "By this time," he continued, "We'd put most of the Nazi spies in the bag before they got very far. Blundering lot of idiots most of them. Put 'em in the bag then took the bag down to Camp XX."

Curry told them Camp XX was not about getting spies to face the firing squad. "It wasn't so much about termination as playing them back to Nazi Germany." Certainly, the staff tried to de-gut them, fillet them, clean them out, but the aim was not to see them ending up on the Tower of London Rifle Range. "They were treated well. The object of the exercise was to get them working with us. Any odd bits of information on the side were a bonus."

Most of the captured spies, and they had caught the bulk of

them – mainly because they were brought into England and Wales in such a ham-handed fashion – finally bowed to the inevitable and sent their messages in their prescribed way. "The information sent was, of course, the stuff we gave them. I only know of two who refused to cooperate. Alas, they ended up on the Tower's Rifle Range at six o'clock in the morning. Not a glamorous end for the Fatherland and Führer."

Curry worked at Camp XX for three months. After that he went on a couple of courses, was upped to major and now operated as what he described as "a floating go-between in the intelligence community".

"And where're you floatin' at the moment?" Tommy's drawl became worse and Curry started to show a shadow of annoyance.

"I drift between the MI6, MI5, Camp XX and the boys in Baker Street, Tom. You know who the boys in Baker Street are?" Like throwing down the gauntlet.

"Would they have anything to do with Sherlock Holmes or Dr Watson?"

"Close," Curry smiled and told him to try again. "After all, Tommy, you've got a sister in the business."

Suzie, as much as she tried couldn't stop the flush creeping from her neck onto her cheeks. She had spent that one night of unfaithfulness to Tommy after seeing him with another woman, in close heads-together conversation. Only later did she discover the truth, that it was his sister, Alison, back on a brief visit from doing something incredibly hush-hush. The tune of 'This Can't be Love' ran through her head and her cheeks became redder.

Tommy sucked his teeth. "Must be an off-shoot of one of the other funny groups, organisations, departments, whatever you call them."

Curry said, "Okay," loudly as though Tommy had made a

bold stab at the answer and landed close to the truth. Then he laid it out. "The boys in Baker Street're various sections of the SOE – Special Operations Executive: the people who are at the sharp end of setting Europe ablaze, which was what Winston asked them to do. They're not just in Baker Street of course but that's as good a generic address as any for them." For a moment the pale grey eyes caressed Suzie, once more making her feel uneasy.

"And who do I work for?" he asked, as though either Tommy or Suzie had formed the question in the way they looked at him. "Well, you might say England, or Winston – and that would be right – but the true answer is the CIGS: General Sir Alan Brooke himself, my old boss, now elevated to head soldier. Chief of the Imperial General Staff, and the word is that he'll be a Field Marshal by the New Year."

"Always said you'd go far, young Shepherd," Tommy muttered. "Lonely up there at the top is it?"

"Tommy, tell me you'd rather be working with me at your back. The alternative would be the hairy great coppers with Special Branch. Not a nice thought."

Tommy, Suzie noticed, didn't meet his eye, sucked his teeth again, noncommittal. At last he said, "Then tell me why I have to work with you, Curry?"

"Because I'm dealing with security for COSSAC."

"And what's COSSAC when it's home?"

"Chief of Staff to the Supreme Allied Commander. A post that has operated since April without a Supreme Allied Commander."

Tommy nodded. "Yes."

"But they'll appoint one soon enough," Curry smiled. "And next year he'll be bustling along in front of us all, but there are two reasons why you should be particularly interested in all this..."

"Do tell," Tommy, face set in a rictus, acid in his throat.

Curry nodded, as if to say he understood Tommy's caustic manner. "Please, I want you to know what's going on. What I'm going to tell you next is totally classified. It mustn't leave either of your brains…"

"Oh, come on…" Tommy began.

"COSSAC lives, moves and has its being down in St James's Square. Norfolk House, know it Tom?"

"I know where it is. Pinky-red building."

"Good," Curry's normal attitude of languor changed and the words now cracked like bullets passing overhead. "Good, because every couple of days or so there are meetings at COS-SAC: forty or fifty senior officers, colonels and upwards, under General Frederick Morgan. These men have been planning the greatest battle so far in this damned war: the invasion of the occupied continent, Hitler's Fortress Europe."

"Really?"

"Yes, really, Tom. These men know when, where and, to a great extent, how the invasion'll take place. So they sit on the greatest secret alive in this country at the moment. And, Tommy, maybe you'll sit up when I tell you that Lieutenant Colonel Tim Weaving was a member of that planning committee. Tim Weaving was a keeper of many of those secrets, so it's sort of important if he died being tortured. Think about it."

During these last words, Curry Shepherd had taken a few steps back towards the door. Now he had reached it, and with a little mock bow and flourish he said, "I go. I come back."

He hadn't been out of the door for more than five seconds before Suzie realised that she missed him.

Chapter Five

THEY WENT OVER to The Bear Hotel – Tommy, with Suzie and Cathy Wimereux, together with Dennis Free, while the rest of the team found their rooms at The Blue Boar, opposite the Post Office. Tommy, Suzie thought, had used his considerable charm on the lady at reception to get rooms facing onto the Market Square and so close to one another that, to use his own expression, he'd know when she changed her mind.

For some reason she couldn't quite comprehend, Suzie was feeling unusually indecisive, and had done so for some time. Not that she had to make any immediate decisions, but deep within her she felt uncertain about life: about her life at the moment within the Metropolitan police, and her long term life with Tommy. The last wasn't new as she'd been putting him off for the best part of a year, and felt guilty about it. Tommy was the man who had made her into a woman and taught her to love – not just in the physical sense, but in the more lasting and profound way, expanding her mind, helping her to reach higher, to stretch out towards unexplored horizons, teaching her to laugh. Laughter was important she discovered. But Tommy was a good deal older than Suzie. She wondered if this was at the root of the problem.

Cathy and Dennis Free were banished to quarters in the rear of the hotel, but Tommy said all four of them would lunch together in the large dining room. "One-ish." He told them. The others, at The Blue Boar, would have to fend for themselves.

While Tommy was welded to the telephone in his room, giving instructions and talking to Scotland Yard, Suzie was content to slip away and join Cathy Wimereux for a pre-lunch glass of sherry in the long Coffee Room: the place where she had taken tea with Tommy on their visit back in August.

For the first time that day Suzie relaxed and found herself

pouring out her reasons for joining the Met, talking about her rise to a responsible position in the Reserve Squad.

She had joined the Metropolitan Police almost in a fit of pique. In the late 1930s her beloved father had died in a road accident within sight of his Georgian house, Larksbrook, outside Newbury. With his death the spoiled idyll of Suzie's pampered middle class life came close to destruction. A year later, her mother, Helen, announced she was going to marry for a second time, her choice being the totally unsuitable 'Galloping Major' as Suzie and her sister Charlotte called the portly, strutting, fussy little Ross Gordon-Lowe DSO.

Charlotte was already away from home, married with two children – one of them gravely handicapped – and Suzie, goaded by her dislike of her mother's new husband, and after a furious row with him, took the easy way out by enlisting in the Met ("I can always arrest the little bugger"). She rose quickly through WPC to a posting with CID as a Woman Detective Sergeant, and from there to Tommy Livermore's Reserve Squad, discovering on the way that she had been earmarked for promotion by an unlikely cabal of senior officers with an eye to what would most benefit the force in future years.

Cathy already knew about the events of Christmas 1940 when Charlotte had tragically died, the children now cared for by Helen and the odious Gordon-Lowe.

Now in spite of some pointed questions, Suzie did not go into the details of her long affair with Tommy Livermore, and the fact that she shared her London bolthole in Upper St Martin's Lane, with her boss. Suzie, however, got the impression that Cathy already knew most of the details of that side of her life and merely wanted them confirmed.

It was only when Tommy and Dennis Free arrived for lunch that she realised how Cathy had quietly loosened her tongue and drawn out her life story with a minimum of fuss, proving that Cathy Wimereux was a skilled and cunning copper: one to be watched, Suzie thought.

At just before one o'clock they sat down to lunch under the careful ministrations of the head waiter – in fact the only waiter – the saturnine Harris who, after he'd served the first course, told Tommy the manager would like a word.

"I'm free at the moment if he'd like to interrupt my lunch." Tommy snapped as Harris removed his soup plate. Like the Demon King in pantomime the manager – a short, plump man in need of a haircut, and with a moustache that seemed to be wearing him instead of vice versa – arrived in the dining room just as Tommy looked at the menu to identify what had been set before him by way of an entrée. The menu said *Jambon Extraodinaire*.

"It certainly is most extraordinaire," Tommy muttered as the manager gave a small cough to indicate he was there, shifting from foot to foot beside Tommy's chair.

"Yes?" Tommy barked and the manager coughed again.

"Detective Inspector Livermore...?" he began and Cathy raised her head, ruffled as though she had visible hackles rising rapidly. "Detective Inspector?" she all but shouted, while small spots of crimson appeared on Suzie's cheeks: she never could stand public unpleasantness and they both knew the Detective Inspector error would illicit rage from Tommy.

"Detective Chief Superintendent if you don't mind," Cathy glared at the preening little manager, very much aware of DCS Livermore's reputation for accuracy and his treatment of fools: Tommy Livermore, it was said, became riled more easily than a bull faced with a cardinal's hat.

"Don't worry about it," Tommy, who would normally be furious, turned on the quiet charm, immediately angering both Cathy and Suzie.

"What can I do for you?" The terrible smile aimed straight at the manager and neatly at the two women detective sergeants at the same time, a trick performed with oily skill.

"Well, Detective Chief Superintendent..." he began and Suzie, now furious at her Chief's decision to play things out of character, tried to score one for the girls by muttering, "Detective Chief Superintendent, the *Honourable* Tommy Livermore..."

Tommy shot her a glance containing several daggers as he unlocked his eyes from her's and told the manager to speak up.

"It's simply the ration books," the man smiled a ludicrous smirk. "We don't know how long you're here for, sir, and we need the ration books." Hands spread wide, like a man claiming to be at the mercy of petty bureaucracy – which of course he was.

Again they all waited, the pause laced with the hiss of a smouldering fuse.

"Think nothing of it," the terrible smile again, then, for reasons of his own, Tommy lapsed into a kind of stage cockney, "Down the nick," he grinned, eyes glittering. *Darn the nick.* "Down the bottom of Mill Street. That inspector down there, give him a bell, eh? Tinkle him and he'll see to it, right? Got an entire office up the Yard to deal with the petty restrictions of wartime: ration books, identity cards, rail warrants all that bumf. That Inspector – Turnbull. He'll see you right. Right?" Which was good coming from Tommy who, when in a hotel, was not above sending for provisions to be driven in from the Home Farm at Kingscote Grange, where his parents, the Earl and Countess of Kingscote, lived out their gilded country lives.

Tommy liked to disappear into characters of his own invention: west country folks who called you, 'my dove' or 'my robin'; Geordies who sprinkled their conversation with 'hinnies'; 'bottles of beer'; and 'why ayes'; and of course, the cheeky cockney sparrow they'd just heard. "Know what I mean?" He added now.

"Certainly, sir. Yes, sir." The manager backed away, adding that there was a nice rabbit stew for tonight, as though hint-

ing that Tommy Livermore would be served with the lion's
share of the rabbit which was a kind of mixed metaphor.

"Don't worry about that," Tommy called, a little loudly. "If
it's rabbits you need I'll have some sent over from my father's
farm. Just say the word." He turned towards Cathy and spoke
in almost a whisper, "Remind me to give Billy a bell. He can
call the farm and we'll have a consignment of dead bunnies
down here quicker than you can say 'twelve bore'."

Several people looked up from their food and scowled. The
word had already got out of course. Mrs 'Bunny' Bascombe
lay dead in her cellar and her husband, Bobby, the hero winner
of the VC would be coming home from the desert to bury her.
Not really done to joke about 'dead bunnies'.

Billy was Billy Mulligan, Tommy's executive sergeant, who
dealt with the business and office side of the Reserve Squad.
Like Brian, Billy had been familiar with the Kingscote estate
long before Tommy Livermore even considered becoming a
copper.

Lunch finally having been digested, with the aid of a cup of
filthy coffee, they walked back down Mill Street, Suzie and
Cathy pondering Tommy's pronunciation of 'darn' for 'down'
when he was in his cockney mode. "That was a real meal,"
Suzie said. *A reel meel*, one of Jack Warner's catch phrases, like
Mind my bike and *My bruvver Sid*.

Cathy grinned and said, "Very tasty, very sweet." Another
catch phrase, from a double act who spent their time talking
about food. Nan Kenway and Douglas Young: proper *à la carte*
they were.

"Chief?" Cathy said, a little loudly.

"That was me last time I looked," Tommy responded with
one of his charming smiles. From where Suzie was standing it
looked as though a flirtation was going on.

"Well, Chief," Cathy moved closer to him and Suzie bris-
tled. "That fellow Shepherd."

"Yes."

"He's from the Home Office isn't he?"

"Some kind of funny, yes." Tommy said.

"Well, don't know what he told you but he'd been down to have a look at the bodies."

"He did?"

"Yes, the local DS – Stimpson is it? Yes, Stimpson told me. He had some official pass and Stimpson let him have quite a long gander, Chief."

"Really, let's not let on that we know. Right?" Tommy flashed his smile. The terrible one.

"That was a character out of that Tommy Handley show wasn't it?" Tommy turned to address Suzie as they came to the big watermill, just past *The Shears* public house at the bottom of Mill Street.

"What character?" Suzie asked, bewildered at Tommy's sudden change of subject.

"Curry Shepherd. When he left us. Here, in the nick before we went to lunch."

She tried to strain her mind back a couple of hours. Curry Shepherd. The three of them with Shirley Cox after they had arrived back at the nick. Oh, yes, she recalled Curry leaving. "I go. I come back," he had said.

"Yes, Chief. Yes, he said that fellow's catch phrase. Yes, 'I go. I come back.' Fellow from ITMA."

It's That Man Again – ITMA – the country's all time favourite morale-boosting, must hear (Thursday evenings 8.30 pm BBC Home Service) radio show, far and away ahead of even the American *Jack Benny Show* now broadcast on Sunday lunchtimes. *ITMA's* endless fund of catch phrases were repeated by people in queues, shops, waiting rooms, school play grounds and offices, everyone buoyed up by the many comic asides the show engendered – "Mr. Handley!" as Miss Hotchkiss bore down on the infamous Minister of

Aggravation and Mysteries (at one time the Mayor of Foaming-in-the-Mouth); "I don't mind if I do, sir," from the bibulous Colonel Chinstrap; the cleaning lady, Mrs Mopp's "Can I do you now, sir?" and "I go. I come back." Ali Oop's exit line.

"Ali," said Suzie.

"Ali who?" asked Tommy.

"Oop," Suzie said.

"Of course," Tommy grinned. "After you, Claude." He quoted.

"That was Claude and Cecil." Suzie wondered if it was Tommy who was disturbing her. Why should it be? But he *was* changing. His attitude and manner altering. Why? No idea. She could read him like a book and if he'd stuck in his usual groove of not suffering fools gladly he would have gone off his chump over lunch. The manager of the Bear Hotel would normally have been blown out of his own dining room. Ten times out of ten Tommy detonated in the face of people behaving like idiots, or being what folk these days called 'Little Hitlers'. But not today. She heard his voice in her head, "Don't worry about it." Quite out of character – except when he was on a charm offensive. So, could it be Tommy who was causing her uncertain confidence?

They made their way into the Mill Street Police Station, heading straight for the office they were setting up as the Murder Room, Tommy calling out to the desk sergeant that they'd like to interview Colonel Weaving's sergeant if it wasn't too much bother. If the unstable anger was gone, Suzie thought, at least the sarcasm was alive and doing well.

Shirley was waiting for them looking pleased with herself, the office neat and orderly.

"Got yourself a billet, WDS Cox?" Tommy asked, walking around, moving things about.

"Very lucky, Chief. Yes."

"With the others at The Blue Boar, eh?"

"No, Chief. Private house."

"Really?" Tommy back on his normal form, expecting Shirley to volunteer information. "Private house, eh? Another police officer?"

"Matter of fact, yes, Chief. Inspector Turnbull, Chief. He has a kind of flat in his house. Offered it to me."

"Of course Sergeant Cox. Churlish to refuse, eh?"

"Quite, Chief." Shirley agreed, and Curry Shepherd came into the room without knocking and hardly opening the door; sidling noiselessly in as though wearing brothel creepers as Tommy remarked later.

"Ah, you come back." Tommy said now.

"What?" Curry smiled. A bit of a supercilious smile, Suzie thought, then realised that under her clothes she was blushing and that she couldn't keep her eyes off Curry.

No, she thought. No. This is stupid. Curry Shepherd cannot be causing me this sense of indecision. No. No. And she heard her long dead father singing, 'No! No! A thousand times no; I'd rather die than say yes.' Like he used to when they had family get-togethers around the piano.

Almost under his breath, Tommy began to sing the closing lines of the *ITMA* signature tune:

> *When there's trouble brewing,*
> *It's his doing,*
> *That man,*
> *That man again.*

With Cathy's help he had arranged a table with two chairs on one side and a single chair facing on the other.

"Thought we'd talk to the late Colonel Weaving's sergeant. 'One who found the bodies. Fancy that, Curry?"

Curry nodded. "Fine. Yes. Actually I've already had a few

words with him myself."

"Really?" Tommy sounded as though nothing in this world interested him less.

"Ali Oop," Suzie said, not meaning to say it aloud and immediately feeling like a Bateman cartoon with them all staring at her.

"Ali what?" Curry asked.

"Oop," she explained. "ITMA character. You said the catch phrase when you left. 'I go. I come back.'"

"Did I?" Curry looking blank.

"Needs to lie down in a darkened room," Tommy said, and the door opened again with the desk sergeant bringing in a short, blocky man with a tanned face, eyes that seemed out of proportion to the rest of him and a troublesome lock of hair that kept falling over his eyes, needed it cut off really.

"Sergeant Gibbon," said the desk sergeant.

Sergeant Gibbon was in uniform, the lion with blue wings on his left breast – glider pilot – the Pegasus airborne badge on his arm above his sergeant's stripes, below the parachute wings on his right shoulder, and his maroon beret sporting the Glider Pilot Regiment badge, the laurel wreath surrounding an eagle in flight and looking nasty enough to deserve its popular name of 'shite hawk'. Not that you saw it much out and about. The Glider Pilot Regiment was not what you might call highly visible. The sergeant dressed exactly as Lieutenant Colonel Weaving, apart from the rank badges.

"Come in, Gibbon," Tommy showing deference to a fighting man, standing up ushering him in. "Do sit down," indicating the chair opposite at the table. "You got a Christian name at all?"

"Yes, sir. Roy..."

"Well, sit down, Roy."

"...But people mostly call me 'Monkey'. Monkey Gibbon, sir, if you see..."

"Yes, very droll." Unsmiling: always a danger sign with Tommy.

Gibbon sat and the weak December light caught his face revealing him as a clear-eyed, hard-skinned man sitting silently, still, that watchful calm manner often present in good fighting men who have learned the art of remaining motionless for long periods, alert and listening.

Tommy said, "Must have been bad. Unpleasant."

"Most unpleasant, sir."

"What was most unpleasant?" Tommy showing he could be tricksy.

"Finding the Colonel and his lady, sir."

"Right. Go on." Then, almost to himself, "*His* lady?"

"How I found them, sir?"

"Good idea Sar'nt Gibbon."

"I was due to pick him up at six o'clock, sir. This morning, six a.m. Punctilious he is, sir. The Colonel. Most punctilious. He was, I mean, sir. The Colonel *was*."

"And you were there in good time?"

"I was there at a quarter to six, sir. When he didn't come down by six-fifteen I got out to investigate. Went up the steps and found the door ajar. Just loose, you know, sir. Open about half-an-inch. Maybe less."

"So you went in?"

"Pushed the door open and went in, sir, yes. I felt there was someone there so I called out. 'Colonel Weaving,' I called. Felt someone was upstairs and it didn't feel right. You know how it is, sir."

"No," Tommy said with some kind of finality.

"Well, you can be out in the field, or clearing a house and you get this kind of second sight. Makes you twitchy, taps into your nerves, like. I was carrying a weapon, here, sir," he swivelled slightly to reveal the holster on the left side of his webbing belt. Left side for the cross draw, lanyard attached to the butt going up and looped around his neck, under the lapels of his battledress blouse.

"So I drew my weapon and went up the stairs, slowly, making hardly any noise."

"How exactly do you manage that, Roy?"

"Training, sir. Rubber soles on the boots. It's the way you test each stair and transfer your weight to the riser. Takes practise. Sometimes the full foot, sometimes just the toe. Even an old staircase can be traversed without a creak if you're careful."

"And at the top?"

"I was wrong. There was nobody there. Upstairs anyway. I went through each room, as thought I was clearing it, ready at each door."

"Nice bathroom, isn't it?"

"Very nice, sir. Very tasteful. Victorian isn't it, sir?"

"The whole house is Victorian, yes."

Inwardly Suzie smiled, knowing the sergeant was taking Tommy for a bit of a ride. She got the impression that he knew the house pretty well: had been there before.

"Bathroom was the last room I did," Gibbon continued. "I was just coming out when I thought I heard a noise from downstairs. I was on that landing again like a thunderflash, convinced someone had been through the hall. And they had. The door, the front door, was open wide. I had almost closed it. But it was as though I could sense someone had passed through the hall and out of the door. You know, as though I'd seen them."

"You went after him?"

"I didn't say it was a him..."

"No, but..."

"It probably was, but I don't know how many. I don't see how one person..." he trailed off."

"Go on. You can't see how one person..."

"When I finally came across the bodies. I couldn't see how one person on his own could've... Well, could've..."

"Could have killed them?"

"Quite, sir."

"You were on the landing. You knew someone had left the house while you were up there: in the bathroom?"

"Yes, in the bathroom, sir."

"You went down. Went after them did you?"

Gibbon nodded, head down, shaking his head, then nodded. "Of course, sir. Of course I went down, went after him...them. Out into the street, onto the pavement but there was no sign of anyone. I walked down to the Royal Oak and out into the road. Crossed the road. Nobody. Either way there was nobody about."

"What was the time?"

"Must've been six-thirty, maybe a little after that. I can't say I looked. I went back. There'd been nobody else out in Portway. The whole place was deserted. I mean you could see a fair distance. Cold though: very chilly. It was dawn, sir."

"Coming up like thunder," Tommy mused. Then, "And you went back into the house?"

"Of course, sir. I did notice the door to the cellar, on the left hand side before you go down the passage to the study and the kitchen. That was open, that door."

"You didn't investigate?"

"Not straight away, no, sir. I went into their front room and the dining room, then down the passage, looked in the study and the kitchen. Even went into the larder. The kitchen table had been laid for breakfast. Must've done that the previous night, last night."

Tommy nodded.

"Then I went back and down the stairs to the cellar. I found them down there."

Suzie thought of the Colonel's head, like a bloodied loofah.

Thought of it and yet again. Closed her eyes to banish it from her head, but it stayed there.

"And then?" Tommy asked.

There was a pause and Sergeant Gibbon didn't look straight at anyone: looked down, then a glance to his left and right. A big intake of breath. "It shook me up, sir. Shook me up. I had to dash up the stairs again. Threw up in the downstairs toilet."

"You recognised your commanding officer then? Colonel Weaving?"

"Immediately."

"Even though he was lying on his face with the back of his head smashed in?"

"Immediately, sir."

"And you also recognised Mrs Bascombe? Emily Bascombe?"

"I did sir. Yes."

"You knew the lady well?"

"I knew her enough to recognise her. Yes."

"You knew she was engaged in an affair with your CO?"

"Oh, indeed, sir, yes I did."

"When had you last seen her?"

"Monday, sir. Monday 13th December, sir. When I brought the Colonel down and dropped him off. She asked me to come in for a cup of tea."

"Her actual words?"

"You want to come in for a cup of char, Monkey?' was what she said."

Tommy nodded. "How many people knew of the affair between Colonel Weaving and Mrs Bascombe?"

"I couldn't say, sir. I never discussed it with anybody else. It wasn't common knowledge, I'm sure. I never heard it off anyone else, except the odd jocular remark."

"Jocular remark?"

"Yes, sir. Like, 'The Colonel's fond of Wantage. He got a pusher there?"

"A pusher?"

"A young woman. A bint. A bit on the side."

"And how would you answer that?"

"I wouldn't sir. Like I said, it was jocular. I would never discuss it. Only with the Colonel."

"You had known him long? The Colonel?"

"About two-and-a-half years, sir. Since early '41. I was with him at the formation of No 2 Commando. We both did the course together at Achnacarry. Then we were both sent to the Central Landing School, Ringway. Did the parachute course together, then worked on the ground training course, formulated it. He was a Major then. There was Sarn't Mulford, Sarn't Alexander, and Sarn't Long – Pete Mulford, Pete Alexander and Chris Long. The officers were Major Weaving, Major Hutt – Shed, they call him, Shed Hutt – Captain Sharp, Wilson Sharp, and Captain Puxley, Bomber Puxley. We were all commando trained and had done the required jumps. We worked out what kind of course we should set up: training after the parachute course. Landed from the air, then fought on the ground. We worked out the best training. A lot of street fighting as I recall. A lot of section in defence and attack. A lot of working in pairs, map reading, navigating on the ground. Major Weaving was very antsy about the possibility of being dropped way off the LZ…"

"LZ?"

"Target. Landing Zone."

Tommy nodded and Sergeant Gibbon continued, "When he did the night jump, Major Weaving landed a mile or so away, in a pond. Didn't like that."

"Yes, I can see the danger…"

"It's all bloody dangerous, Guv'nor. They can shoot at you in the air and on the ground. It's dangerous coming down and dangerous when you get down."

"Yes, I understand, Sarn't. Unpleasant."

"Thinking about it's unpleasant. But, finding my boss and his lady like that. Well..." he shook his head once more and swallowed hard.

Eventually Tommy asked if these same, named, officers and NCOs were still together.

"Some of them, yes. We'd just got things set up for ground training when we were all – officers and NCOs – sent off to train as glider coxwains."

"Coxwains?"

"Original name – Glider Coxwains. Didn't last long. Glider pilots took over."

"So you did your training together, you and Colonel Weaving?"

"The lot, sir, yes. EFTS, then Glider Training and last of all the conversion to heavy gliders."

"And you were with him through it all?"

"Close as a sergeant can be to an officer, yes. When we were moved to Brize for him to take command of the Heavy Glider Conversion Unit I became his Orderly Room Sergeant. Then Sarn't Major Hardy arrived and took over the Orderly Room and I became his personal sergeant. Like his driver and bodyguard."

"A sort of unofficial post?"

"Not really. Colonel Weaving was the boss. He could appoint who he wanted. He got the people he wanted at Brize."

"Who?"

"The people he'd trained with. People whose measure he knew."

"Names."

"I already give them to you. Sarn't Mulford, Sarn't Alexander, and Sarn't Long. Officers are Major Hutt, Captain

Sharp and Captain Puxley. The Old Firm, the Colonel called it."

"And they're all at Brize Norton?"

"The lot, sir. Well Major Hutt's been on leave, so's Captain Puxley. I think Major Hutt's been called back – I telephoned the Orderly Room about an hour ago - and Captain Puxley's expected back tonight. I think that's how it stands. Oh, and there's Sarn't Major Hardy, Pearce Hardy. Bit of a nob, sir. They say he's an Honourable, like yourself, sir."

"You're well informed." Tommy reached for his cigarettes and Cathy leaned over to light one for him, using her lighter that she said some boyfriend had made for her. "*Turned it on a lathe,*" she'd said. Suzie wondered if he'd turned Cathy on a lathe as well.

"Anyone the Colonel didn't get on with? Among his officers and NCOs I mean."

"Absolutely not, sir. The kind of unit we had would eventually have to fight together – *will* eventually have to fight together. There's no room for petty squabbles or bits of resentment knocking around. No, we were a team and Lieutenant Colonel Weaving was the boss. We all obeyed him and worked with him. No rancour, no bitterness. I don't know about his private life, sir."

EVENTUALLY TOMMY FINISHED it up, told Suzie that he wanted her to make a thorough check on Tim Weaving's background, "Parents, siblings, mistresses, children, houses, guineapigs, the lot: the full calamity." Tommy smiling with the kind of smile you see on determined, but dead, people.

Sergeant Gibbon was heading straight back to Brize Norton and before he left, Tommy rang the aerodrome and let them know that he would expect to be there, and would like to interview the Glider Pilot Regiment training staff tomorrow. He spoke to Captain Sharp advising him that he would like to interview each of the officers and NCOs in turn, and learned they were expecting Major Hutt back later in the evening, and Captain Puxley before midnight. Tommy made a strange, knowing face and took the others off to the murder site, Dennis Free lugging his camera equipment with him. "Dinner at The Bear, Suzie. Seven-thirty on the dot." Eyebrows arched, "No need to dress." Then a throaty little laugh, kind of suggestive, but Tommy was always being suggestive.

Suzie huddled over one of the telephones, making notes and tracking down the numbers of half a dozen departments she needed to speak to at the War Office: people who would give her everything, she was assured, from Tim Weaving's shoe size to the state of his liver.

It had gone six o'clock when she was on her third call to find, yet again, that her quarry had already left for the day. She wrote a report on what she'd managed to get – mother and father still living, near Kingsbridge, beautiful Devon, close to wild Dartmoor (which they'd already known because Tommy had spoken to them after a local officer had broken the news). In her head, Suzie sang –

'When Adam and Eve were dispossessed in their garden up in heaven,
They planted another one out in the West,
'Twas Devon glorious Devon.'

Her dad had sung that when they holidayed on the west coast, and she didn't care if the words were right or not.

Weaving had another girlfriend, Annie Tooks, private income, flat in Knightsbridge; and yet another who sounded a bit of a tart, little flat near Shepherd's Market. Made a note of it, Julia Richardson. Siblings? One brother and one sister, Ralph and Dorcas. She had just signed the report, put it in an envelope and placed it on Tommy's desk when the door opened hesitantly and Curry Shepherd slid into the room.

"Suzie," he said, with that same charming somewhat scep-
tical manner that seemed, to Suzie, to be like an engaging stut-
ter of his personality. "You want to...to know about Tim
Weaving?" He had a grin, ear to ear and his eyes were lit up
like the proverbial Christmas tree, the little candles flickering
away in the bottomless grey of his irises.

"That's want Tommy wants," her heart was doing little
jerky fast beats and she was again blushing under her clothes
while she imagined her breathing was becoming too fast for
comfort. In her head she saw the Harvard aircraft she had seen
with Tommy, the one flying low over the Market Square on
that cloudless sunny Sunday afternoon.

"Well, old horse, come hither because what I don't know
about Timothy Arthur Weaving ain't worth knowing. Fancy a
jar of something, where we can talk in comfort...er...heart, as
Tommy would say?"

"Well, a crystal goblet's more in my line, Curry."

"Mine as well and I know a nice little place where we won't
be disturbed."

Chapter Six

HE CAME UP from the underground and marched into the gloomy confines of Paddington Station. Marched was the correct word. When he was in uniform he moved smartly, shoulders square, spine straight, looking every inch a man with pride and confidence, oblivious to the filth hanging everywhere.

Even the air smelled dirty, full of grit and soot while the drabness seemed to transfer itself to the people all around: the soldiers, sailors and airmen, the elderly porters and officials of the Great Western Railway who ran the place. Then there were the civilians with their bloodless faces. Lord how he hated them all. The soldiers in their rough uniforms, sometimes dazed or drunk, rifles slung on their shoulders, going on, or returning from, leave or to a new posting. Tired.

To Sadler these men were civilians dressed up as soldiers, not the real thing, and how they had run from the Panzers in 1940: the Panzers and the Stukas who played their efficient game of leapfrog across France, Belgium and the Low Countries in that glorious early summer.

Now he saw others, the sailors with their neat little suitcases, wearing their square rig uniforms with the sailor caps that used to proudly bear the name of the ship in which they served, now reduced to a dull gold simple *HMS*. And the civilians? All looked fatigued beyond their limits, their faces greyed out, as though they were auditioning for the part of a corpse. Blind leading blind, he thought.

As he moved steadily towards the noisy public bar on the main concourse, Sadler cursed and fought a battle deep inside himself. Why in heaven's name had he taken such a risk? Two dead and the police climbing all over Wantage. What on earth had possessed him? A kind of bravado? The need to share what he was doing with others?

The killing didn't worry him, except for a few nasty

moments with the woman. Possibly it was the need to show off, to declare himself to Linnet? After all he couldn't possibly have done it without Linnet. His friends in Occupied Europe didn't know about Linnet because when he first suggested it – in an encrypted signal – they slapped him down.

If I find a suitable recruit, who could assist in my work, have I the right to use him without reference to you? The answer came back, volleyed on the return: *On no account recruit anybody. Trying to recruit would put your own status at grave risk.*

And now what was the result? Two lives for nothing. The woman knew nothing and the man, Tim Weaving, was brave. Yes, everybody cracks in the end, but you require more sophisticated methods than either of them had to hand. In the end what had he got? The code name of the operation. *Overlord*, which they almost certainly knew already; and the fact that airborne troops would take part, several thousand airborne troops. By parachute and glider. For God's sake, the OKW (High Command of the Armed Forces) would be thick as glue if they didn't know that already. After all they had led the way, and demonstrated it in May 1940, at the 'impregnable' Belgian strategic fortress Eben Emael, together with the three major bridges across the River Meuse; as well as in Holland. Then again in May '41 when they captured Crete using only airborne forces.

The last little obvious piece of information he had ripped out of Weaving was that the *Overlord* plans also contained a vast deception operation, crammed with strategic and tactical moves of misdirection. But on all these points there was no detail: no collateral; nothing to back up the bare flimsy information.

He sighed, pushing his anger away; aware of the stupid mistake, but forced to go on.

They always sent a different courier. Sadler used to be amazed that there were so many women in England who supported the Nazi cause: the women were all British, ghosts like himself. Then he realised, quite quickly, that they supported no Nazi cause, they did it for pin money and had no idea what it was about. He also saw they were all friends of Julia's, and Julia thought she was working for the Swedes anyway.

Odd about Julia because it was through Tim Weaving that he had first met her. "Smashing girl," Tim had said. "Must take you to meet her she's a really splendid popsie. Not a tart mind you: nice girl, good girl. Only does it for friends. Has no enemies, eh? I'm engaged to her actually," and he laughed like a drain, and in many ways she was a good girl, good family, top drawer, good clothes, spoke beautifully, had this wizard flat, wonderful taste, never wanted for anything. You could take her anywhere.

To keep him operational the Abwehr wanted him to believe they had a considerable supporting cast floating around him, to make him more confident, keep him happy. First there was the way in which contact was made: not as secure as he would like, a FLAXman telephone number: Julia's number. The first time it had been Julia herself and after that he saw her occasionally, just for a spot of the usual. Then he was told to meet in a certain place, and abide by rituals and safety precautions, like those ordered for tonight.

The rule was to meet in a crowded place, as now in the humming main bar on the concourse at Paddington Station, noisy and brash, stinking of beer and deep within a cumulous of grey, choking cigarette smoke, a lot of uniforms interspersed with homeward bound shuttlers from as far away as Reading or Oxford grabbing a fast drink before doing the return journey to their chosen provincial bolt hole; terrified of the night.

And there she was, perky little hat, dark coat designed and made by someone with more than a passing knowledge of military tailoring; black leather bag on the small table, blue paper packet of Players cigarettes angled precisely against the ashtray next to a copy of the *Evening News*, and the leather gloves poking from the open bag, the sign that it was safe to approach. He also had a copy of the *Evening News*, folded and held in the right hand, while she smoked cautiously, holding the cigarette between neatly manicured fingers, the nails a startling crimson, the rings precise, in particular the intricate gold Greek puzzle ring on the little finger of her left hand – the final identification.

Folded inside his copy of the *Evening News* was an envelope with the information neatly typed in a series of coded groups.

He had been told to call her Dorothy, which he did now, sweeping down on her and planting a kiss, flamboyantly continental, on each cheek. "Darling," she said quietly. "How lovely. Thought you'd never get here."

"Usual," he grinned. "Bloody train was late, but I've got the whole weekend."

"Isn't that marvellous. You said so on the phone."

"Darling," he said and they locked eyes as he slid his copy of the *Evening News* on top of her's, ready to make the switch now that they'd recited the coded passwords.

"Want to stay here or go on to the hotel?" he asked, and she started to gather up her things, including his newspaper.

The information would go to Julia and from her to the Swedish Embassy. From there it would pass to a particular person in the Defence Ministry at Stockholm. From Stockholm the coded groups would be sent swiftly to Hamburg and Berlin. Much good would it do them.

CURRY SHEPHERD HAD a car. It was parked round the corner from the nick in Mill Street, an expensive, dull green Vauxhall Ten. "The wonderful thing is I can get as much petrol as I want," he told her, handing her into the front passenger seat.

They drove out along the Oxford road to what he said was a roadhouse called The Noah's Ark. In her imagination Suzie pictured a roadhouse as being somewhere glamorous, smelling sweetly of sin and illicit whatever: the scent of wickedness. Roadhouses, often referred to in B Pictures from Hollywood, conjured up all kinds of immorality that made her blush again under her clothes and wish she could, perhaps, settle the indecision she felt about Tommy Livermore.

He drove for about another mile and she asked him, "So, what do you do in the real world, Curry?"

"I do exactly what I told Tommy. I go between spies and spies and spy-catchers."

"You honestly do that work? You're a kind of spy?" Surprised.

"Oh, indubitably." He put on the sing-song voice of the actor Robertson Hare who used expressions like that to great comic effect. *Oh yes. Indubitably. Oh yes. Oh dear. Oh my, yes.* Made you smile even to think of it.

"And how do you qualify for a job like that?"

"The same way your average big footed copper qualifies for being in the Branch." He meant Special Branch which used to be called the Irish Branch – the mailed fist of MI5 as someone once called it. "I joined up and got posted to Military Intelligence."

"Just like that?"

"No. I'd been in the Corps at school," he meant the Officers Training Corps, which, at the advent of war, was renamed the more classless Cadet Corps. "Went in and they immediately started to make me an officer."

He had done a couple of months basic training – as they called it – then started his officer training. "A lot of that was square bashing. Square bashing, and a bit of arms training: the rifle, the Bren, the Sten, two inch and three inch mortars, hand guns – Smith & Wesson .38s, Browning .9mm, and the big Colt .45s; the old heavy machine guns, the elderly, water-cooled Vickers gun, the Lewis gun, grenades, rifle launched

grenades, then the PIAT (an acronym for the weapon's targets: Projectile, Infantry, Anti-Tank). Platoon in defence and
attack; map reading; on, on, on, kill, kill, kill. "They made us
recite that like doggerel."

Curry began to giggle then chuckle.

"Was it that funny?" Suzie asked, a trifle disturbed by the
sudden levity.

"On the parade ground we had a Brigade of Guards Sarn't
Major," Another giggle. "Had a chip on his shoulder: inferior-
ity complex, wanted to be better than us prospective officers.
Bit like Tommy."

Suzie's ears pricked up but she said nothing.

"He hadn't had the most exhaustive education, the sarn't
major, but he'd put himself through an English Language
course at night school. Thought it was a degree." Yet another
giggle. "Used to say things like, 'What you think I am lad?
The Akond of bloody Swat?' I thought that was hilarious. The
Akond of bloody Swat."

Suzie giggled. Paused. "What did you mean about Tommy?"

"Tommy getting passed over... You knew that, surely?"

"No," she said in a little voice and in the darkness Curry
glanced towards her.

"Oh lord," he said. "I'm sorry. You close to Tommy, then?"

"I suppose you could say that."

"Oh, bugger. Sorry." Another pause. He told her that he
was commissioned in the Intelligence Corps, then went on a
round of courses. "Enemy documents; photographic interpre-
tation; surveillance." Then a stint with MI5. "When they were
housed in Wormwood Scrubs. Bloody funny. The 72 bus con-
ductor used to sing out, 'All change for MI5'. Then, in 1940 I
went onto General Brooke's staff, Corps Intelligence Officer."

"What d'you mean about Tommy being turned down for a
commission?"

"You don't want to know."

"I think I do," almost physically feeling her ambivalence to Tommy.

Curry pulled the car over and stopped.

They had arrived – he put on the hand brake – a lowering dark barn-like building just off the main road. "All change for the Noah's Ark," Curry mumbled.

"I think I do need to know," she repeated.

"How long you known him?"

"Tommy? 1940. Late 1940."

"At his most vulnerable then. Desperately wanted MI5. Thought he had all the right attributes."

"And he was turned down? Tommy? MI5?" Incredulous.

"Let's go and have that drink."

"No. Tell me this. I think I need to know."

"It's changing room gossip, Suzie. Christ, I wasn't even in the UK then. I was scurrying around in Belgium and France trying to work my passage out of Occupied Europe…"

"But when you got back?"

"Yes, it was the talk of the town. Churchill, hot as hell and slashing his way through Whitehall, booted General Kell out of MI5."

"Who?"

"Vernon Kell, captain in the Staffordshire Regiment, put in charge of MO5 – as it was – in 1910. Architect of MI5 as we know it today. Routed out the Kaiser's spies in the '14-'18 war, plagued the Communist Party of Great Britain, IRA, British Union of Fascists and a number of half-brained subversive organisations through the '20s and '30s. Built up MI5 from two people to what it is now. So, Vernon Kell, legendary head of MI5 – General Kell as he had become – leader of the Security Service over three decades got the order of the boot. Winston sacked him, and they say it just about destroyed him, the General. Problem was that the PM didn't get on with Kell, and Kell, like a lot of people, didn't trust Winston. Anyway

MI5 didn't have a happy year – they thought the sinking of the Royal Oak in Scapa Flow in October '39 was an act of sabotage. That led them on a wild goose chase. And there was the explosion at Waltham Abbey – Royal Gunpowder Factory. So, Winston had Kell up in his room at the Admiralty, read him the riot act and chucked him out. Died last year. Friends and allies say he was broken-hearted and it was down to the PM."

"So?"

"So, Tommy's father's a friend of Winston's. Jimmy Livermore, Second Earl of Kingscote thick as thieves with the PM. Tommy wanted to be the big white chief of MI5, just as he wanted a military commission that he thought would go with the job. Believed he had all the qualities of a security Panjandrum. Knew it all. Tommy can be pretty much a vain bugger when he wants to be: very sure of his own view; always believes he's right." Another pause, three beats. "Bit like Chamberlain really."

Suzie found herself nodding in agreement in the dark – one of Tommy's unlovable traits.

"Any old how, Kingscote the elder began to pull strings and eventually the PM saw Tommy; heard him out; then told him there was no way he would appoint him as MI5's big cheese. Said Tommy was too visible – Dandy Tom: all that stuff in the papers. 'You catch murderers not spies, and you do it with a lot of – what's the American word? – You do it with a lot of razzmatazz: personality stuff: publicity in the newspapers.' Winston's supposed to have said. 'No! No! Tommy, sorry but you're not the right material for clandestine spy catching.' Made him look a bit of a fool because old Tommy had been shouting his mouth off in the sacred corridors of New Scotland Yard – 'You're going to have to get yourselves a new boy with my talents because I'll be a secret squirrel soon enough.'"

"Yes, let's go and have a drink," Suzie thought she'd heard enough and Curry didn't demur. Got out, handed her from the car and held on to her elbow, like a real gent, guiding her to the entrance.

The only thing illicit at the Noah's Ark was possibly the bottles of whisky and gin. Otherwise it was rather ordinary with Christmas lights stretched around the bar, a waiter who needed a better suit, and a five-piece orchestra sawing away. Suzie was an expert in that kind of music, three strings, a piano and drums, like Mummy used to enjoy at Benthalls. She liked the Christmas lights as they were a relatively new thing. Suzie thought about her childhood and what a risk they ran with the little lighted candles on the tree in the hall.

"What about something to eat? Curry offered, and Suzie said she was supposed to be dining with Tommy and the others at The Bear. "It'll be better here," Curry told her, his right hand in the small of her back, making her glow like a flarepath.

"Maybe I should ring him," she looked up at Curry realising she was being what her mother would call a *coquette*, but Mummy was given to little French words and phrases.

"Maybe you should." Curry smiled. "But don't use me as an excuse. Tell him your great uncle's turned up from Birmingham."

"How did you know I had a great uncle in Birmingham?" Genuinely surprised.

"It's my job." A nod to the waiter who was leading them towards a table. "My stock in trade, you might say."

"Of course it is." Suzie turned and looked the waiter in the eye. "You got a public telephone I can use?" Flashing a radiant smile.

The waiter, in his threadbare grey suit, looking almost as old as the itch, led her to an alcove where she shuffled through her handbag for coins, retrieved her notebook with The Bear's number in it. Dialled and finally got Tommy.

"Where are you, heart?" he asked, and in her head she saw his brow furrow. "Been waiting ten minutes."

"Listen Tommy, there's been a development. My uncle Rupert's turned up."

"Where?"

"Here. Wantage. Insists I have a meal with him. I think he knew one of our victims. He's going to take me out to a place he knows. Got a car and a petrol ration."

In The Bear Hotel, some ten miles away Tommy Livermore coughed then said he'd been looking forward to seeing her. "You know we're doing Brize Norton tomorrow? Leaving before dawn. Well, nine o'clock. Got all the boys and girls champing at the bit, heart. Get in touch when you're back in the hotel." He was irritated, she could tell. Irritated and possibly being overheard.

"I may be late, Tommy. But I'll be at breakfast. I promise."

He sounded reluctant but finally let her go, saying they'd a lot to talk about tomorrow.

Suzie returned to Curry Shepherd and their table near the small string orchestra, going through their repertoire of gems from Gilbert & Sullivan, 'The Maid of the Mountains' and 'Chu Chin Chow', with a couple of popular foxtrots thrown in for good measure: 'Moonlight Becomes You', 'Don't Sit Under the Apple Tree', and 'I Couldn't Sleep a Wink Last Night' played alarmingly slowly.

The waiter stood facing the wall trying to get the cork out of a bottle with a penknife.

"He buy it?" Curry asked.

"Me?" Suzie said, "I could sell ice cream to the Eskimos."

He had ordered – "Actually there wasn't much of a choice, you either had the rabbit pie or the rabbit pie. He told me it was very good, local delicacy. Oh, and there's some kind of soup for starters. Veg I think he said. Or it could have been hedge. Hearing, you know. All those bombs and all that." Touching his right ear. "Mutt and Jeff," he said.

"Yes, I know."

"And I know you know," another grin. "Several bad nights during the Blitz, I gather."

"Don't talk about it," the smile going out of her eyes.

"One in particular," he persisted. "One when you were a tethered goat while the bombs dropped. A tethered goat that Tommy staked out to catch a murderous loony."

"I told him my uncle Rupert had turned up," changing the subject, seeing pictures in her head: that dreadful night just after Christmas 1940 when Tommy had put her in great danger, then took all the credit for capturing a multiple killer.

"But your uncle's not Rupert, he's Charles."

"Mmm." She agreed, nodding, letting him know she was building a little web of lies. "Tommy's met Charles so you never know..." A shade surprised that Curry really did know about uncle Charles.

The soup arrived smelling good, chicken with a lot of herbs and carrots in it.

"You're a bit like Tommy, aren't you? Know how to give a girl a good time. His speciality was the Ritz."

"It's the education, you know," Curry picked up his spoon. "We did restaurants and wines in the Lower Sixth. Chat-up lines in the Fifth."

The soup was good. And hot. After a moment she asked if he was really concerned about Colonel Weaving and, "...what was it..?"

"COSSAC. And yes. Yes. You see I knew Tim Weaving. Knew him quite well."

SADLER FOLLOWED THE girl he called Dorothy. Put her in a cab and luckily picked up another just afterwards. Great luck because there were a lot of Americans around who easily snaffled taxis in London.

Sadler was relieved to find there were no surprises. Her cab went through Shepherd Street and dropped her off near the corner. He paid off his cab and walked through, eyes adjusting to the dark. He stood back and watched her ring Julia's bell, saw the thin stream of light as she was let in.

He walked back, at ease now in the blackness, keeping off the main streets until he reached Piccadilly, crossed over and just missed being mown down by a grey double-decker bus looming out of the dark. Sadler jumped and it missed him, leaving him on the other pavement trembling with fear. He hated the dark.

Eventually he found himself in St James's Square, looking across the central garden with its bare trees just seeing the red brick Norfolk House. Thinking that's where I have to be; that's where I need to be, inside COSSAC, clear the board of all their plans for their wretched *Overlord*, and save Europe for the Führer.

A Humber staff car pulled up in front and a woman driver went in, returning a few minutes later with two senior officers who got into the back. Before she restarted the engine, Sadler heard the officers laughing and wondered what they could find so amusing.

As he walked away he thought that now he must use all his energy to infiltrate COSSAC. Do the job they'd sent him to do. Whatever it meant.

THEY HAD FINISHED the meal and now leaned forward, better to hear one another over the studiously picked out melodies of the Famous Five as they had dubbed the orchestra. Suzie heard the words in her head, and tried to blot them out:

Dearly beloved how clearly I see,
Somewhere in heaven you were fashioned for me.
Angel eyes knew you,
Angel voices singing to you…

"So, how well did you know him, Curry?"

"I vetted him. Made sure he was clean for COSSAC. Went back into his life."

"And what did you find?"

"Lovely fellow; grammar school boy made good. Sandhurst. Career soldier. Commissioned in the Royal Warwickshire Regiment. Good leader of men; knew about disposition of troops in the field. First class officer. MC during the battle of France. Got his majority soon after the Warwickshires remustered after Dunkirk. Then he volunteered for everything going: commando training, then all the dangerous stuff, parachute, glider, the whole business."

"Paragon," said Suzie. "Must've had something wrong: Achilles Heel?" she thought, they've got me talking their lingo now: all quick bursts of information.

Curry nodded. "Achilles Heel," nodded again. "A whole Achilles Foot as it happens. You know what his problem was. Saw it yesterday."

"A woman? Emily Bascombe?"

"Women. *Women beware women.*"

"What?"

"Name of a play, Suzie. Webster I think. Someone soon after Shakespeare. We did him at school as well. Knew a fellow once..."

"Knew a fellow once, what?"

"Knew a fellow once who said you should read *Hamlet* every few weeks. Thought it had everything in it. Good as the Bible, this bloke used to say."

"Really? And Colonel Tim Weaving had the itch?"

Curry nodded. "And scratched it regularly. Had several of them at one time but seemed to settle on this one. On your Emily. Knew it was trouble, he did. Spouted a lot of stuff about love..."

"But you okayed him? For the vetting? For COSSAC?"

"Of course. He was okay unless some female spy seduced

him, and that wasn't likely with me keeping an eye out. Most unlikely as the Abwehr doesn't seem to know about selecting its spies. They're all pretty duff. I should say *seemed* pretty duff."

"Things've changed?"

"They've been like bloody Laurel and Hardy up to now. As fast as they came in we picked 'em up. We had one guy walked into a railway station and asked where he was, and another, in Ireland, who asked what time the next train was due when there hadn't been a train for thirteen years. You get complacent when that happens a few times."

The orchestra did a flourish, then a hesitant segue into 'It's a Lovely Day Tomorrow'. Suzie winced.

"They've been amazingly cooperative. Faced with death or a quiet life being played back they don't choose death. We're playing back all but two of them. That's the trouble I suppose. Straws in the wind."

"Straws in the wind?" Suzie repeated.

"We've had a few pointers. Picked up some clues that they're running someone who's aimed straight at COSSAC and the invasion plans. Christ, Suzie, I shouldn't even mention this to you, but you saw Weaving and his girlfriend. They'd been through the wringer, been tortured. Someone was trying to extract information from them – at least from Weaving. Whoever did it either got what they wanted or went too far, killed him by accident and had to wipe out Emily Bascombe because she knew too much. This is urgent, Suzie. Very urgent, with a capital Urge because time is shrinking."

"How urgent is a capital Urge?"

"Work it out – less than two weeks to Christmas, which means two and a bit weeks to the New Year which is when we expect an announcement about the Supreme Allied Commander. When that's out of the bag the invasion plan'll be almost set in stone and there'll be those who will want to reorganise it, make changes, argue over it. I mean if Monty's involved – and he has to be one way or another – he'll want to alter the whole shooting match just on principle. There'll only be a handful of weeks to bed it all down and decide on the date – May or June by my reckoning. It's getting bloody close, and if they *have* got someone on the loose, and if he gets into COSSAC... well, there's the element of surprise up the spout: might as well not go at all. I mean we'll be right up the Swannee."

"Then why're you telling *me* all this?"

Curry gave a wide smile, engulfing her. She thought he looked so much younger when he smiled, and he seemed to know exactly what she was thinking. "You surely knew my people wanted you moved?" he said, heavy on the incredulity.

"Moved. Where moved?" she was almost angry.

Curry spoke low. "We did. We wanted you. They also wanted to give you the George Medal, after that business in '40, but Tommy Livermore wouldn't hear of it."

Suzie's jaw drooped. Just before she had been co-opted onto Tommy's Reserve Squad, in 1940, she had learned that a team of senior officers, Tommy included, had put her on a list of young female officers set aside for special grooming and responsibility. They were, they said, 'looking to the future', to a time when women police officers would automatically have bigger accountability, play a greater role, within the Metropolitan police force when, at that time they were regarded as simply secretaries, or women to run errands for more senior officers. On Suzie's first posting to a busy CID team her senior officer had asked her, "How d'you make a good cup of tea, Sergeant?"

"Tommy blocked the George Medal? They were going to..?"

"Said he didn't want you to get above yourself. Also said that, while demanding a certain amount of courage, the incident was in your normal line of duty. That's absolutely true. I saw the papers myself."

"Normal line of duty?" voice rising so that Curry put his hand across the table and took hold of her wrist to quieten her. "Have you any idea what I did, Curry?"

He nodded, knowing that she'd been set up as a target for a psychotic killer who had almost strangled her. It had been in all the papers.

"I was in hospital for almost two weeks. Couldn't talk properly for three."

"He did say that you showed great pluck."

"You sure that was the word he used. Curry? He was sleeping with me...that was his problem. Moved in with me. Probably thought I'd wear the gong on my nightie and it would get in the way."

"Sush," he stroked her hand and smiled at her as though she was a small child who could only understand simple things.

"I'll pluck him," she said, her mouth twisting. And the orchestra came to the end of 'It's a Lovely Day Tomorrow'. "I'll pluck him alright."

The orchestra was taking a welcome break and the players glanced in Suzie's direction as they left the podium, the drummer giving a little end-of-set riffle on his snare drum.

"Suzie," Curry in his calming voice. "Suzie, don't go off at half cock."

"I'll make bloody certain that he never goes off at bloody half cock ever again."

"Suzie."

"I can hardly believe it. The bastard."

"Suzie, it's true. But there's no point in having a big set-to about it..."

"Why not?"

"Because I'm not supposed to know, and you can't say where you heard it. For one thing..."

"Oh, you bloody public school boys are all the same. Why don't you just drive me straight back to Wantage and I'll resign from his bloody Reserve Squad. Resign from the Met."

"There's no need for you to do that. No need for you to resign. We can simply have you transferred. My boss'll welcome you with the proverbial open arms."

"Who's the 'we' in 'we can simply have you transferred'?"

"War Office Intelligence Liaison. Couple of dingy offices near Baker Street tube station. Plenty of dust and the odd popping gas fire – the usual appurtenances of people in the spy trade."

"I wouldn't be brought over just to clean and make the coffee?" her hand raised in warning.

"You'd be out in the field. May even be dangerous."

She frowned, then nodded. "Give me a couple of days. I'd like to pick my time for leaving. Stage the dramatic walk out. Know what I mean?"

"I know exactly what you mean," said Curry Shepherd with a grin.

They drove back in silence until they got into Grove Street where he stopped the car out of sight from The Bear across the Market Square. Feeling very daring, Suzie reached up and kissed Curry on the cheek, just a swift peck during which she wondered what the real thing would be like.

She crossed the Square and let herself into the hotel; picked up her key then went over the cobbles to climb the narrow stairway leading to the Coffee Room, preparing to negotiate the tables and get into the corridor leading to her room. She reached the top, blinked and took one step forward when someone moved in the blackness ahead.

"Who's there?" she asked, loud enough to sound like the voice of authority.

"Oh, Skip. Thank heaven it's you." Shirley Cox was beside her.

"What the hell?"

"I had to come over with a report from Ron and Laura. Delivered it to the Chief, but I've hung on hoping to see you. I tried your door..."

"What is it, Shirley?"

"Just thought you'd like to know. The Chief's in his room alright, but he's not on his tod. She's in here. Cathy Wimereux, our gallant new sergeant. Very cosy it looked."

Chapter Seven

"NICE TIME WITH Charles?" Tommy stayed behind his newspaper, one hand on the toast rack, the remains of his bacon and tomato pushed to one side. Suzie always reckoned Tommy as a messy eater, particularly when there was Worcester sauce around. The paper's headlines were divided, the main story, taking up half the front page, concerned General Henry (Hap) Arnold of the 8th US Army Air Force declaring that they were almost ready to start a 24-hour 360-degree bombing campaign on Germany, from North, South, East and West. He had said, "We're going to hit them every day, and the RAF's going to do it every night." The other story was confirmation that Field Marshal Rommel had been appointed C-in-C of 'Fortress Europe'.

"Charles who?" Suzie asked, pulling up a chair: sitting.

Tommy put the paper down and helped himself to another slice of toast. He didn't look at Suzie. "Your uncle Charles. Dinner with him last night, didn't you say?"

A waitress in a full length wraparound apron poured coffee for Suzie.

"No. I told you I was having dinner with my uncle Rupert."

"Who's he? Don't know him. Never heard of him, heart." Still did it without looking.

"He's my great uncle on my mother's side."

"Ah." Exaggerating the nod. "I spoke to the ma last night."

"Oh, shit," Suzie, brought up by Anglican nuns, thought.

"*My* ma, that is."

Sigh of relief.

"All very smart, she'd been with Pa to have tea with Mr and Mrs King. Buck House and all that crap, eh?"

This time *she nodded*. He still wasn't looking at her. At one point the Countess of Kingscote, Tommy's ma – once described as overbearing as a land mine – had been a lady-in-waiting to the Queen so afternoon teas, or lunches, at Buckingham Palace were regular occurrences which Tommy loathed.

"Loads of gossip," he said. "Talk of an arranged marriage between Princess Elizabeth and Philip of Greece, but the best is that they're very worried about the balcony. Structurally unsafe so it's being strengthened with concrete because they want to use it when celebrating the victory. A jot presumptuous I thought. Lot of dying to be done before that day."

"Lot of gongs to be won as well," it was out before Suzie could stop herself. Oh shit she thought again and was sure that Tommy stiffened without looking at her.

"Yes, heart. Yes, I suppose so. How was it at the Noah's Ark? Any good at all?"

So he knew. "You have your spies everywhere," she said.

"Just like you, heart. Everywhere from what I hear."

Oh, very comical, yes. She was saved from answering by Cathy Wimereux sliding into the seat next to Tommy and giving a breathless "Good morning," throaty but underplayed and leaving Suzie in no doubt about what had been going on while she had been with Curry.

Cathy wore a biscuit coloured skirt with a jacket top – the latest Utility design with a bit of light blue piping round the lapels. Her old gold hair had a sheen to it, smooth as bloody silk, Suzie thought. Like that bloody complexion, sodding peaches and cream.

"Right," Tommy pushed his chair back. "In the Murder Room at nine sharp." Stood up. "I'll be briefing the Squad on what today's going to be all about, if you'd care to be there Susannah."

He looked at Suzie for the first time that morning and she saw the glint of anger in his eyes. Like a death ray, she thought. Like a death ray that you'd read about in kids comics. But she couldn't define whether the hatred was for her or himself. It had been a long time since she'd seen a kids' comic: back when she was living at home and her brother James was there in the school holidays. Now James had followed his uncle Vernon Fox's lead and was at the Royal Marine Depot, Deal – a Y-Scheme candidate, potential officer.

Tommy turned, squared his shoulders and strode towards the restaurant doors, back straight yet somehow different: a view of him she never remembered seeing before, a stiffness of gait, the angry way he cocked and held his head.

In the thirty seconds or so that it took him to reach the doors, Suzie's mind was peppered with a collage of images from her recent past with Tommy Livermore: the first meeting, then the first dinner they'd had in The Ritz when he told her that she was on a list of women earmarked for promotion against the future; their first kiss, the delicious love they'd shared; the secret things, hiding it all from other people; the moment he had made her a woman, had taught her the arcane language and physical tricks of love; his body; the delicious feeling of being in thrall to him; the devotion she had felt; the long days of immense summer pleasure and the short days of winter bleakness as he had started to let his true self show from inside the carapace that was his reality together with his extraordinary vulgarity.

Inside, Suzie reeled as if she had been punched in the face. For a long time she had been trying to find a way of finishing it, but now that it had happened all she felt was anger. She turned her head, glaring at Cathy Wimereux. She still had Tommy's last words echoing in her ears: "In the Murder Room at nine sharp. I'll be briefing the squad on what today's going to be all about, if you'd care to be there Susannah."

"Well Cathy," knowing that there were tears forming in her eyes Suzie bit her lip. "Well, did he debrief you last night?"

"Suzie…I…I…"

"Don't bother," she spat out quietly. "I've only been living with him for the past three years. You're welcome to him," and she rose from the table and stalked out, thinking this was all a bit adolescent. Like people in their teens when it was almost a matter of life or death to know who loved whom, who was out and who was in.

Last year Tommy, in one of his amazingly gentle moments had written another poem for her, left it under her pillow:

> *You wonder in the night,*
> *How much I care and why,*
> *You wonder if it's big or slight,*
> *You probe and gouge with silent cry*
> *Not realising that you've become*
> *My day, my night,*
> *My everyone.*

She thought of that now, and the dozens of other little fractured poems he'd written for her, to her. Head down she thumped out of the restaurant, almost flat-footed, and bumped straight into Curry Shepherd, obviously on a recce, searching for her.

"Whoa!" Curry put his hands on her shoulders. "Whatever's the matter, Suzie? Seen a ghost?"

Her lip trembled, then she steadied herself and took control again. "No, but Tommy…Well, I don't know if it was him or me…but…"

"Come and sit down," he edged her towards one of the tables out in the Coffee Room and before she knew it, she was seated and the waiter, the omnipresent Harris, was bending over the table, "Madam didn't have any coffee. Shall I get one of the girls to serve it here?"

"Yes, please" Curry made a gesture to indicate the sooner the better.

"That waiter gives me the twitch," Suzie fumbled for her

cigarettes. Curry leaned over and lit one for her.

"So what's up?"

"I think Tommy spent the night with our new sergeant – Cathy Wimereux. Not that it matters," she spoke low, almost a whisper, a catch in her throat. "But he knew where I was last night, so presumably he knows we were together, and..."

"It doesn't matter."

"I think I should be the judge of what matters..." Sharp, sounding confrontational when she didn't mean to be.

"Suzie, Tommy received this at around six o'clock this morning," Curry opened his dispatch case, that looked like the one Suzie had used to carry her music to school, and passed an official-looking sheet of notepaper to her just as one of the waitresses set a small pot of coffee on the table and asked for her room number.

Suzie mumbled the number and took the paper from Curry.

"It was brought down by despatch rider and they had to wake him up. I gather he didn't take too kindly to that."

"Not at his best first thing," Suzie gave what she supposed was a brave little smile, then started to read the paper he'd handed to her.

```
TO: Detective Chief Superintendent
Tommy Livermore.
FROM: Commissioner Metropolitan Police,
New Scotland Yard.
DATE: 16th December 1943
RE: Woman Detective Sergeant Susannah
Mary Mountford.

With effect immediately the above named
officer will be transferred from the
Reserve Squad to special duties War
```

```
Office Intelligence Liaison Group. She
will still be allowed all privileges
within the Reserve Squad such as infor-
mation concerning cases under consider-
ation of the Squad, attendance at
briefings, special instructions, inves-
tigations etc.
Also, effective today, Woman Detective
Sergeant Mountford is promoted to Woman
Detective Inspector.
```

The signature was scrawled at the bottom of the order, plus a few words neatly written in distinctive green ink. *Tommy*, it read, *this is a significant move and promotion aimed at putting the Met in a very favourable light in backing up the Military. I am sure you will be as pleased as we are that DI Mountford has made great strides, leading her to such an important posting. She will, I know, be a credit to the Met.*

Suzie mumbled again and gasped. "WDI? Woman Detective Inspector?…"

"I have the promulgation of your promotion here," Curry slid a sealed envelope across the table. It was addressed to DI Susannah Mountford and was thick, bulky and with that weighty feel that, in spite of paper shortages, was still a characteristic of officialdom.

"Tommy knew all this before…?"

"Before you saw him, yes. We'll go to his briefing and follow things up, keeping a watching brief on whatever happens today."

"But who am I responsible to?…I…"

"To me in the first instance. Finally to Colonel Partridge, the boss of WOIL. I hope to take you up to meet him later on. Maybe this evening. Elsie Partridge, that is. Good man. We're all responsible to him."

Couple of dingy offices near Baker Street tube station. Plenty
of dust and the odd popping gas fire – the usual appurtenances of
people in the spy trade. Bloke called Elsie?

"Baker Street?" she asked.

"Quick learner."

"Did you get me transferred, Curry?"

"Not me personally, no. Elsie Partridge thought it was
about time after I spoke to him last night."

"So you gave it a little push?"

"Possibly. Look, I've got this for you," he handed her a flat
leather wallet, flicking it open to show her ID as a member of
War Office Intelligence Liaison under the crown and crossed
swords of the army insignia.

She took it and studied it. "So, I'm what Tommy called a
secret squirrel?"

"You're what he calls a Funny, and that's probably how it'll
feel for a while."

She grinned, "Do I get inducted, like in the Free Masons?
Rituals in dead of night? I get cleared for top secret stuff?"

"Some, only we call it 'Classified'." He grinned back.

"Go ahead then, tell me all," she sipped her foul coffee and
grinned, beginning to feel a little better.

"Nothing to tell you as yet, except what I've already told
you, that we're concerned about Tim Weaving's position, his
access to COSSAC, whatever he might have had in Classified
information regarding *Overlord*..."

"*Overlord*?"

"Ah, yes, that's your first bit of inside guff. *Overlord* is the
code word for the invasion of Occupied Europe, and that's
about all you'll have for the time being. Oh, you have signed
the Official Secrets' Act haven't you?"

"Every copper in the land has to sign it, Curry. Yes."

"Good, then we're all set for Tommy's briefing. Finish
your coffee, go and get yourself prettied up and we'll go down

to Mill Street nick as you coppers call it."

"I *am* prettied up," she said with a slice of anger.

Chapter Eight

EVERYONE WAS THERE – the whole team – seated at desks, and on desks, with Tommy standing by a recently acquired blackboard looking like a Prep School master. There were seven names written on the board:

Sergeant 'Monkey' Gibbon
Sergeant Peter 'Mulfy' Mulford
Sergeant Peter Alexander
Sergeant Christopher Long
Sergeant Major Pearce 'Kissme' Hardy DSM
Major 'Shed' Hutt MC
Captain Wilson Sharp
Captain 'Bomber' Puxley MC

"Come in, gentlemen," he said when Curry and Suzie opened the door. He wasn't smiling and he stressed the *gentlemen* like the old joke about the butler walking in on the master and a chambermaid.

Dennis Free was a gent, got up and offered Suzie his chair. "Thanks, Dennis, we'll stand at the back." Generous smile and a nod of the head. She followed Curry to the back and they leaned against the wall like a couple of oiks waiting for something to happen, to give someone a kicking but that rarely happened these days.

"I've already explained you're not with us any more, WDI Mountford." He hadn't had much fun explaining it judging by the acid in his voice. "But I have told them you're still on this case with the Funnies. Welcome."

He turned back towards the blackboard and, as though he'd suddenly remembered something – "Oh, yes. I've also told the Squad that you're too precious to lose, DI Mountford, so I've made an application to the Commissioner.

I'm asking to have you back and I'm offering the Funnies WDS Wimereux in your place." Smirk and twinkle.

Suzie and Curry smirked back and as though by pre-arranged signal they both silently shook their heads; went on shaking them.

She saw the particular glint in Tommy's eyes, recognised it and thought, Jesus, he's jealous, bloody jealous. He thinks Curry and me...beast with two backs...Golly. Probably wouldn't say no come to think of it, if the light was right and there was a following wind.

"Something you want to share with us at all, Mr Shepherd?" Tommy digging a grave for himself.

"Major Shepherd, please, DCS Livermore, sir."

"Oh, of course," any charm had gone, replaced by sarcasm laced with a tincture of cynicism.

"All right," he pronounced it *orl right*. "Royal Reserve Squad and the Royal Funnies," trying to be amusing. "You've heard this before. Received wisdom is..." that was a favourite of Tommy's, 'received wisdom,' "received wisdom is that when you get a brutal murder the first people you take a look at are the family. In this case that's Mr and Mrs Adrian Fletcher Weaving who're living out retirement in glorious Devon – he's in the Home Guard and she's doing auxiliary nursing which ain't bad for late sixty-year-olds. His brother Ralph's a CPO in the Royal Navy, aboard HMS Formidable while his sister's Land Army, farming away like Old McDonald in Somerset, not going too fast for you Major Shepherd?"

"I'm keeping up remarkably well, DCS Livermore. Sheep go baaah and the pigs go oink, that's how it goes I believe."

"Congratulations." Pause, another smirk. "So, I think we can reject Colonel Weaving's side of the family as possible suspects. Regarding Mrs Bascombe there is the question of her husband, Captain Robert Bascombe VC. Well, I don't suppose our Bobby Bascombe would be too pleased to know that his wife was doing the post horn gallop with Colonel Weaving, but, alas, Captain Bobby's decorating a POW Camp in Germany at the moment and I should imagine the War Office is searching its collective intelligence regarding breaking the news of his wife's death to him. Not easy at all."

Tommy looked round the room as though he'd just set some weighty problem that called for profound knowledge of integral calculus. "So, I doubt if hubby could have arranged for someone to come here, to Berkshire, and batter the adulterous couple's brains out."

Suzie thought, Lord help us, as if Tommy Livermore's patent and pompous schoolmasterish manner was being revealed to her for the first time. Then her mind whirled and she saw again the broken bodies in the cellar of the house on Portway, wondered about the minutes that led up to the deaths, thought about the anguish, the fear and pain that must have swept through the two wretched people who died, bludgeoned to death, in that alien, cold and hostile vault.

Among the pictures in her head she wondered about pain, she, who had never felt excruciating hurt, only the bumps and knocks of childhood, the petty violence – the Chinese burn, the Indian rub or the penny stamp, all in the arsenal of school bullies, yet nothing like the horror of the real thing which ended only in death.

"So, not having any leads *en famille*..." Tommy started again, more composed, putting the nasty little digs to one side. "We have to move to the slightly wider family, the family of the Regiment, the people serving immediately under him at Brize Norton." His hand swept down the list on the blackboard. "And here we have them, the officers and NCOs of the Heavy Glider Conversion Unit – the people we're going to talk to today, people who're going to help us with our enquiries."

He looked around, slowly catching each face, giving Suzie a long stare so that she finally felt she knew what the word lupine meant.

"I don't want to go in there mob-handed," he continued, looking a shade smug. "So we're all going." Laugh. Oh, Tommy you are a wag, Suzie thought.

"What I suggest is that WDS Wimereux and I do the interviews, with Ron as muscle." Ron Worrall nodded agreement. "The rest of you should mix with the customers and talk with them – nice and gentle, make mental notes, keep your eyes and ears open. I want to hear if anyone sounds like they had problems with Colonel Weaving: or if there was ill will of any kind." Nods from around the room and Tommy asked if anybody had queries.

Dennis Free asked, "We going to divide up the officers and NCOs, Chief?"

"No," the self-satisfied smile again (Oh what a bastard, Suzie thought). "What I thought we'd do is put the officers on the hop; make arrangements to interview everyone in the sergeants' mess, eh? Good, eh?"

Murmurs of 'good' and 'yes,' everyone happy and bright, what a clever bloke the Chief is. Good on you, Chief, and someone else asked if the Glider Pilot Regiment had separate messes for their people, there being piles of Brylcreem boys at RAF Brize Norton. Originally, in 1940 the fighter pilots of the Battle of Britain were the Brylcreem boys after the sleek advertisements for the hair cream showing a pilot with polished hair, glossy, lustrous. A 'corker' as Suzie would have called him. Now any aircrew seemed to be referred to by this sobriquet, while most other ranks and non-flying personnel were 'erks'.

There was ten, fifteen minutes chatter during which Curry asked how they could help with the questioning of the GPR officers and NCOs. This made Tommy treat him to the long state, the evil eye look. "Well I suppose you've got to be there,

Major Shepherd, but if I had my way you'd carry out a completely separate investigation..."

"Don't want to duplicate it," Curry drawled, a little loudly, as if he was spooked by Tommy's suggestion, but Tommy's eyes flicked away, not really meeting Curry's.

"You'd better sit in with us, then," the invitation came with ill grace.

Later Curry said that he imagined old Elsie had spoken to the Commissioner, or to Tommy Livermore himself.

"Elsie?" Suzie asked. They were driving to Brize Norton – forty miles or so from Wantage – following Brian driving the Wolseley, with Tommy and Cathy, Tommy in the front passenger seat, Cathy behind with Laura Cotter, all girls together and the Chief being as witty as hell, talking about how they'd go through the GPR people like the proverbial dose of salts. Suzie knew because she'd been there too many times, going off to scenes of crimes with Tommy all worked up, ready to take on the world, a bit of a show-off.

"Elsie?" she asked again.

"Our boss," she knew that already, his eyes watching the road and the brake lights of the Wolseley ahead, as he needed to for it was cold and freezing fog drifted in patchy waves over the hedgerows across the road. The other car was behind them, making up the little convoy, Dennis Free at the wheel with Shirley Cox beside him and Ron Worrall in the back.

"Leonard Cyril Partridge." Curry supplied, "Known by his initials just to confuse folk. L C Partridge equals Elsie Partridge. Likes to be known as Len Partridge, a deeply secret man; been everywhere, spent time with MI5 and the Secret Intelligence Service, sat on the right hand of God in Special Operations Executive; all round good egg and won't stand any fiddling from Tommy Livermore."

"Really?" pleased.

"Yes, really. Elsie Partridge got out of Berlin in his socks in

September '39; interviewed Hitler under the guise of being a journalist for some imaginary far right magazine he invented. Called it Excalibur. Asked the Führer impertinent questions; says he's full of himself, can't understand why the people fall for the load of rubbish he feeds them, plays on the pure German race business. According to Partridge the real brains is the little club foot Goebbels."

"Do I get to meet him?"

"Goebbels?"

She laughed, "No, Elsie Partridge you fool."

"Watch it!" This time he did turn his head; looked straight at her, smiling. Lovely smile. "Beatable offence calling your senior officer a fool; and don't let the gaffer hear you calling him Elsie. Bit touchy about Elsie."

"When do I get to meet him?" she repeated.

"Sooner than you think."

"When? And do I salute or anything?"

"Nice if you call him sir to start with, and you'll meet him tonight if Tommy gets on with this. How is he with inquisitions?"

"Bit long winded. Calls them interviews, though – 'officers from Scotland Yard are talking to a man who is helping with their inquiries' – you know how it goes."

"Yeees," slow, drawn out. "We call that an inquisition, as in The Spanish, but we don't use the Rack or the Iron Maiden. You an Iron Maiden, Suzie?"

"Not iron. More steel I suppose."

"I had heard. Suzie Mountford, Steel Maiden."

"Not even a maiden I'm afraid. Was once, back in days of yore."

"Days of your what?"

"You've been watching too many Abbot and Costello flicks," she said, grinning broadly, loving this kind of surrealist backchat.

"Who's on first?" he asked, quoting from the comedy couple's best-loved sketch, repeated almost in its entirety in pubs and school playgrounds: as well-known as the catchphrases of ITMA.

She chuckled.

After a minute or so he again asked about Tommy and his inquisitory techniques.

"He once said something very vulgar about questioning procedures, but then Tommy was/is vulgar."

"He is?"

"Extremely. You should know, you were at school with him. Tommy never stopped being a vulgar little boy."

"I wouldn't have known that. School was only a couple of years. He was seventeen when I was fourteen. Those few years are an entire era when you're that age. Gets better when you're older, but I don't think I could ever be on close terms with Tommy Livermore." Another longish pause. "What was this particular vulgarity?"

"He said that the object of questioning a suspect was like getting to the far end of a fart. But then it's one of my mum's favourite expressions as well."

Curry spluttered. "I don't call that very vulgar. Not when put against some of the things you have to hear."

"No, it's not when you put it against what Tommy used to say and do. I lived with him, Curry. Well, just about lived with him from 1940 until recently."

They drove on almost in silence and Suzie found herself leaning against the door, away from Curry. Are all men basically the same, full of cheap crudities? Sniggering at sex and body functions? She couldn't believe they were all tarred with the same brush. All of them? Never.

She was wearing her severe dark blue suit, with the skirt a fraction too short, but over it she had the very military cut greatcoat, burgundy with little metal D-rings on the belt, like a trenchcoat and long skirts she could wrap around her thighs and legs. It was a coat that gave her tremendous confidence: the one her mum had bought for her at Fenwicks.

It was almost eleven-thirty when they arrived at the main gate of RAF Brize Norton, only they did not have gates beside the sold concrete Guard Room, they had a red and white striped pole, like you saw at some continental level crossings. An RAF Regiment sergeant, spiffy, and knowing it, in his blue beret and greatcoat, leaned down and talked to Tommy through the passenger side window. Curry stayed back, foot resting on the brake, gear in neutral and his eyes flicking up to the mirror, taking in the grey Wolseley to his rear with Dennis Free at the wheel.

"They're not taking any chances," he said as the sergeant hurried off into the Guard Room and an airman with a rifle watched the cars, some menace in his eyes put on especially for the occasion.

"Tommy hasn't got the password for the day." Suzie said.

"Betcha."

"That the password?"

"No, but I bet you know it."

"Haven't a clue."

"Piece of cake," Curry chuckled.

Suzie said, "Advance piece of cake and be recognised," and they both chuckled as the sergeant came doubling out and called for the red and white pole to be raised, then bent down again to give Tommy more instructions.

"Telling him where to go, giving him a map," Curry muttered.

"I'd tell him where to go," Suzie stated, entering into a conspiracy.

They followed Tommy's Wolseley as it turned right and skirted past the more permanent buildings of the RAF station, the barracks, parade ground, officers' mess backed by three big hangars, two old Armstrong Whitworth Whitley bombers and a big Short Stirling parked off the perimeter track, as were three Horsa gliders, while a twin-engined Oxford was coming in over the far hedges, the first aircraft to use the aerodrome that day, now that the fog had started to lift.

Beyond the hangars a cluster of more temporary buildings sprawled out towards the north – Nissen huts and larger pre-fabricated, wood and block structures, marking where the Glider Pilot Regiment's Heavy Glider Conversion Unit was stationed. They threaded through the roadways until the Wolseley turned off to the left, stopping by a larger hut marked, above the door, HGCU sergeants' mess.

Almost as soon as the cars came to a stop, an officer with Major's crowns on his epaulettes, came out of the door followed by a warrant officer. Both had welcoming smiles plastered unconvincingly on their faces.

"Bet that's Major 'Shed' Hutt and Sergeant Major 'Kissme' Hardy." Curry already had the engine switched off and his door open, determined not to be left out so that Suzie had to leave the car in a sort of undignified flurry, gathering the skirts of her burgundy coat around her and almost trotting to keep up. The other car disgorged its passengers who had somehow pushed ahead – probably told by Tommy to thrust themselves forward: instructed to keep together.

They arrived at the small knot of police officers just as Tommy was doing the introductions. "Oh," he sounded reluctant as he flapped a hand in the direction of Curry and Suzie, "These are two people from one of the Home Office Organisations."

"Curry Shepherd, Major Shepherd," Curry stepped forward, hand outstretched adding, "WOIL".

Major Hutt said, "James Hutt, how d'ye do?" sounding like an old time squire up at the big house, rode with the hounds in winter, fished and blew game out of the sky for the rest of the year. "How's that agin?" he asked referring to the WOIL.

"Jumble of letters to confuse the innocent," Curry burbled, "and this is Woman Detective Inspector Mountford, on attachment to the Home Office."

"Jolly good," Hutt smiled, sounded perky, smoothed his little waxed moustache, allowed his eyebrows to lift while the grey eyes did an alarming twinkle meant to give the impression that he was a lonely bachelor who was no end of a dog. Aloud he said, "Sarn't Major Hardy," and the tall warrant officer leaned forward to go through the hand-shaking routine like his commanding officer before him. The sergeant major touched hands with everyone, smiled and spoke with a seriously wha-wha accent rarely heard except at point-to-point race meetings and in old country houses.

"Jaas, wawcome," he said which Suzie translated as yes, welcome, then Major Hutt stepped in with something about hoping they'd all lunch in the officers' mess, "When you've finished what you've got to do that is. Not going to take long, is it?"

Tommy took over with what Suzie thought was unseemly haste. "It'll take as long as it takes." Sour. "Ought to get cracking soon as possible, eh?" a splash of self-importance.

"I say," said Jim Hutt, whom they called 'Shed' Suzie remembered. "I say. Aren't you that copper whose always getting himself in the papers? Call you 'Dandy Tom' don't they?"

Tommy didn't like this, Suzie could tell because the colour came out, high on his cheeks. Dandy Tom, the papers called him because of the sharp, almost Edwardian, cut of his suits and the manner in which he approached murder cases. Tommy Livermore loved his colleagues seeing him talked about in the papers as Dandy Tom, but he didn't like it so much when what he referred to as 'civilians' called him by the nickname.

Suzie saw Curry Shepherd give a little leer and knew he was aware of the joke.

Inside, the hut was laid out like a club, a small place just for men to come and enjoy themselves: tables and chairs dotted around, a bar to the left, steering its way out of the wall then turning and running down the room, backed by shelves with bottles and beer pumps nearest the customers. A tall grizzled man stood behind the bar, ready to serve drinks.

"That's Pop," Major Hutt said with a big smile and Suzie saw Tommy nod at the barman as though he was doing everyone a great favour by acknowledging him. Pop gave a little smile, quick and far from humorous or friendly. Suzie thought, 'Hallo, that's an old friend. Been in more nicks than a notch. Probably done some bird as well for he had that shifty way of looking at the assembled police officers.'

Looking round, Suzie saw that as well as Major Hutt and Sergeant Major Hardy there were two other officers, both captains, three pips on their shoulders plus four sergeants, among whom Monkey Gibbon grinned, drawing attention to himself. She tried to put names to the NCOs but, of course, couldn't until Hutt started to do the honours. The small, chubby Captain was Puxley, "Branwell, but the chaps call me 'Bomber'".

"Why would that be Captain Puxley?" Tommy, officious and unsmiling. Puxley, from the look of him was the oldest present, late thirties, maybe even forty.

"Spent some time in the RAF. Flew bombers, well doubt if you'd call them such today. Flew Heyfords damned great things, big biplanes, two huge engines, three Lewis guns, loads of bombs. Handley Page Heyfords, last of the biplane bombers. Bit outdated nowadays."

Suzie realised that Captain Puxley wore RAF pilot's wings on his khaki battledress, not the crown and wings of the army and glider pilots.

"And I suppose your people were stuck on the Brontë family." Tommy looking pleased with himself because he had recognised the name Branwell, the only Brontë male sibling. "Right," he raised his voice, having been told by Major Hutt that they would be doing the interviews in the small room next to the dining room, through a door at the far end of the building. Out of deference to the acting CO's name Tommy refrained from calling it a hut. "Right, let me just explain what all this is about."

They listened politely as he gave them almost the same spiel as he had given back in the Wantage nick: first people they always spoke to after a murder were the family. "You are Colonel Weaving's family to all intents and purposes," Suzie had to admit that he was good in this kind of situation. A pompous prune, possibly, but a good prune, gently easing things along. "We're all aware of how you feel. We know about loss of a leader, seen it before, dealt with it on several occasions," he went on. "We are sensitive to your bereavement; conscious of how you must feel; you all worked with Colonel Weaving over a lengthy period…" Heads nodded across the room and there were murmurs of agreement.

"So," Tommy ended, "let's get these little interviews over as quickly as we can, then you'll all be able to get back to the vital work you're doing here." He nodded and looked round.

"He's good at all that," Suzie told Curry later. "When he talks to a dozen or so people he ends up looking around and actually having eye contact with every one of them. Got it off an actor, he told me; actor who used that trick when taking his bow, taking a curtain call."

Tommy gestured towards the door that led into the room at the rear. "Why don't you be the first, Major Hutt? Do you good, get it over with. Few questions, nothing difficult." He signalled to Dennis, flicking his hands, getting Dennis, Ron, Cathy, Curry and Suzie to pull chairs around a centrally placed table while he dragged what looked to be the hardest and most uncomfortable chair in the room to a spot in front of the table. The chair didn't look too safe with a broken back, a small seat and one leg obviously shorter than the others.

Suzie remembered him talking, teaching her about interview technique. "Always get your suspect at a disadvantage: put him on a stool, or the most uncomfortable chair you can find, and put it in the worst possible place – in a draft, in the sun on a hot day – but make certain he or she is totally discombobulated."

She didn't even know it was a real word until she heard Tommy use it: discombobulated.

Now, suddenly they were off into the inquisition, no warning, no preamble, just Major Hutt sitting there, too big for the rickety chair, Tommy, Cathy, Ron Worrall, Curry and Suzie behind the table.

"Major Hutt, been on leave I gather?" Tommy said with a smile.

Like the smile on the face of the tiger.

Chapter Nine

SHE HAD TO admit Tommy was good at the question and answer routine: incisive, pauses in all the right places, immaculate timing. Tommy's teaching on pauses was that you could elicit an answer to an unasked question by just saying nothing, pausing for longer that usual. He also said you should watch the suspect's hands: *Tension or movement in the hands often reveals more than the answers to your questions.* That was one of Livermore's rules of interviewing.

"Major Hutt," flashy smile of greeting, sincere as a harlot's kiss. "Been on leave I gather?"

Shed Hutt had this annoying habit of smoothing his moustache, finger and thumb of his right hand reaching over, smoothing it left, then right, finishing with a little flick, forefinger against the right waxed spike.

"Yes. Got recalled when the CO was killed. Should've had fourteen days. Had ten, then summoned back with the old telegram. Boy on a bicycle. Not easy where I was."

"And where were you?"

"My people's place in Scotland. 'Bout twenty miles west of Aberdeen, Castle Killeenon. They're down south at the moment – the parents – so I had it to myself."

"Anyone bear this out?"

"The servants knew I was there. Didn't see much of me but they knew. I saw the ghillie, MacFarjeon, and Mrs Crochette, housekeeper. Local police knew I was there as well." He paused and Tommy let it hang for a moment. Suzie counted, 'Nine...Ten...Eleven...'

"Oh, yes and I met old Bomber Puxley at Paddington. On the station. Had a drink in that big public bar. Travelled back together matter of fact. Both shaken by the news. Colonel Weaving's death. Bad show."

"The death was a bad show, or Colonel Weaving was a bad

show for getting killed with his inamorata?"

"Death of course. Tim getting murdered. Terribly bad show."

Tommy nodded.

"And you met Captain Puxley on Paddington Station?" Cathy stepped in. Hair looking a bit washed out, Suzie thought, losing its sheen, needs seeing to. Cathy probably needs seeing to as well.

"Yes. In the public bar, getting a drink." Hutt didn't even look at Cathy Wimereux: pointedly turned his head away.

Tommy seemed to show some interest in this. "Bomber Puxley? What's the full story on him, Major Hutt? Full strength on Captain Puxley."

"In what way?" Hutt appeared flustered, frowned, eyes unsettled.

"He's older than the rest of you for a start."

"Well that's true, yes, but he's done all the courses. Did his nine jumps and all that."

"Former officer in the RAF isn't he?"

"Yes, but...Oh, I see. Yes."

"Yes. Serving officer with the RAF and now with Airborne Forces. Strange isn't it?"

"Suppose it is. Old Bomber went into the RAF on a short term commission. Straight from university. Cambridge. He was with the University Air Squadron, early in the '30s. Came out in '38. Yes, I believe he had words with his CO. Said something stupid in the mess and this wing commander took exception: said he'd put up a black, serious black. Old Puckers was in the Volunteer Reserve. They had him in front of a board in '39 just before the balloon went up. Asked him a lot of drivel about what he'd said and told him this Wing Co had advised he should be stripped of his commission. Not allowed back."

"Really?" Tommy took off his specs and sucked one of the

earpieces. "What had he said? Must've been something pretty bad."

"Yes, I believe it was. But old Bomber always speaks his mind. Comes out with the most frightful things. Load of balls really of course. Bomber just likes having a go at people."

"And on this occasion?"

"What? What he said to produce the wing CO's ire? Haven't a clue. Never asked. Bomber's a bloody good officer: fine pilot. Wouldn't dream of asking him."

"Left the RAF under a cloud then?"

"Not that I know of. He got angry I gather. Angry because this stupid wing commander became so prickly. Said if that was how they felt he'd rather transfer into the Army."

"And that's what he did?"

"Royal Artillery I believe. Got a gong for being brave as hell in France. Near Dunkirk. Then flew Austers observing for the guns for a bit, then, when we got Airborne Forces going, he was sent to us. I first met him at EFTS. He helped out with teaching people to fly Tiger Moths. Became one of what Tim Weaving called the Old Firm."

"And he's still only a captain?" From Cathy Wimereux.

"Yes. Well. Sizeable black I suppose."

"Anyone here didn't get on with Colonel Weaving?" Tommy turning on a sixpence.

"Not like Tim? Not an enemy in the world, Tim – except Jerry of course, mutual that I should think. This is an NCO Regiment, Chief Super. NCOs and officers only. Have to be at least a sergeant to apply. Everybody, Officers and NCOs worshipped Tim Weaving. We all hoped to go on serving with him when the HGCU was disbanded."

"And when'll that be?"

"Probably in the spring. We're all going off on more leave over Christmas. Skeleton staff here. Then new course starting in January: sixteen new boys, done EFTS. Sixteen glider pilots'll bring the Regiment up to full strength: six-week conversion onto Horsas; pray the weather's okay for flying. End of January that'll be. Should have a new CO by then. Fact is we're expecting one any time."

"And you can think of nobody here who had any grudge against the Colonel?"

"Good grief, no. Nobody at all, sir. No, not one man." With a flourish he produced two sheets of paper. "Typed up these for you actually. Little pen portraits of all the staff here. Help you on your way, what?"

"Right Major," Tommy all business, taking the sheets and running his eye town the typed contents then passing them along to Cathy. "Would you ask Captain Puxley to come through?"

Then a thin smile and a shake of the head. "No, hang on a moment. One more thing. Emily Bascombe, Mrs Bascombe, wife of the VC. Anyone know about her? Any little rumours about Colonel Weaving and Mrs Bascombe? Any gossip?"

Major Hutt looked away, stared at the floor, then shrugged, lifted his head and put his eyes on Tommy's face like someone aiming a lethal weapon straight at a target. "Emily Bascombe," half whispering. "Yes, a lot of people knew about Tim Weaving and Emily Bascombe. There's always talk. Especially in the mess – officers or sergeants' mess. It was all sort of jokey. Nudge, wink. People talk and people knew but didn't actually carry tales out of school. I happen to know that Colonel Weaving had an Achilies' heel. Ladies, that was it, and I also knew that Tim Weaving was engaged to another lady. Met her on several occasions. Julia Richardson. Flat somewhere behind the Athenaeum I think. They were officially engaged. She came here for some function, ring on her finger – bells on her toes shouldn't wonder. Lovely girl: the colonel's fiancée. Piece in the paper and everything – *Mr & Mrs William Richardson have pleasure in announcing the engagement of their daughter Julia bla-de-bla-de-bla-bla to Lieut Colonel Timothy John Weaving, Glider Pilot Regiment. Bla-de-bla...* Expected a wedding this summer to be honest, but knew he was doing a bit of the old dog with Emily in Wantage. Didn't approve, but what can you do, Chief Super? What *can* you do? Tim sewing his oats I suppose."

"Anyone else mention it?"

"Little asides. You know how it is. People thought Tim was no end of a lad. Liked him anyway, whatever. I don't think anyone blamed him. Eat drink and do the other thing, for tomorrow we may die – as we may all do. And Tim was right wasn't he? Died, what?"

Tommy looked quite grave for a moment. "All right Major Hutt. Send in Captain Puxley would you."

Shed Hutt stood up and flung Tommy a terrific quivering salute. Do himself an injury throwing his arm around like that, Suzie imagined and Tommy instructed Ron to cut along (that was what he said) and tell Dennis to check up on Major Hutt's parentage: "Castle Killeenon and all that. Make sure that's where he was all the time. Be certain that he didn't slip back to Wantage and take out Tim Weaving in the middle of the night, then nip back and run into Puxley on Paddington Station."

Ron went off and Tommy looked towards Suzie. "Susannah, when you were working for me yesterday, did you include this Julia Richardson among Weaving's nearest and dearest?"

"She was on my list, Chief, yes." The 'Chief' slipped out, could have bitten her tongue when she saw Tommy's wry smile. "Address, telephone number, the full treatment."

"Good girl," Tommy Livermore said with oily condescension that made Suzie want to spit: preferably in his eye. Christ you can go off people.

Branwell Puxley smiled a lot, went with his chubby and

ruddy face: pleasant, very friendly but the constant smile was infuriating. Suzie could well understand why the wing commander had got umpty with him. Didn't matter what he had said, the smile would do it every time for Suzie.

"Well, Captain Puxley. Been on leave, I hear." Tommy repeating himself.

"Indeed, yes sir. Very pleasant."

"You came back with Major Hutt?"

"Only from Paddington. Met up with him at Paddington Station. Poor bugger had been recalled from leave because of the dreadful business with Colonel Weaving."

"You spent your leave where?"

"Norfolk."

"By the seaside, eh? Or on the broads?"

"No, not quite the seaside."

"Your people live there?"

"No, Chief Super. No, I've got a nice little cottage quite close to Cromer. Well, four and a bit miles from Cromer. A hamlet, few houses, a pub, not even a church. Thorpe Market; south of Cromer. Dot on the map."

There was a lengthy pause during which Puxley simply looked around and smiled, staring up at the ceiling and generally gazing about. It appeared that he had said all he was going to say on the matter of living in Norfolk.

"Tell me, Captain Puxley, you've spent a fair bit of time in the services."

"Yes, sir. Seven, almost eight, years with the Royal Air Force."

"You left the RAF?"

"I did, sir."

"Under a cloud was it?"

"There was this wing commander..."

"Yes, please tell us about the wing commander."

"Fanning, that was the wing CO's name; dead now, his

Wimpy went into the drink, late '40. Whole crew got the chop. Fanning was a flaming arsehole – I'm sorry ladies – Fanning was a navigator and the brevet they wore at the time was an O with a wing attached, hence the flaming arsehole – excuse me again ladies. But I think what you really want to hear about is my clash with him."

"It was the cause of your leaving the Royal Air Force, I believe."

"Indeed it was. Summer of '38 I was dining in the mess, sitting next to Wing Commander Fanning. We'd been converting from the ponderous old Heyfords. Converting to Wellingtons, the old Wimpy. We all thought there weren't enough of them. Lovely aeroplanes but a bit short of carrying power, bomb loads: less than 5000lbs of bombs. The wing CO asked me what I thought of the Wimpy."

"And you told him?" Tommy squinted up; moving back in his chair as if cowering from whatever Puxley was about to say.

"I told him they were great to fly, but if push came to shove I'd rather be with the Luftwaffe because they had more aeroplanes, more guns and more bombs. What we need, sir – I said – is the Luftwaffe mentality. Quantity and quality, not a mixed bag."

"Bet he loved that," Tommy was smiling and not expecting Puxley to whip forward and bring his fist down hard on the table.

"This was 1938, Chief Superintendent, sir. 1938!" He leaned forward and brought his fist down on the table again, making Tommy jump. "Every one of us knew war was only a matter of months away. At the end of the year we were pretty much all amazed that Chamberlain had bought us extra time. And what did we have? What did we have in the way of bomber aircraft? We had the Wellington, fine; we had the Handley Page Hampden, tiny bomb load and an odd design; we also had the Armstrong Whitworth Whitley, slow, cumbersome, relatively small bomb load. Of course we still had some Heyfords which were hopeless, we also had some of those bloody great Bristol Bombays, twin-engined with a fixed undercart, slow as a wet week. I mean put against the bombers we knew Jerry was developing, well – the Heinkel 111, the Dornier 17, the Junkers 88 and the 87, the Stuka – all up and coming in '38. Against those we were, at best, mediocre. And I told him so. He threatened to have me court martialled. Exploded there and then, in the mess. Terrifying." Again his face lit up in that bubbling smile. "Put the fear of God into me, but when something like that happens it's like a red rag to a bull. I gave him some more. Looking back I can't believe what I said to him," he chuckled.

"Well?" asked Tommy and Cathy in unison.

"I told him that as well as the planes being better, I thought the Luftwaffe uniform was smarter than ours. I'd seen 'em, 1937. Had some leave, went over to take a look. A month in the summer. Saw some of the younger chaps doing their gliding – got interested in that actually. And saw some of the new aeroplanes as well. Good fighting machines. Not long range but most serviceable. Funny, I heard kids talking back in England, saying that German aeroplanes had to land every fifty miles to tighten up the nuts and bolts." A big chuckle at that. "Have to admit though, Jerry seemed to have the airforce thing buttoned up. Damned impressive. Knew what they were doing." He paused and nodded. "Yes, that's what I said to him, even the uniform's better than our kit."

Tommy nodded, "Let me guess. He said you'd best go and wear it then."

"Something like that. Told me to get out of the mess. Said I was a bloody Nazi spy, ought to be shot." Count of around ten. "'Course I was as pissed as a newt."

"You'd have to be," said Tommy. "But what about Colonel Weaving?"

"What about him? Rarely pissed. Only seen him pissed the once, actually. Ringway when we got our parachute wings. He was singing 'There's a hole in the elephant's bottom'. Elephant! What we called the Whitley: had a hole we jumped out of, where the lower gun turret used to be, the dustbin turret, looked like a dustbin lowered under the kite. Put his arm round me, 'Bomber,' he said, 'Bomber we're all bleeding mad jumping out of aeroplanes. Crazy.' Stewed as a haddock that night, old Tim. The mess sergeant marched in with his staff and they took the pictures off the wall. We were playing rugger at the time, using a fucking great shell case as a ball. 'Scuse me ladies, I'm a bit bilingual tonight."

"How did you feel about him? He was your CO."

"Tim? Best man I've ever served with. Salt of the earth. Officer and gentleman. All the usual."

"No reservations?"

"None."

Suzie suddenly realised what everyone else in the room had known from the moment Captain Puxley had come in. Branwell 'Bomber' Puxley was stewed as a haddock already and it was only twenty minutes past the noon hour.

Christmas is coming, she thought by way of making an excuse for him.

Tommy grimaced as if saying he didn't believe Tim Weaving could possibly be such a paragon of virtue and excellence.

"What about his love life, old Tim?" Tommy asked.

"You mean little Emily?"

He nodded. Suzie thought that's what they mean by nodding gravely. "Yes, Bomber. Yes I mean his love life with little Emily and little Julia and also little Annie Tooks in Knightsbridge. Bit of a Lothario, old Tim, eh?"

"Man's got to do what a man's got to do." Puxley smiled, swaying happily in the uncomfortable chair.

"In triplicate?" Tommy asked.

"In quintuplicate if he's a mind to. Specially these days when the evil Hun's on the warpath."

"Be that as it may. Surely there were some objections."

"Padre possibly. Maybe some of his flock. But who are we to cast the first stone?"

"Know of anyone at all who was deeply offended by Colonel Weaving's peccadilloes?"

"Narry a one."

A long pause followed, stretching it seemed almost to infinity.

"Right, Captain Puxley. Like to get Captain Sharp to come in if you wouldn't mind."

"'Nother good bloke, Wilson Sharp." Puxley said. "Good bloke to have on your side." He saluted Tommy, but not with the panache Shed Hutt had shown, then set course towards the door on what appeared to be a swaying floor.

"Dennis is checking out Major Hutt," Ron Worrall said quietly. He had returned to his chair while Branwell Puxley had been regaling them with the tale of his clash with the late lamented Wing Commander Fanning.

"Good show," Tommy drawled. "Damned good show, Ron," in imitation of their recent interviewees, indicating that he wasn't totally enamoured of the officers he had met so far. Suzie felt that wasn't fair, these men were bloody brave, how would Tommy face up to leaping out of an aeroplane or landing a glider in a hostile field?

Captain Wilson Sharp was tall, tough, bronzed and dark-haired. In the right light you could have called him saturnine, and he appeared to come from the same school as the officers already interviewed, except without any smartness. There was no snappy salute to Tommy, just a raising of the hand, fingers touching just above the right eyebrow. Suzie thought she could be watching him greeting a farmer on his tractor on a winter morning in some Berkshire village.

Sharp, she told herself, had been the officer temporarily in charge while Hutt and Puxley were on leave: so take heed. Tommy asked him if things had been busy while Major Hutt was away.

"We did a little flying in the past couple of weeks," Sharp's voice had slight traces of an accent, country, a mild burr, possibly the Hampshire or Berkshire burr, but way back in the mists of time so that it had been overlaid with standard middle class pronunciation. Tommy would know where he was from, for Tommy prided himself on being a real Professor Higgins when it came to accents. He'd certainly suss that Wilson wasn't top drawer. If he was lucky maybe he'd even place him within ten miles of his native town, village or hamlet. Wilson Sharp certainly did not come from a city, even Suzie knew that.

"Flying eh?" Tommy sounded as though this was an odd thing to be doing from an aerodrome.

"Some of the lads from the previous two courses came back for a refresher on the Horsas: four days, towed take-offs, circuit, cast off and bumps. Chap called Bartlett bent a Horsa. Overshot at Grove and ended up across a road. Sergeant Alexander nearly had a litter of pups sitting next to him. Said he was screaming at him that he was too high all the way down. Didn't do any good. Then a Sergeant Franks almost accomplished the same thing but Sergeant Long, Chris Long, took over and landed. Next time round Franks did the same thing; bloody useless so we had a long talk and he got himself posted back to 6th Airborne. Did the decent thing, but an absolute prune; useless, but he'll just about manage to jump and fight."

Sergeant Franks almost accomplished the same thing. Almost accomplished? Suzie queried to herself.

Sharp raised his face, grinned at Tommy and asked if he

could do anything to help.

"Possibly. Actually I'm just checking up reactions to Colonel Weaving's death."

Sharp nodded, bobbing his head as if he was an acolyte in church, bowing to the celebrant during Mass. "What can I tell you?"

"He seemed to be well-liked, Tim Weaving."

"Very well-liked. Couldn't ask for a better CO."

"That's what they all say. Seems too good to be true."

"No, sir, that's Colonel Tim. He *was* just about too good to be bloody true. Did everything a soldier should do. If he'd lived and we'd gone into battle with him every man here would have followed him right into the jaws of hell, and that's a fact."

"Jaws of hell, eh? Nasty place jaws of hell."

"It is, sir. I've been there and it's not at all pleasant."

For a couple of seconds Tommy looked as though he had been ridiculed. "That's the style," he muttered as if he could think of nothing better to say. Then, "What's that like, Captain Sharp? Jumping out of an aeroplane?"

Sharp gave a little rasping noise from the back of his throat. "Bloody terrifying. Anyone says he's not frightened of jumping, every time he does it, is either mad or a bloody liar. Like going into action, that scares the blazes out of you, but once you become involved you get on with it: the same with jumping, terrified one minute, then when you're working the shroud lines, stopping yourself from oscillating, trying to guide yourself in for a soft landing, spilling air out of the canopy, then it's not frightening any more – except of course when it's for real and they're shooting at you from the ground. It's all a dicey business, Detective Chief Superintendent. Dicey as buggery."

"Mmm. Once you become involved, you say. What does that mean? Once involved going into action? Mean once you begin killing people?"

"And doing your best not to be killed, yes."

"What about Colonel Weaving and his lady friend in Wantage?" Tommy reaching the final questions.

Wilson Sharp threw it back in his face, "What *about* the Colonel and the lady? Never did me any harm so I don't know what you're getting at."

"No moral feelings about them?"

Sharp laughed, humourless, cynical, dismissive even. "You ask that while this war's going on around you? Moral feelings? Ask the kids dead in the Western Desert, or killed on the beaches of Dunkirk or in at cock-up at Dieppe. Ask them if they've got any moral feelings about anything. Morals're too expensive for me. I just don't have moral feelings any more. Have you thought about the morals of what's going to be left when it's finally over: thousands of young men turned out into a cold world trained only in the profession of death. Good for people like you I suppose. Great if you're a cop."

Tommy grunted and busied himself with his notebook. Finally he asked, "Night of 14th/15th December, Tuesday and Wednesday?"

"Seems like a thousand years since I've been out of camp."

"Including Tuesday and Wednesday?"

"Including all the days of the week."

"And everyone else'll tell me that?"

"Ask anybody. I've been here holding the fort for ever."

Sharp didn't even wait for Tommy to tell him he could go: just touched his forehead again and walked out, his heels ringing their disgust on the wooden floor.

It took them another hour-and-a-half to talk with the remaining NCOs starting with Sergeant Major Hardy whose voice was far too lardy-dah for any of them. "Did you bloody hear him?" Tommy shrieked when Hardy has left. "More cut glass than Waterford."

Indeed, the Sergeant Major seemed to have appropriated not a so-called upper class accent, but an accent he had made up for himself. Some of it approximated what is known as upper class pronunciation – 'girls' became 'gels' and there were odd bits of French littering his speech, notably *bouleversé*, *coupe de foudre* and *hors de combat*.

Suzie didn't believe a word the man said – among other things he had confirmed all the alibis – and Major Hutt's thumbnail comment on him was tersely 'Jump happy'.

Monkey Gibbon was wheeled in and proved to have become cocky, having had his moment with Tommy in the Grove Street nick at Wantage. Now he started to call Tommy Livermore 'Guv'nor', which Tommy didn't like; preferred 'Chief' which most of the Reserve Squad called him.

"Lay off the 'Guv'nor', Monkey," Tommy told him, "or I'll lay off the Monkey and call you Sergeant Gibbon, then I'll see to it that you decline and fall, both."

Pete Alexander proved to be running slightly to fat; definitely pudgy and seemingly not quite in the same world as Tommy, thinking very hard and struggling with some questions while smiling a faraway smile. Major Hutt's notes declared that he was *a s/h pilot but his conversation belies his skill. Lives in his own head.* Tommy said that 's/h' was a very vulgar rating for a glider pilot and Suzie had no idea what it meant.

Alexander confirmed that the Major and Captain Puxley had been on leave and that everyone else from the GPR was highly visible at RAF Brize Norton. On the night of 14th/15th December he had personally eaten in the sergeants' mess and then gone to the pictures in the Garrison Theatre. "Saw a thing called *Road to Morocco* with Bing Crosby and Bob Hope. That Hope's a fair caution," slow and the sly smile again, remembering the film, humming under his breath, 'Like Webster's Dictionary we're Morocco bound.' Didn't seem to care a jot that he was being interviewed.

He also told them that Mulfy Mulford and Chris Long had eaten in the mess that night. But when Sergeant Mulford came in – medium height, salt and pepper hair with Hutt's evaluation saying, '*straightforward man, obeys orders sometimes without thinking*', the reality didn't quite marry with the Major's assessment: Mulford appearing to be nervous to the point of twitchiness.

Eventually Mulford began to hum and hah over the where-were-you-on-the-night-of-14th/15th December question.

"What's up Sergeant Mulford?" Cathy asked, belligerent and confrontational. "Come on, tell us what's wrong."

"Can I get Chris to come in? Chris Long?"

"Will that help you?"

"He's my mate and we were together that night."

Long was a short man, a classic 'Lofty'. Short, curly headed and miserable looking. Tommy got him to bring another chair over and sit next to Sergeant Mulford. Then he went through the whole spectrum of questions, bouncing them from one man to the other. All was straightforward until they again got to the one about where they were on the night of 14th/15th December: the night the Colonel and Emily Bascombe were killed in Wantage.

"We weren't in the camp." Mulford blurted.

"We were out," said Long, very quickly.

"But we were together." Mulford again.

"What's your problem?" Tommy asked, doing his gentle voice.

"It's against standing orders," Mulford told them.

"Not allowed to sleep out overnight." Long looked even more miserable.

Tommy again asked what their problem was.

"Well, it's difficult, sir. It's something we'd rather not talk about in front of the other blokes."

"But you were together?"

"Yes, sir. You see it's a mixed class, women as well as men so the others might think we're a bit odd. Maybe even think we're. Well, queer."

"But we were asked," Long took up the convoluted story. "We didn't like to say no. I mean we saw no harm in it."

Tommy took in a deep breath, "No harm in what?"

"Happened just after we were posted here," Sergeant Long nodded. "We was down the pub. Brize pub, The White Hart. Met this fellow. Taught art. Taught drawing and painting. Watercolours and oils, both...Name of Morrison."

"Every Tuesday evening, down the Church Hall. Men and women. Mixed class. Problem was he needed models."

Tommy chimed in. "So you became nude models for this art class."

"That's cold that church hall. Wind whistles round your..."

"There's nothing wrong in posing as nude models."

"Well, we didn't want the rest of the lads to know. They'd have taken the... pi...mick...know what I mean?" Mulford looked definitely self-conscious while Chris Long just shrugged and appeared to be blushing.

"How late did it go on for, the class?" Cathy asked.

"Couldn't have been all night surely?" Ron puzzled, joining in.

"What else was going on," Tommy seemed to be smirking. "You said you were out all night."

"Well, there's these two Land Girls. Twins." Mulford didn't meet his eye. "We call them Topsy and Turvy. Real names're Topsy and Tessa, and Mr Raines – that's the farmer they work for – he's given them one of his tied cottages. They made it really nice...Did it up, got some nice sticks of furniture."

"And from time to time you'd stay in this cottage?"

"That's about the strength of it, sir." From a gloomy Chris Long behaving like Eyore in Winnie the Pooh.

"We stay with them. Sometimes. Not every time..."

Mulford about to over elaborate.

"We'll have to talk to the ladies." Cathy on her high horse.

"Oh, I don't think they'd like that," Long shook his head and looked even more down in the mouth. "See Tessa has this fiancé out in Italy. With the 8th Army."

"Yeah," Mulford added. "Fighting like buggery."

SADLER KNEW WHO the dangerous ones were. When he'd gone into the room for his interview the snotty plainclothes copper had introduced everybody: his Detective Sergeant with a weird name, Wimerew or something, and a Detective Constable called Worrall. Then the two sitting slightly apart. "My colleagues from the Home Office," the copper said, flapping his hand wearily towards them, man and a woman: the man tallish and tanned, young with eyes that seemed to bore into you, the woman a nice piece, good legs, neat tits, but had copper written all over her, way she moved and looked. Suspicious blue-green eyes, restless.

They were spy chasers if he knew anything about it. They just sat and listened, watched, the pusher staring at his hands. Didn't ask questions, but listened and watched intently. Watchers were fucking dangerous and he knew immediately that he'd have to do something about them. Go talk to Linnet. Linnet could fix it, set it up and do it now. Now, now this minute.

There'd be a stink of course and the coppers would be chasing around for days. But how could they possibly find out. If they were any good they'd only work out who Linnet was. Trail'd go cold after that.

Couldn't touch him, Sadler.

THE OBSEQUIOUS SERGEANT MAJOR Hardy was hanging around the mess when they finally wound up the little conference following the last interview. Cathy had been told to find out where the Land Army girls lived. "Track 'em down," Tommy told her. "Embarrass the hell out of them. No doubt it's all okay, but we've got to follow up the nookie." Tommy being really unpleasant.

He also took Ron to one side and told him to liaise with Dennis Free and check on all the other alibis. "Apart from that strange sergeant major, these are intelligent men. Put all their stories through a sieve. If necessary we'll come back and take them through it again tomorrow, okay? This is where Colonel Weaving lived and worked and I don't trust all this best-soldier-whoever-breathed lark."

Ron was to double check on anything he felt uncertain about.

In the mess bar, Dennis Free, Shirley Cox and Laura Cotter hung around trying to avoid talking to the Sergeant Major who loudly informed Tommy Livermore that there were a couple of jeeps outside waiting to ferry them to the officers' mess. The way he said it sounded more like, 'A payer of japes waiting to ferrayew...'

The jeeps were manned by RAF drivers because the GPR had only one jeep, the CO's transport, usually driven by Monkey Gibbon.

Curry and Suzie climbed into the rear of the second vehicle.

"We'll give it one drink and a ham sandwich then we'll ease out," Curry said. "I've got a few ideas of my own and we can always come back with Tommy tomorrow. Priority is getting you to meet Elsie Partridge, right?"

"Whatever you say."

The mist and fog had burned off leaving a clear cobalt sky, a beautiful morning with a sharp tangy chill in the air. Out on one of the frying pan hard-standings a Wellington ran up its engines, making the air tremble. Someone had said that the Wimpies at the Operational Flying Training Unit at Harwell used Brize as one of its satellite aerodromes.

Suzie couldn't follow the route to the officers' mess, and

when they finally arrived in front of the semi-permanent building she took a deep breath, looking around in an attempt to identify exactly where they were. The building fronted the main road, some fifty yards away: high barbed wire fences ran along the perimeter, and traffic, mainly military, hummed defiantly past. On the other side of the road, over the hedge, a long and wide meadow sloped up towards a horizon dotted with clumps of trees and, to the right, a group of buildings huddled around a grey stone church.

Suzie took in the view and was just turning away to follow the others into the mess when something caught her eye, a shimmer, unnatural movement among a group of low trees and bushes some two hundred yards up the slope away from the road.

She was aware of the first two cracks and thumps and her mind took in what was happening. Tommy, in an idle moment, had fully explained the theory of crack and thump. It you are being shot at the crack is from a bullet cleaving the air somewhere near you; while the thump is the actual discharge of the weapon.

She heard two cracks and two thumps, followed by a third one.

Then something hit her with force on her back, knocking the breath out of her and she went sprawling to the ground, her head glancing off the jeep's bonnet. For a few seconds her world filled with electric blue pain.

Chapter Ten

SHE CAME BACK as though from several fathoms, breathless and lying on a leather settee in a neat room with paintings of aeroplanes on the walls, a big fireplace with a marble surround, that seemed out of place, and windows looking out towards the road. In the distance she saw a white coated orderly hovering with a glass on a silver tray. Nobody else around except for Curry Shepherd.

"You okay, Suzie?" he leaned over her and she moved experimentally, feeling bruised around her back and shoulders. "You okay?" He asked again.

"You get the license number of the truck?" It was a line she remembered from a Laurel and Hardy film. Curry gave a little half laugh, unconvinced.

"What happened," she asked. "Where are the others?"

"We got shot at."

"Where am I...?"

"In the GPR officers' mess ante-room."

"Where'm I hit?"

"You're not."

"But something knocked me flying. I heard the crack and thump and..."

"You know about crack and thump?"

"Yes. Why? Is it a secret from women? Where'm I hit?"

"Haven't met a girl who knows about crack and thump before."

"You have now. One of the many mysteries Tommy unveiled for me. Where'm I hit?"

"You're not."

"Something knocked me to the ground. Of course I was hit."

"No. That was me. I wanted you to get down: avoid the bullets. Whoever was doing the shooting was trying to remove *us* – you and me, Suzie. Nobody else. *We* were the targets."

"Crumbs."

"Crumbs indeed."

"So I'm not wounded?"

"No. Probably bruised a bit. I leaped on you from behind."

"Chance would be a fine thing," she muttered.

"What?"

"I said it must have been a near thing."

"It was. He fired four shots. The last one put out the jeep's engine."

"Lucky you didn't bring your car over then. Where is everybody?"

"The shots were fired from half way up the meadow opposite. Everybody's gone to get the would-be assassin. Every officer here and Tommy with his people. I reckon the sergeant instructors as well, and a posse of RAF Regiment. Armed to the teeth."

She tested her back again, wiggling her shoulders against the leather, shifting slightly. "I think you're right," she looked up and wiggled some more. "No, I don't think I *am* wounded." Wiggling as far as she could move back. He looked terrific, bending over her, his hands on either side of her shoulders. He doesn't half look jolly good, she thought. Toyed with the idea of giving yet another wiggle of encouragement, decided against it.

She felt warmish under her clothes, shifting her thighs gently, rubbing them together a little, hardly moving.

You want to kiss me, she thought. Then, aloud he asked if she was sure she was okay.

"I'm okay." She pulled herself into a sitting position and thought, well that's that. All over now. He's out of reach. Gone and never called me mother.

"Want a drink?" Curry asked. The mess orderly came over with the silver tray and the little glass with the amber liquid.

"Drop of brandy? How about that? Drop of brandy'll do you the world of good."

Curry took the glass, leaned over again and held it to her lips. Her mouth, then her throat filled with fire and she spluttered.

"Sorry," he grinned. "Probably not used to brandy."

"I'm very used to brandy," a challenging flair in her eyes. "When I was little some stupid nun made me help carry chairs over the Lax pitch to the Pav in the freezing cold. Said it'd do me the world of good, brace me up. I got home that evening with chilblains, fingers swollen and red raw, me shivering. Daddy gave me some brandy. Just a sip but I never forgot it. Warmed me up a treat." Those wonderful days of safety. Peter Pan had the right idea.

She took another swallow, felt the fire course down her oesophagus and explode in her stomach, making her feel much better so she sat up, struggled out of her burgundy coat and handed it to the mess orderly who sprang forward to help her but Curry beat him to it and passed the coat on to him. She was sitting properly now, feet on the floor, skirt adjusted and everything.

"We could make our getaway," she tried.

"Yes we could, but I rather think they'll want to ask questions. At least Tommy will." He frowned as though remembering something important. "Funny, I was with Tommy when we first learned about crack and thump. School. The army came over to give the Corps a day's training. We had to dig a slit trench then stand in it in pairs while they fired over our heads. I was with another boy called Osteritter: Bugs we called him because he was an amateur lepidopterist or some such, Bugs Osteritter. That was quite a thrill, having live rounds fired over our heads. Different when it's for real of course."

"I know, we've just had it done."

"Lax?" he said, going back a snake. "You used to play Lacrosse, didn't you? That's what Lax is, right?"

"A very dangerous game, but the nuns said it was character building."

"The nuns played?"

"No, we had a Games Mistress, Miss Druit. Used to hang around the showers and changing rooms, flicked our bottoms with a wet towel when we misbehaved. Sometimes when we didn't. A real sadist that woman. Miss Monica Druit."

"And the showers and changing rooms were in the Pav, right?"

"Absolutely."

"Just wanted to get the lingo straight. Like to be able to follow you." He grinned to show he was having a bit of a joke.

She swigged down the last drop of brandy and was relieved that her throat seemed to have become accustomed to the spirit: cauterised it she presumed. "Who'd want to shoot at us, Curry?"

"That's the big question; don't really know the answer. Got an idea, but not quite certain."

"It was just *us*? Nobody shot at Tommy?"

"Just us. No doubt about that. Tommy was almost at the mess door. There's no justice anywhere, Suzie. Neither a jot nor tittle."

"Narrows things down though, doesn't it?"

"You mean it possibly puts Colonel Weaving's killer here, with the regiment?"

"That's what I was getting at."

"Unless the weapon was from outside the aerodrome. But on the whole it probably narrows the field. Why us though?" He shook his head and twisted away, standing up as they heard voices coming into the mess entrance hall. There were people outside, Suzie glimpsed them through the big windows and they began to come into the ante room: Major Hutt with

Tommy, followed by Bomber Puxley and Wilson Sharp with the remainder of Tommy's crew bringing up the rear.

Curry immediately asked if they'd had any luck.

"Found where the blighter was lying: in that little stand of trees, half way up." Tommy's face was red and his breathing irregular. *Making you run for your money*, Suzie thought and had a picture in her head of Tommy stripped to gym shorts and vest, wearing white gym shoes, doubling around a field being shouted at by a fiery little PTI, all bounce and swearing.

"What was he shooting at us with? A Bazooka?" Bazooka was a new word to Suzie. She had read about the Americans having an anti-tank weapon called a Bazooka, but hadn't a clue what it was.

"I've got Ron digging the bullets out of the mess wall. Then we'll know. Bazooka would've done for you." Tommy actually looked at her as he spoke. "You alright?"

Oh, he still cares, she thought. "Yes, I'm fine."

"Whoever it was he was a careful bugger. Cleaned up after himself. Took all the cartridge cases with him. Picked them up."

At that moment Shed Hutt came up, rubbing his hands together in that swift concentrated manner some men use to cloak nerves when addressing a woman. "Well, well, how's the little lady then?" Big smile all teeth and tonsils.

"I am not a little lady," she began, a healthy dollop of rancour sliding into the way she spoke, causing Major Hutt to take a couple of steps back. "I'm sorry, sir," she added, "But I'm a trained and tested police officer and I don't like being addressed as a 'little lady'."

"Sorry, I'm sure," Hutt took another step back. "Only anxious for you. How you're bearing up, that sort of thing. After all, you nearly caught a packet, almost bought it."

"Thank you, but shouldn't we get on? Pin down who was shooting at us." Pause, count of four, "and why?"

"Some idiot with a gun having some fun, my guess," Tommy joined in, swaying back on his heels. "Not a good shot after all. Think it was an impulse: out potting rabbits and saw some people moving below him, thought he'd have some fun."

Tommy had raised his voice. Wants everyone to hear him, Suzie imagined, wise in the ways of Tommy Livermore. Shed Hutt drifted off towards the bar.

"You're not really asking us to believe rubbish like that, Tommy?" Curry moved in quite close. From where Suzie sat it looked almost threatening.

"Of course not young Shepherd," all but whispered. "But we should try and keep these brown jobs happy."

Curry turned towards Suzie. "I'll go and get the car and we can start making tracks for London."

"You leaving us, then?" Tommy sounded happy about the prospect.

"Only temporarily. Back before you know it."

"Need to talk to you both, privately before you go. Right?" Tommy smiled as if to cover the seriousness of what he was saying.

Nearby, Bomber Puxley had overheard them, "Not leaving without something to eat, I trust. Small mess this, but we do ourselves proud." He bent down and laid a forefinger alongside his nose, "Pinched the best cook on the 'drome." Grin, two-three, eyebrows up, two-three, relax.

"A little something eggy on a tray'll do for me." Suzie made sheep's eyes in Curry's direction and he was just turning away when there was another bustle in the hall, the ante-room door opened and a dazzling figure appeared.

He was around six foot two or three inches tall, broad and muscular in the shoulders slimming towards the waist, immaculate in a tailor-made battledress with two or three ribbons over his left breast pocket, above them the Army wings, plus the parachute wings on his right sleeve, Airborne flashes high below his shoulders. On his epaulettes were a crown and pip, signifying Lieutenant Colonel. He had the face of a gentleman farmer, ruddy cheeks and clear eyes while his head was thatched with a beautifully maintained, crisply cut, crop of corn-coloured hair.

When he spoke it was with the voice of the old sea captain Billy Bones out of *Treasure Island*, combined with the Angel of Death, both of them Eton and Cambridge.

"Well, well, well," he said. "Here I am at last."

"Good grief," Shed Hutt gasped. "Barty Belcher in the flesh."

"And with a bump-up, young Shed; bump-up to half Colonel and your CO to boot. Your new CO, come to take over from the late lamented Timsy Weaving." Big smile flashed all around the room, taking in every last one of them. Then, "I spy strangers," looking at Tommy hard.

"Bart Belcher," Tommy said. "Long time no see, Bart."

"Hon Tom, eh? Not seen since we all got kaylied, last day of school." He fixed Tommy with a pursed smile, stern and as though he knew something about the Detective Chief Superintendent that nobody else knew. "You investigating the demise of the former Commanding Officer of this shower, or just on a social jaunt?"

"Here on business, Bart," cosy and on good terms with Belcher. "Do you speak true? Are you the new CO of the Heavy Glider Conversion Unit?"

"Very much so," he saw Curry and the smile momentarily froze on his lips. "Joined the cops have you, young Shepherd? I heard you were dead."

"Gross exaggeration, Bart. Out of proportion when put against the facts."

"Glad to hear it. Where's my adjutant?" looking towards the door.

"Here, sir." A second officer appeared, a captain, spruce,

bandbox smart with all the same badges and brevets as those worn by the Colonel.

"Captain Carter," Belcher introduced him. "Leslie Carter. Thought it best to bring my own man, because all you chaps are going to be pretty busy. Now, listen, this is an order I'm taking all officers to London tomorrow: meeting at COSSAC. Talked to them today and they tell me they can use all the brains I can bring up. You can come back here when we're finished in London, make ready for going on Christmas leave, right? And you'd better make the most of it because I've a feeling you're not going to get much leave in 1944." Thin smile all round: quick, off and on. "Shed?" He called, a little loud.

"Sir?"

"Immediately you're back from leave you'll give me a quick course on the Horsa – me and Les Carter, both."

"Piece of cake, sir."

Nobody seemed to know Captain Carter and Curry whispered to Suzie, "Grammar school, I'd guess, wouldn't you?"

Then, before they knew it, Tommy was between them, arms outstretched resting on their shoulders and propelling them to a quiet corner away from the knot of officers gathered around their new CO who was buying drinks at the bar.

"You know something I don't, Shepherd?" he began.

"Such as?" Curry had dropped his smile, all grave and serious now.

"Such as why anyone here might want to do away with you, and Suzie here? She's of special interest to me as you probably know by now. Has been for the past three years."

Curry nodded. Waited for more.

"Someone tried to chop you two," Tommy continued. "And for what it's worth I think it was the same person who killed Tim Weaving. The same persons, I should say because there are at least two of them."

"Who went off with you in search of the sniper, Tom? From among the officers here?"

"The whole bloody lot, Curry. All three of the buggers, led by Shed Hutt. Some of his sergeant instructors were around as well. Didn't see how many, but I did see that affected bloody Sergeant Major join them, coming down the hedgerow on the far left, carrying a rifle. All of them were armed to the teeth. Damned Commandos and Airborne they're like private armies, got weapons from everywhere, British, French, German, American. You expect them to appear with stuff nobody's seen since 1911." He drew a quick deep breath, "and watch Belcher, their new Commanding Officer, rogue elephant that's what he is, always was. Known him since the year dot. Don't trust him. He's a vain braggart. Know what he did when he got his MC? Telephoned the News of the bloody World, that's what he did. Fella doesn't get much lower than that."

Curry gave a curt nod. "We'll go and get my car then, Tom. Got an appointment in London." He hadn't seen Colonel Belcher come up behind him.

"Can't go yet," boomed Belcher. "You're guests here, got to show you a bit of regimental hospitality, what. They tell me the catering's reasonable here, and..."

"We really should be getting away, sir," Shepherd very firm and earnest.

"You know best, young Shepherd," reluctant and a shade put out. "I provide anything for you? Transport? How you off for transport?"

"A lift over to the sergeants' mess might help, sir."

"Drink? Have a drink before you leave? How about you young woman?"

Suzie declined with a matching show of firmness, so, finally an RAF driver ferried them back to the sergeants' mess where Curry's dull green Vauxhall Ten stood, lonely in the large parking area to the side of the wood and block building.

Thanking the driver they watched him turn the jeep around and head back towards the officers' mess.

"Is this so terribly important, me meeting Elsie?" Suzie asked.

"Not really, but it's important we get ahead. You've worked and played with Tommy Livermore. What'll he do next? In your opinion what'll he do?"

"Well, to his mind he's made one pass through the family: the regiment, people Weaving was working with. He'll see the real father and mother, and the sister, but not yet. He'll go for the other girls next. Julia Richardson, the fiancée, and, what was the other one, Anne Fooks?"

"Ann Tooks. Yes. More or less what I thought, and that's important. We should see them first, before Dandy Tom gets at them."

"Game's afoot, Watson, eh?"

"A foot, a yard, a couple of miles. Let's go."

They took two steps towards Curry's car when it erupted in a ball of flame, a deep, throaty explosion that seemed to come from somewhere near the engine, a deep single horrible amplified drum stroke, then the blast blowing towards them like a cyclone, hot and full of deadly shrapnel.

For the second time that day, Curry threw himself on top of Suzie, pushing her onto the ground.

As she rolled and climbed onto her feet again, breath knocked out of her, trembling with shock, Suzie gave a little strangled cry. "Oh bugger," she intoned. "Bloody nylons."

Chapter Eleven

SUZIE WAS STILL trembling when they got her back to the officers' mess, her legs wobbly and unable, for a time, to take her weight, let her stand or walk. Curry just looked pale: both of them aware they'd been quite near death – "Another five paces and you'd have bought it," Tommy said – and their hands shook trying to hold the big enamel mugs of tea. Suzie, with a wan smile, said that another two steps and she'd have needed ODO-RO-NO – a deodorant much in demand.

Finally she stood up from the big sofa in the ante-room, then sat down again quickly, feeling she didn't exist, that inside she'd been excised, as though all the muscle in her body had been sucked out by the explosion, her bones fragmented and her mind expunged. She had been all but eliminated and, for a moment only, knew it was as though she'd never been born.

Colonel Bart Belcher came in as they were lifting the mugs in two-handed grips, gingerly getting them up to their lips, swallowing and gasping, burning their mouths.

"Strong, hot and sweet?" he enquired of the mess waiter who had, on Shed Hutt's orders, brought the tea.

The mess waiter told him, yes, and the colonel said, "Best thing for shock, strong tea with plenty of sugar." While he was speaking a RAF doctor, squadron leader, came bouncing in, saw the colonel's insignia, bounced out again, deposited his greatcoat then came in for the second time and asked the colonel's permission to look at the patients.

"We're okay, doc," Curry said adding, "Aren't we, Suzie?"

"Right as rain," Suzie wasn't all that convincing.

"I'll be the judge of that," the doctor confident, brim full of medical knowledge, walrus moustache and a barrelful of laughs.

"The doc'll be the judge of that," Colonel Belcher added unnecessarily. Suzie wondered if he was a bit of an unnecessary man, didn't like him.

"Need somewhere to examine them," the doc looked around searching for a likely door and the mess sergeant came out from behind the bar and said they could use his little office. "I've got this caboose round the back," he told them. "You're welcome to use that."

The doctor thanked him while Suzie was ready to give him an argument because she knew caboose was the wrong word but somehow didn't want to take him up on it when the time came.

The doctor smiled at her. "Take you first, Miss...er...Miss..."

"Mountford," Suzie supplied, then tried to get up, couldn't at first because her legs wouldn't do the trick, so the doctor put an arm round her shoulders and lifted her up, walking her along until they got into the mess sergeant's office where the doc gave her a swift going over, all the little tests.

"You seem to be okay?" it wasn't quite a proper question. "No bruises? No abrasions except your knees. You'll be as right as rain."

They had got the pair back to the mess in an ambulance that had turned up the same time as a fire engine and a squad of RAF Regiment men. The car was a blackened skeleton by the time they put the fire out, and an armaments officer was soon probing about giving notes to a corporal with a clipboard.

Tommy was poking around with Shirley Cox and Dennis Free following him like a couple of trained guinea pigs, sniffing out devious bits of electrics trying to work out whether the explosion had been triggered by fuse, or timer.

Back in the mess, Curry Shepherd went into the doctor's, makeshift surgery after Suzie came out, still unsteady on her feet.

The doc did almost the same things he had done with Suzie, felt all over for suspected broken bones, did a few tests, tried the reflexes with a little rubber hammer, looked into his eyes with an ophthalmoscope, and his ears with a little light – his auriscope – talked all the time, happy-happy, then got him to spread his hands out in front of him, palms down, fingers open, watching them moving about as though they had a mind of their own, the fingers waving around like an aspen leaf in a force nine gale.

"You're going to have to take it easy for a while," the doctor cautioned.

"Got to get to London, doc," Curry said, concerned and showing it. "Imperative."

"Well you're not driving yourself there," the doctor looked grave. "Out of the question." He said. "Why've you *got* to go?"

"Important meeting. Essential."

"Essential in the sense that it could endanger the war effort if you didn't go?"

"Absolutely. It is *that* serious." Curry performed a weaving motion with his body, like a boxer preparing for a fight.

The doctor swallowed, then did a slow nod, "Well you shouldn't drive yourself for at least twenty-four hours. Bloody dangerous if you did."

"Then I'll have to resort to that old Navaho Indian trick of begging and pleading for transport."

Curry picked his way back into the ante-room where Suzie was sitting up, still drinking tea and being chatted to by Tommy Livermore who was leaning forward, one hand on her arm, Cathy Wimereux and Dennis Free stood quietly by the door, keeping to themselves, not eyeballing Tommy, a bit sheepish.

Tommy was saying he was concerned for her. "Almost had your head and horns blown off so you must be feeling a bit shaky..."

"I'll be okay, Tommy. I'll be fine..."

"Look, I'm sorry. Right? Really sorry." She knew he wasn't talking about the shooting and the explosive device.

"If you're talking about us, it's been coming for a while,

Tom. I think we've both come to a decision." Idly she thought *this goes deeper, deeper than death*, then considered that was a bloody silly thing to think: sounded pretentious and stupid.

"Doesn't make it any easier."

"No, but…"

"Just watch out." Quiet, almost a whisper. "People in Curry's line of business can be dangerous."

"Tommy, I'll be fine."

"Can't be too careful."

"She's just told you, she'll be fine…" Curry was standing right beside him.

"I'm sure, yes" Tommy looked unconvinced.

Suzie said something about having to get to the meeting in London. Tommy raised his eyebrows, "And how're you going to bloody get there now Curry's car's gone for a burton?"

Curry said he'd find a way, he'd fix it, talk to the colonel, and Tommy shot back a crack about secret squirrels having more pricks than a secondhand dartboard. Unpleasant. For a moment Suzie thought they might exchange blows, but Tommy just glared at Curry, who glared back and Suzie tried to glare at both of them.

Eventually all the glaring got too much and Curry said he had to arrange the transport. "You be alright?" he asked Suzie.

She nodded, and reluctantly he left the room.

"Tommy there's nothing between us – Curry and me, I mean." As if she had to explain.

Tommy grunted.

"Curry didn't ask for me," she began. "It was his boss, apparently. Tommy, us…well, it's just come to a natural end…I had a great time, you made a woman of me and we worked well together." In the back of her head she heard an old song,

It is best to be off with the old love,
Before you are on with the new.

And she didn't even know if they were the right words, just hearing a memory, her mother and father singing it around the piano, Daddy playing like he always did when they had family parties at Christmas. *The Indian Love Lyrics* and a song they really loved called 'The Beggars'.

> *How jolly are we beggars*
> *Who never toil for treasure,*
> *We all agree in liberty*
> *And poverty befriends us*
> *Come away,*
> *Come away,*
> *Let no evil care be found,*
> *Mirth and joy,*
> *Never cloy,*
> *While the sparkling wit goes round.*

And she began to cry, big breathless sobs so Tommy moved towards her, ready to be of comfort, but she pushed him away. Just stayed there knowing it was all a mixture of the shock of being shot at and then the bomb in Curry's car and her half-decision to end it all with Tommy who had been so wonderful and then proved to have some habits she didn't like and wasn't really the man she thought him, or the one painted in the newspapers – Dandy Tom Livermore. All men, she thought, most men anyway, were the same. Feet of clay she supposed.

After about twenty minutes Curry returned to tell them the colonel had arranged a RAF staff car and driver to take them to London. A little cocky, Suzie thought, bit full of himself, showing off that he could handle a little thing like getting transport.

Tommy asked them both to sit down, wanted to tell them something: and began –

"What happened this afternoon...the shooting, then the

car blowing up. Well, no accident, not even a warning. Someone wants the two of you dead. Curry, if you know something I don't, for heaven's sake tell me." He paused, his eyes moving between Curry and Suzie, then settling on Curry who had remained standing.

"I only know what we've all worked out, Tom."

"Listen," Tommy took Curry by the shoulder and forced him to sit close to Suzie. "Listen to me. You've been shot at and almost blown to pieces, the pair of you. And you, young Shepherd, have been much too sanguine about it. Whoever's doing this is dead serious about it. They're not playing around. They mean to kill you."

"I'm *not* sanguine."

"You are bloody sanguine. Too sodding relaxed, Curry."

"I'm about as relaxed as a bayonet, and Tommy it's just a hint, an idea, a theory. I've already told you. COSSAC."

"Well tell me again, young Shepherd. Lay it out."

Curry looked at his feet, then told him what he'd already carefully laid out for him in Wantage: the connection between Tim Weaving and the biggest single secret in the United Kingdom. "You'd agree that the cellar in Portway House had the feel of a torture chamber?"

"Of course."

"Then follow the logic, Tom. *You're* the great detective."

"You mean the next front? The invasion of Occupied Europe?"

"Give the man a toffee apple and a stick of rock. Exactly. What I said before, Tom. People who turn up at COSSAC a couple of times a week have their hearts, minds and every other bloody organ full of the details for the invasion. Planners at the War House have them as well, but they're split up in little bits. Some know the exact landing places, some know the composition of the troops, others know the overall picture once a break-out's confirmed. It's a huge bloody operation. Naval specialists and RAF specialists; how the beaches are going to be supplied, and how petrol and ammunition can be brought over. Jerry would give his eye teeth for a few bits of it…Come to that old Rommel would give anything for details."

"And you think some skulking spy beat Weaving to death trying to prise out some of the details?"

"Absolutely. I've already told you, Tommy."

"And the woman, the woman in Portway House – Emily Bascombe – she was done away with just because she was there?"

"Naturally. What's wrong with that?"

"You want to know what's wrong with it?"

"Yes."

"Too bloody melodramatic if you ask me. I mean it doesn't take the brain of an Oxford geography don to work out that the most straightforward way is to assault France across the *Pas de Calais*. I suppose you land infantry along a front from where? ten-fifteen miles either side of Calais; bombard 'em from the sea and air, drop gliders and parachute troops a few miles inland, make a bridgehead and break out into France. That's what I'd do."

"Yea, but they're not asking you, Tommy. There's a shade more to it than that. The logistics are enormous."

Suzie caught a glimpse of Curry's face, the grey eyes were on fire as he continued. "I'm supposed to have my eye on the security of all those officers working things out down in St James's Square. One of them goes under a bus, I'm unhappy. One of them dies being put to the question I'm bloody devastated."

"Well…" Tommy Livermore sucked his teeth, obviously still unconvinced. "As an old policeman I tend to take a different view."

"You mean you think a friend of Captain Robert Bascombe VC has come in, done for the wife's lover then done for the wife. Dear Bobby, I did it all for you. Lots of love Tiger."

"At the Yard," Detective Chief Superintendent Livermore said slowly, and with a shade of pomp and circumstance, "At the Yard we tend to go for the domestic motive every time."

From the doorway, Dennis Free signalled the staff car had arrived for Major Shepherd and Woman Detective Inspector Mountford. A WAAF corporal hung around the hall outside the ante-room, and a couple of RAF officers stood around, one of them a squadron leader, medium height, corn-coloured hair, a flourish of a moustache below a chiselled roman nose. A pilot, handsome with a clipboard and some kind of form that required Curry's signature. The squadron leader grinned happily at Suzie and said they were all set to go now in a nice deep basso profundo voice that gave her a tiny sweep of goose pimples down the spine, but not for long. There and gone like a wink.

As they were leaving Tommy quietly said, "Three-oh."

"What?"

"Calibre of the rounds we took out of the car and the mess wall. Point three-zero, which as like as not means it was an M1 Garand. American rifle."

"Narrows it down then," Curry with his hand on the doorknob, grinned broadly. "These days a man can hardly walk the length of his own shadow without tripping over a Yank. So it really narrows it down."

IT WAS A COUPLE of hours later that Sadler met Linnet in the public bar of The Eagle and Child in St Giles, Oxford. They had both changed into mufti: unusual because you did not easily change into civilian clothes, even off duty. This was how it was in wartime Britain. People had been known to look horrified at the sight of fit and able-bodied men out of uniform. In any case it was not the done thing: a member of HM Forces was, in the main, proud to be a fighting man or woman.

They sat together in the corner of the saloon bar sipping

their weak beer and talking quietly. All the beer in England was pretty weak, it wasn't simply the prerogative of the Bird and Baby, as countless undergraduates referred to The Eagle and Child.

"So what happened with the timer?" Sadler asked.

He could understand four rifle shots missing, but they had worked out the lump of plastique, the detonator and the fuse. Sadler had rung Linnet from the mess as the car pulled away taking Shepherd and Mountford over to the car park beside the sergeants' mess.

They knew the drive took approximately three minutes. Make it five, giving them time to walk over to the vehicle. All Linnet had to do was set the timer for five minutes and dump the neat little bomb under the bonnet, using the magnetic clips, before the pair arrived. Plastique bombs were ten a penny at Airborne camps.

"They stopped," Linnet said. "They bloody stopped to talk by the edge of the parking area. Stood chatting away as though they had all the time in the world. Then, boom! They were nowhere near it, the buggers."

Sadler finished his beer and stared into the glass as though he could read something terrible in the dregs.

I am the prince of fools, he thought. Madness, all of it, and Tim Weaving had been the beginning. He should've remained in control instead of being so damned stupid. And the business on the aerodrome, what had that been about? The shooting and attempted bombing? Initially everything had started on an impulse.

They had been driving a mile or so following Tim Weaving and passing Portway House Linnet said, "He's in there. Now, he's in there."

And he thought, why not? and bounded out of the jeep and bounced up the steps...one...two...three...fit and hale and hearty, lifting the heavy brass knocker and the door opened.

There was Emily Bascombe, provocative, cocking her hip and wearing that interesting crooked smile, and – "Excuse me, madam, is Colonel Weaving here?"

Tim stepping into the hall from the right, from the front room, the drawing room if you thought you were as smart as that.

Tuesday 14th December, 1943. 11.30 in the evening.

Timmy not at all pleased but polite as ever.

"What d'you want?"

"A word, sir."

"Better come in. All right Em?"

"Of course."

Close the door behind you but leave it a smidgeon ajar. Nothing ostentatious, just around half-an-inch, then follow old Tim into the front room. The patterned carpet and stained polished border; luxurious blue velvet curtains, ceiling to floor, keeping the light in, well-lined; a three-piece suite covered in matching blue silk; a nest of tables; two standard lamps with cream shades; the picture over the mantelpiece, cows pausing in a rocky stream, behind them the hills, reeds and grass. Two other pictures, head of Erasmus and one pen and ink drawing of some Italian campanile rising from a huddle of buildings by a shoreline. Could be Switzerland not Italy. If not Como, then Magiorre or Lugano.

"Sit down —." called him by his name. But Sadler didn't sit.

"Well?" Tim Weaving asked, made no pretence that he was displeased, angry even, turning away as Sadler went through the curtains into the bay of the windows, signalled Linnet, turned and walked back.

Weaving now irritated, like someone with a head full of lice, "What the hell're you doing? Are you drunk or something...? Mind that bloody blackout."

Emily coming in, quite stunning in a green dress, narrow skirt, pinched waist and buttons down the bodice.

Tim Weaving turned back to Sadler just as he hit him with the ball of his fist, spun him then chopped hard in the back of his neck, put him down, out for the count.

Emily starting to scream but Linnet coming in behind her, right arm crooked around the throat, right hand on left bicep, left hand behind the head: you do not have to be strong to use the left hand to get purchase and the right forearm to subdue the throat. A quick death, very fast.

She was on the floor, lifeless by the time Sadler had the handcuffs on Tim Weaving. Always carried the handcuffs. Some ladies loved them. Got them from a Military Police sergeant when he was doing the EFTS and having a splendid ride round the park with a WAAF flight officer.

"Somewhere quiet," he told Linnet sharp, commanding. Linnet found the cellar. Within the half hour the night had become troubled far beyond sanity.

"Mr Ling! Mr Ling!" the barman of the Bird and Baby, called at them, leaning forward. "The telephone call you were expecting, sir."

Linnet disappeared behind the bar, hunched over the telephone, muttering.

"Beryl's lost them," he told Sadler when he returned. "Bloody lost them."

Beryl was the name of the WAAF corporal who had driven Curry Shepherd and Suzie Mountford to London. Owed Linnet a favour.

Chapter Twelve

CURRY TOLD THE WAAF corporal to drop them in Piccadilly.

"Anywhere special, sir?" She asked, bright corporal Beryl Collins.

"Oh," face screwed up, hesitant. "Oh, over there, near the Regent Palace Hotel."

The blackout was more relaxed now, at the end of 1943, unless a warning sounded; certainly easier to drive at night with the glimmer lights in the streets.

Suzie's head whipped round in the direction of the Regent Palace and she could see from here there were crowds of people about, the Piccadilly Commandos out in force, with plenty of customers, mainly Yanks. These prostitutes, some only enthusiastic amateurs, did a great trade with the Yanks who were more able to afford the girls than the British soldiers.

Her heart sank as the young corporal went round the Dilly and pulled up in front of the hotel. A sludge of memories filled her mind. A couple of years ago – '41, just after the Americans came into the war – she was working undercover for Tommy, attached to the CID at West End Central police station.

She had come into the Regent Palace one day when trying to track down some villains who had gone AWOL from the army and were now doing odd building and decorating jobs. While there she bumped into an immensely attractive RAF Spitfire pilot, Wing Commander Fordham O'Dell, and had spent a night with him, believing that Tommy had been unfaithful to her. It was the only time she ever cheated on Tommy, but now, as they drew up outside the hotel the memories of that time were vivid, *son et lumier* in her head. There, two years ago, she was playing around with the idea of leaving Tommy, and now she had done it.

She wondered what had happened to Fordy O'Dell whom

she'd first interviewed with his flight at Middle Wallop, just before Christmas 1940 when she was on her way to spend that terrible Christmas Day with her sister, Charlotte, in Hampshire. The Christmas when it all went wrong.

They climbed out of the car, a Humber painted matt RAF blue with a roundel on its offside front mudguard, and Curry signed the chit Beryl presented to him. "You can lose yourself 'til tomorrow morning, corporal," he told her and the girl nodded unhappily, saluted and got back behind the wheel.

"Don't go into the hotel," he told Suzie, lowering his voice. "Get lost in the crowd up here," nodding towards Sherwood Street, running alongside the hotel, taking her elbow and propelling her away from the entrance.

As she turned her head, Suzie was aware of the WAAF corporal fiddling around in the driving seat before starting the car again and slowly moving away.

"Into here," Curry told her as they approached a doorway. "Hard against here, out of sight."

"What's up?"

"You didn't notice?"

"Notice what?"

"That girl, the corporal driver."

"What about her?"

"She was very interested in where we were going. I slowed you down to let her see we weren't actually going into the hotel."

"So?"

"I want to see if she comes looking for us."

A few minutes later, as they stood silent in the doorway, watching tarts and their clients go by, Curry said, "There you go, she's looking as if her life depends on it." Sure enough the RAF Humber cruised past, the corporal's head stretched forward, eyeballing the pavement, craning, trying to spot them.

"Well?" Suzie still puzzled, then seeing the problem. "You

mean she was told to watch us? She's searching for us because someone's told her to?"

"That's about the strength of it. I think we should have a word with her as soon as we get back to Brize."

"We're going back?"

"Oh, in due course, yes. We can't really telephone 'cos we've no idea who may have asked the girl to pinpoint us, and I want to know who did the asking."

They went down into the Piccadilly underground and took the Bakerloo line on to Baker Street, Curry silent now, reflective. The regular, expect-em-same-time-every-night air raids had finished, yet people still automatically went down into some of the larger underground stations, spending the nights there; tiers of bunks were apparent in many of the stations, set back against the curved walls at the rear of platforms, though the chaos and stench of those early days of the Blitz were long gone.

At Baker Street they went up into the cold night and Curry led her along to Ivor Place, where, he told her, War Office Intelligence Liaison had an office on the second floor of a small commercial building.

Three organisations identified themselves on brass plates to the right of the door, each with its own bell push on the left of the plate. *Spindlers Surgicals Ltd.*, appeared to be on the ground floor; *War Office Annexe G8* was on the second floor; and at the top was *Bran Hoffman & Co (Sales)*. Later, Suzie discovered that all three ventures were really part of WOIL. Taking no notice of the bell pushes, Curry let them in with his own key, going up the uncovered stairs two at a time and walking straight in through what looked like the door to a flat on the left of a small landing. Suzie followed him and they walked straight into what had originally been the flat's hall, now converted to a general office: linoleum under foot, two metal tables, facing each other, telephones, a couple of type-writers and a pair of metal filing cabinets against the one empty wall.

A redheaded girl with wide hips and a confident manner turned from the filing cabinet as they entered. "Curry," she said in a somewhat proprietary manner. "You've just missed him – the boss that is, and...oh, hello," as Suzie came in.

Curry introduced them. The redhead was Ruth, "General factotum," he said.

"General bloody dogsbody more like." She wore a dark red suit, the skirt well cut so that it showed up the outline of her thighs as she walked with her fine, firm strides.

"Keeps us in order, does the typing, filing, takes the telephone calls, makes the coffee and adds a hint of mystery to the place."

"Not *all* the typing," she said, shuffling papers and taking a file over to the desk. "I share that..."

"With a little blonde who comes in a couple of times a week..."

"Every other day," Ruth corrected. "And she has a name. Jocelyn."

"Very posh, yes." He laughed, pronouncing it *powsh*. "We share her with somebody."

"We share her with her husband who's a wounded hero."

"That's the one. Where's the boss gone?"

"Elsie's across the road," which Curry told Suzie later meant he was over with the SOE people in Baker Street. Special Operations Executive, the people at the really sharp end of setting Europe ablaze as Winston Churchill had commanded: spies, saboteurs, resistance organisers.

"He leave a message for me?" Curry asked.

"Yes, he said come back tomorrow. He'll be in around nine. Very important." Stressing the 'very'. "Longing to see you."

"I bet he didn't say that."

"He said imperative, actually."

"Good. Okay, Ruth, we'll get off and hide in some nearby

woodshed. You here all night?"

"'Course I am. Guarding the Crown Jewels."

"'Course you are."

"They'll eventually give you a key," Curry told Suzie as they went downstairs.

"I look forward to that."

"Then you'll have it ready if some poor sod gets a nosebleed, slip it down his back."

They went out into the night and he asked where she had to go, where she lived?

"Not far. Just Upper St Martin's Lane."

"Come on," Curry said. "There's a good British Restaurant in Baker Street, up towards Oxford Street." He must have caught a look on her face, "If a British Restaurant's not below you."

British Restaurants had been opened by the government early in 1940 to ensure that anyone could get at least one, cheap, good and coupon-free meal a day and the standard was high.

"Why should British Restaurants be below me?" she caught hold of his arm, a little off balance in the dark.

"Hoi polloi eat there, the proles. You were Tommy's girl weren't you? With Tommy it'd be the Ritz, Savoy and clever little Italian places in Soho. Knew all the good eating houses, I'll bet."

"He did, rather, yes." Her mind circled the meals she'd had out with Tommy Livermore. Yes, the Ritz and a lot of clever little places. Tommy always knew where you could get good or different food. There was a French place in Marshal Street he swore ran a regular boat to join the fishing fleet off Normandy, went into Cherbourg with them, picked up homemade sausages and smoked hams, then slipped out after a couple of days. She never knew what to believe when Tommy got going. Later she had reasoned that the good food had something to do with having a private income. She remembered going to a party with him, at the Savoy, and being amazed at the amount of food and drink that were consumed in one evening.

"Why should that make any difference, being Tommy's girlfriend?" she asked now. "Heaven knows I've eaten in all kinds of places: like the canteen at West End Central." Curry gave a little one-note laugh. "And I've eaten in British Restaurants before." She bridled. "On numerous occasions."

The British Restaurant at the top of Baker Street was in fact a very good one in which they ate well. Thick vegetable soup; braised tongue with mashed potatoes and carrots; treacle tart and custard; tea and bread and butter. True the bread was not of the finest texture, more your off-white, battleship grey colour, but it was all edible and cost only one shilling and ninepence each.

"I wonder what the poor people're doing tonight," said Curry.

"Probably eating cake." Suzie with her dopey grin that she was starting to perfect. Then she thought, the poor people, that's a very Tommy remark. "So," she continued, "So, there's Ruth, then Jocelyn every other day. Elsie's the boss, how many others are part of War Office Intelligence Liaison?"

"Full strength's about eight." Curry kept his voice down remembering the warning advertisements – Careless Talk Costs Lives and Tittle-tattle lost the battle.

"How can full strength be *about* eight?"

"Give or take a couple. Sometimes we have to get people seconded to us – special skills people..."

"Like me?"

"Your skills are mainly being a woman."

"You mean you didn't get me in for a particular job?" She didn't care for his last remark.

"We did, actually. That is apart from being allowed an experienced female officer on the strength."

"So what's the special job?"

"Elsie'll tell you."

"You mean you can't or you don't know?"

"Meaning I'm not allowed. I know but Elsie has a better view of the overall picture. How're you going to get home?"

"I'll get home in a taxi – if I can find one. If not, it isn't that far to walk…Well it is, but…How about you?" she trailed off, nowhere to go with this particular line.

"Oh, it'll take me a couple of hours. I've got to get out to New Malden."

"You live out there?"

"Yes, I do. Murderous journey."

"That's ridiculous. What've you got, some sordid little flat?"

"Bedsit with a small kitchen and use of bathroom. All mod cons, as they say. Running hot and cold sausages, place mats, stainless steel cutlery, all those lovely middle class necessities, silver napkin rings, fish knives."

"Dead sophisticated, Curry. You can come home with me if you like."

"Oi-oi."

"I have a spare room. You're very welcome." Being a straight bit of goods, not a flicker, not a smile, no wrong messages. Keep it simple, she thought.

Curry said it would certainly be easier to get into Ivor Place if he stayed at Suzie's flat. "We'd get in easily from St Martin's Lane."

"Well then," grin and shrug. "It's not even *my* flat. Not strictly speaking." She went on to tell Curry about the flat belonging to her mum and the need to keep it dark because of her stepfather Ross Gordon-Lowe. Just in case her mother had to do a midnight flit.

"I mean, he's okay – in small doses – but old Major Ross

Gordon-Lowe DSO is often hard to take. Not absolutely certain that's his real name. I think the Gordon part is actually simply another Christian name," a charitable statement, she considered, because Ross Gordon-Lowe was in many ways a pompous, pedantic old bore.

Now, over the braised tongue and treacle tart, she told the troubled history to Curry Shepherd while he made sympathetic noises.

"In the end, he was quite good though a bit of a prune when it came to Tommy." She bit down on a large slice of treacle tart and sucked in on the custard making a little moan of ecstasy. "Lord, I love treacle tart."

"In what way, a prune?"

"Thought chatting to Tommy was like gossiping with royalty. Oh, and I love the custard. My mum made the best custard ever."

Curry smiled and shook his head, a sign that he was falling for her winning ways, she decided and so asked him if he wanted to avail himself of her spare room.

"Avail myself? Well I've got to say that I could be talked into it. Just thinking about riding out to New Malden makes me tired and depressed."

"I could do you bacon for breakfast," she give him her best smile, the winning one.

"Consider me talked into it then. Do you hoard bacon or what?"

"One of the benefits of Tommy was the by-products we got from the Home Farm at Kingscote Grange, the family seat."

So they managed to get a cab to Upper St Martin's Lane and Suzie showed him around her small flat, and made up the bed in the spare room, hoping he wouldn't use it. And as she went round she kept remembering Tommy because, of course, he was here: the smell of him, his tobacco, his scent; couldn't get it out of her head: little waves of nostalgia.

Then she made Curry some cocoa, which he liked, and drank in the kitchen idly flicking through the Ministry of Food leaflets: *Step lively with Potato Pete or Dr Carrot*, or *Food without Fuel, Kitchen Goes to War* and the others she had neatly stacked on the dresser.

"This looks good," and he read from a recent Food Facts, "Date and Nut Loaf, All Clear Sandwiches. Oh my God, Trench Cake, Mock Fish. Ugh, Rook Pie. You don't really cook stuff like this do you?"

"Made a rook pie last year." Bouncy, all capable woman. "Delicious, but you've got to be careful to use only the breast meat because the rest's foul, bitter and horrid," she scrunged her face up comically.

As they said goodnight on the landing outside the master bedroom door she simply stood there looking a bit pathetic trying to be a woman in need of protection, arms hanging straight down by her sides. Don't act predatory, she told herself. Just look as if you need keeping safe. Head up to him; big eyes. She even asked if he needed anything.

"No," he said.

"Pajamas? I've got some of Tommy's if you..." realising that was quite the wrong thing.

"No," he said coldly. Flat.

"Oh, damn. Sorry." And she was.

Her reward was a chaste kiss on the forehead which left her lying in bed wondering if she had something wrong with her.

Perhaps he's queer, she thought. No, she had learned to spot queers while she was at West End Central. Anyway, it was against the law and she very much doubted if there was one queer copper in the Met, let alone among the secret squirrels.

Tomorrow, she thought, tomorrow they would see Elsie and he'd let her into the charmed circle: tell her about her real job. Then she thought what a slut she was, trying to seduce that nice Mr Curry Shepherd. Jeerusalem, if only.

It was an unfulfilled Suzie Mountford who dropped into sleep that night.

Chapter Thirteen

LINNET DROVE THEM back to Brize Norton, both of them wrapped in their overcoats, freezing and silent in the jeep, their hair collecting rimes of frost in the open vehicle. Sadler thought that it was now they should be talking, out in the open not as they had done in the public house, in the Eagle and Child. It was what Ritter, Klampt and Osterlind had taught him in Hamburg back in 1938. Never talk about the work inside; always get out and away from buildings they said, and he'd disobeyed them. But then he'd disobeyed them in so much: about recruiting Linnet, about the folly of the melodramatic inquisition of Tim Weaving leading to the death of Weaving and his lady friend.

The wisdom of clandestine warfare said that, given time, everybody cracks under a good interrogation; some people crack faster with torture, some dig their heels in and put up the shutters, sometimes seeming to revel in pain. Weaving had been of the latter kind, not even beginning to crack; showing immense courage: giving them only a couple of generalisations before he died because Sadler had become overzealous, angry with the man's bravery. It was so stupid of Linnet, killing the woman like that. Weaving knew immediately that he was never going to leave that cellar alive: and when you know that…well, he had nothing to lose.

Then there was the other idiot thing he had done – trying to kill the two spy-catchers, if that was truly what they were.

He wondered if he was going out of his mind, if he was starting to lose the sacred trust he had sworn to Deutschland and the Führer. In the 1930s, the concept of National Socialism had him by the throat then, and was present in him as though it were mingled with the blood running through his veins. The historians taught that he who rules Berlin rules Europe, and after Hitler came to power the other leaders of

Europe looked like the namby-pamby weaklings they were. Neville Chamberlain, ineffectual, peace at any price, didn't stand a chance against a man of the Führer's vision.

It was said that when somebody asked Hitler why on earth he had signed the non-aggression agreement, in Munich at the end of August '38, the one the British Prime Minister brought back and waved around at Croydon aerodrome – Peace in our time – the Führer had said, "He seemed such a nice old man, so I thought I'd give him my autograph". Hitler had broken the mould as far as single-mindedness was concerned, while the old divisions between ruling classes and proles ground on archaically in England.

Sadler had been totally dominated by the Nazi ideal, for him it was like a drug, or as though he had been hypnotised, which in some senses he had in falling under Hitler's spell. For Sadler it was both the power and the glory. Yet now, and only occasionally, he questioned it, as if there was a weakness, a chink in the steel of his will, a fissure through which doubts assailed him. He became terrified of these suggestions of a loss of faith. He considered that he was like a holy man going through the dark night of the soul. To him it was no real threat, yet on the drive back to Brize Norton on that frosty night before Christmas, things started to go seriously wrong in his head.

He concluded that he might even have the bulk of the information on *Overlord* before the week was out. After all, he needed only the headings: where, when, how and an outline of the logistics. And tomorrow he would be with Colonel Belcher and the others inside Norfolk House, the headquarters of COSSAC in St. James's Square listening to a recital of the outline plan. The Abwehr could work out the strengths themselves. Osterlind had said they were listening to hours of military radio traffic as the British, American and other armies moved around the highways and byways of southern England

and East Anglia.

Then there was the other side of the coin, the dark side. There was a point when the jeep was only a couple of miles from Brize that Sadler actually contemplated throwing the whole thing overboard: giving up, getting himself moved to some non-combatant outfit and then lying low. When it was all over he could seek out his German masters, even at this stage he could not conceive of Hitler's great armies losing. From what he knew about tactics and strategy he was aware that an all-out assault on the Channel coastline of Northern France was a mad, unrealistic gamble. With Rommel in command of Fortress Europe the Allies would be swept back into the bloodstained sea in a matter of days.

He had even heard the rumour that the whole scheme had been hatched by the Americans, and everybody knew that as a race their kind of military thinking was at the best shaky. In the past few days, someone had even said he knew for a fact that Churchill favoured an advance through Portugal.

When Linnet finally pulled the jeep into the park in front of the officers' mess and switched off the engine, Sadler turned to him and quietly told him not to worry the WAAF corporal about losing contact with the two Special Branch officers, or whatever they were. "With any luck, I'll have the information we need by tomorrow night, or the next day." He said, keeping his voice down.

"But…" Linnet started.

"I've had second thoughts," Sadler leaned towards him. "I think what we've been doing is wrong and it's essential now that we keep our heads down, become really invisible like the ghosts we are."

Linnet again opened his mouth, but Sadler shut him up with a simple wave of the hand, got out of the jeep and walked quietly towards his quarters in the Nissen hut backing on to the mess.

Ten minutes later, in uniform, Sadler came into the bar. The CO, Colonel Belcher, was there with a RAF redcap, a squadron leader who had come over to take a look at the breaches of security: the shooting and the bombing of the civilian car.

Sadler shook hands with the squadron leader and said how relieved he was to know there was a professional on the job. He then asked, "Who were those two, Shepherd and Mountford?"

"Couple of funnies," the squadron leader said with his mouth turned down as if to say that funnies were not his cup of tea.

"Really?" Sadler put on his I'm-impressed voice. "What kind of funnies?"

"Funnies is funnies. Intelligence is better left to the cavalry," the squadron leader snorted. "Something to do with liaison with other funnies I understand."

"Never held with funnies," Bart Belcher snarled. "Funnies're irregulars in my experience. Neither fish, flesh, fowl nor good red herring."

"They're certainly fishy," said the squadron leader laughing loudly at what he thought was a profound witticism.

HE WAS AMAZED because Suzie cooked him four rashers of bacon for breakfast – more than one person's ration for a week, unheard of. "Make the most of it," she said, "I've only got eight more rashers left and I don't see Tommy's people wandering down with more for me now I'm a thing of the past."

She had also boiled some potatoes the night before and left them in the cold cupboard let into one of the flat's outside walls and adjacent to a window. It had a door on it covered in tight wire mesh, and the whole cupboard interior and shelves were fashioned out of cold stone. It was the nearest thing Suzie could afford to a refrigerator. Refrigerators were prohibitively expensive and not readily available in spite of the advertisements from the Electricity Development Association telling you that electric fridges were there to help you Wage War on Waste. Next to Curry's four rashers was a pile of fried cold potatoes. Suzie only managed two rashers and a few of the potatoes because she had butterflies of excitement in her stomach: going to meet the new boss.

"Tommy always said something to try and get my angora," she said. "Sometimes I'd put a huge meal in front of him, meat and two veg, and he'd say, 'Tell you what would be nice with this, a few baby carrots'. He was pulling my leg, of course, see if I'd rise to the bait, and I often did. If I'd put rashers and fried spuds in front of him he'd say that a few fried tomatoes would be nice with it. Now, I mean he'd say it, in winter, when you can't get tomatoes."

"He hasn't changed very much. I fagged for him at m'tutor's and when I did his tea it was never right. I'd get him crumpets in winter and he'd want cucumber sandwiches. Like you say, when you couldn't get cucumber. In winter. There's no way of bottling cucumbers is there?"

"Not a chance. Mummy bottles everything she can lay her hands on. She bottles tomatoes but you can't use them for a fry-up. Can only really use them in soups or a stew."

"You're a fount of information, Suzie. Don't know how I managed without you."

They walked down to Charing Cross and got a taxi to the Courtauld Institute of Art, then walked through Portman Street to Baker Street and on to Ivor Place. "Never ask for Baker Street or Ivor Place in a taxi," Curry counselled her. "In fact it's a good rule never to direct a taxi to wherever you're really going. Always check for a tail – surveillance, I mean. You just can't be too careful. It's as well to watch your back wherever you're going. In the business you're in now you should really assume that somebody's got the dogs on you

most of the time. Not necessarily the Krauts, you'd be surprised. Our French allies watch us a good deal. Don't really
trust us. Still think we ran away and hung them out to dry at
Dunkirk. Then there was the Oran business of course."

Suzie nodded sagely, "Of course," remembering that the
Royal Navy had sunk elements of the French fleet off Oran,
when they had refused to join with the British. Many had been
killed.

Ruth was wearing a purple woollen Jaeger dress (*The Best
in Utility*, they advertised) that didn't really suit her, the skirt
a little too long and narrow, meant she couldn't take her usual
long strides. Curry said, "A stitch in time saves coupons, I
see." And Ruth glared at him.

A large tough-looking customer sat near to what Suzie presumed was Elsie's office door.

"Wotcher, Eddie," Curry greeted him and the big fellow,
whose nose was decidedly off-centre, gave an evil grin,
"Wotcher, Curry me old horse. How y'doing?"

"Decidedly well, Ed. Better than some."

"Yea? Well the gaffer's waiting to see you. A band of hope
all ye who enter here." Another grin, still evil and he leaned
over and opened the door for them.

"Ed's the boss's bodyguard," Curry told her.

The first thing Suzie saw in the office was a small portable
organ standing the middle of the room, a pile of sheet music
on the music rest, while an old big wooden desk took up
almost the entire width of the rear wall. On the desk were four
telephones drowning in a sea of paper, and behind it there
seemed to be a reddish glow that turned out to be L C
Partridge.

Elsie was a difficult man to describe, tall, but in no way dis-
tinguished, with a dome of a bald head, ginger hair, in smooth
segments, sleek on each side, above the ears, bright light eyes,
a mouth set in what seemed to be a permanent smile plus an

aquiline nose, big and beaky. He was dressed in a ginger three-piece tartan check suit, white shirt and russet-coloured tie.

When he spoke it was like being captured in an enthusiasm of words sprayed out by a fizzing human bomb, short sentences shot from his mouth, words bubbled over one another, sometimes mixing several subjects into one sentence.

"Ah, Curry, how lovely to see you. My word, and you're the famous Suzie Mountford. Come in, come in. Goodness me you're a pretty girl, I must say. A very pretty girl. Sit down then Suzie. And you Curry. No standing on ceremony here. Come now, sit ye down the pair of you. Sit ye down." Delight just flooded out of him.

They sat and waited. Suzie said later that her waiting was done with bated breath. "For the first time ever I know what bated breath really means – restrained breathing, I suppose. Or abated breathing. Whichever, I waited with it."

Elsie leaned back in his chair, folded his hands over his waistcoat and gave them a benevolent smile. "You've had a rough old time, the pair of you."

"We know," Curry said silkily. Curry, Suzie decided, could do silky quite well.

"Shot at, eh? Then nearly blown to Hades. Oh my as Ratty would have said to Mole – Oh My! Oh My! Oh My! Ah, sorry. Suzie, welcome. Glad to see you here, good to have you on the team." Sounding like some football captain.

Elsie bent his head forward and, for a second, Suzie saw the top of his head was covered in what the Germans call *Sommersprossen* while we, the English, more prosaically call them, freckles.

"Well, Suzie," he continued, looking at her with his pale gooseberry green eyes wide, almost pleading, "What do you make of it? Do you think Colonel Weaving was murdered while being questioned? And, if so, what do you imagine the questions concerned?"

For a moment Suzie had the strange idea that she was being interrogated by a foreigner. "I think he died while he was being tortured, yes, sir." Dried for a second or two and Elsie leaned forward, nodded, saying "Good," under his breath, and again, "Good."

"And the only thing that makes sense is that he was being questioned about the invasion plans." Pause. "I think, sir."

"You think?"

"Yes."

"Curry?"

"I don't think, boss, I know that's what happened. Just as I know we've frightened him, panicked him, because the bugger tried to bury us."

"Quite so, quite so. Yes, I think Curry's right, Suzie. As you said, it's the only thing that makes sense." And he was off talking nineteen to the dozen for it became clear a lot of work had already gone into the case. Tim Weaving died early on Wednesday morning. It was now only Friday yet Elsie Partridge was telling them what men he called Big Peter and Little Trevor had discovered in that relatively short space of time.

"You'll meet Peter and Trevor in due course, Suzie," Elsie leaned forward and grasped her wrist. "Good fellows to have around you in a scrap, eh Curry? But they're also not lazy when it comes to the intellectual stuff, the brainpower, you know. They've been down to see the poor parents in Devon. Weaving's people. They're in a state, I can tell you. Idolised Tim and very proud of him. Odd point, though. Tim was supposed to be engaged to the girl Richardson, what?"

"Julia Richardson," Suzie provided.

"Quite. Precisely. Fount of information you are, Suzie. Don't know how we've managed without you." And behind his hand Curry gurgled and Suzie tried to stop herself smirking, realising that Curry had been setting her up when he'd used almost the same words earlier.

"Well, funny thing, both of you, but the old parents knew nothing about it. One of many girlfriends, they said, the old loves. Engagement? No, bewildered, so Trev, who's very quick on these things, young Trevor steered the conversation into another direction. Cold are we Curry? You shivering, eh?"

"It is rather chilly," Suzie said with a thin smile, not showing her teeth, still hiding the giggles.

"Pop the gas fire on, Curry old love. Put a match to it. Should have done it first thing but don't feel as chilly as you ladies. Probably got more on than you," he chortled, no end of an old dog. "You girls in your little nothings, eh? Ho-ho."

When a match was put to the three-bar fire it lighted with an amazing whumph. "Small bomb that bloody thing," Elsie said. And one of the elements was broken so the heat being thrown out was irregular. It also popped in the old tradition of gas fires in official houses.

"We're looking at two women, girlfriends of the late Colonel Weaving. Anne..."

"Tooks," said Suzie.

"Tooks. Fount of information, Suzie, absolute fount. Tooks has her own money, lots of it and a flat in Hands Place, handy for Harrods, just round the corner. Doesn't seem to have many friends though. Very few callers, bit of a loner. And, of course we've been taking a look at the fair Julia Richardson, lives in Shepherd Street. Amazing area that. Ladies of the night, frail sisterhood, girls' boarding houses, proper slice of sin round there. Damned difficult place to put watchers they tell me. Fellows standing about casually get accosted every few minutes. Some tart comes stooging up, 'Want to come home with me, dear?' I mean what does a fellow say to that?"

Elsie paused for breath and Curry nipped in, "We *have* established, boss... I mean those two girls...We...I've established..."

"Yes. Of course, Curry. Does Suzie know?"

"Doubt it, boss."

"Well," he settled back, fingers linked over the waistcoat. "Clever old Curry here, Suzie. Damned smart, old Curry. Our victim, poor Colonel Weaving, last twelve, eighteen, months, had only *two* lady friends." He looked up, turning the full power of his dark eyes on Curry Shepherd. "Little Trevor spotted it as well, when they went to talk to the parents, break the news, that kind of thing, they said – the parents – he seemed only interested in two. Ann Tooks and the fair Julia Richardson. They said that before Anne he had played the field. I think they meant just about every field you could run across, couldn't do a hand's turn without coming across one of Tim Weaving's girls." He, of course, pronounced it, 'gels,' and Suzie wondered when the hell Curry had managed to come up with the information concerning Tim Weaving's girlfriends.

"Now Julia is the one for company. Don't know if she's just blessed with a lot of friends, but they never stop. Round the clock, young women, mostly calling on her all times of the day or night. Don't know what she's up to, but money's involved somewhere."

Curry grunted and Suzie said, "In that area she might be involved in anything. Even S-E-X." She spelled.

"Interesting really," Elsie Partridge continued. "Interesting that nobody seemed to talk about the woman who died with him. Few people knew."

"They knew at Brize Norton," Curry said.

"And the two who killed them knew. May have known for some time." Suzie nodded and pulled down the corners of her mouth.

"So, what you want us to do?" Curry asked.

Elsie gave a heavy sigh. "Okay. I want you to visit both women." His voice seemed to change down like someone shifting gears in a car. "Not in any official capacity, mind you. Take a bit of getting used to, Suzie. No need to go in showing

Warrant Cards, that sort of thing. Go in as old friends of Tim Weaving. Curry knows the form, so he'll tell you how to do it. Just paying a visit of condolence, eh? What?"

"But what d'you really want us to do?" Curry asked.

"Been thinking about that." Once more his voice changed down. "I'll tell you what I think…" and he talked for around fifteen minutes, telling them, in some detail, how they should go about the visits. He used the word guile often, and also said it would be like taking sweets from a baby; this way they would never know they were being interrogated.

When he had finished talking, Elsie Partridge did one last – and to Suzie, strange – thing. He got to his feet, tapped his pockets, nodded towards the organ in the middle of the room. "How about a hymn? Get the blood going. Good idea?"

"Of course, boss." Curry rose bringing a bewildered Suzie with him. Elsie seated himself at the organ and pumped the foot pedals. "How about 'Fight the Good Fight'," he said and struck a chord, then launched into:

Fight the good fight with all thy might,
Christ is thy strength and Christ thy right;
Lay hold on life, and it shall be
Thy joy and crown eternally.

By the time they reached the last verse Suzie was singing along as lustily as the two men.

"Does he often do that, warble a hymn?" She asked Curry as they drove towards Knightsbridge. Elsie had made a telephone call and Curry's Vauxhall Ten was replaced with another of the same make, dark blue this time.

"Known for it," Curry sashayed through the light traffic. "Embarrassing sometimes if you've got some hairy great knuckle dragger like Ed in tow. Come to think of it, Ed quite likes the odd hymn. Fight the good fight would be a favourite with him."

"Like being back at school," Suzie squinted at him.

"Hardly," he stared ahead.

They reached Harrods and turned left. "Have you thought," Suzie said, "if you're right about Colonel Weaving having been killed by one of the officers from the Glider Pilot Regiment, whoever it is will be sitting in Norfolk House, COSSAC HQ, now, this minute listening to the Classified stuff?"

"I've thought of nothing else since we left Ivor Place." A long pause followed, then, "I ever tell you about the ARP warden who went to a house of ill repute to complain about a blackout infringement? Back in 1940?"

Suzie shook her head knowing something pretty terrible was coming.

"Well, the old Mother Judge came to the door and asked what was wrong. The ARP man says, 'you've got a chink in the second floor front bedroom.' 'You're wrong,' says the Mother Judge. 'He's a Japanese gentleman.'"

Chapter Fourteen

SHE WAS A little woman, small-boned, neat but without the gloss you would expect from someone as independently wealthy as her. When she opened the door to them Suzie was surprised, thought she'd have servants to do things like that, open doors, wait at table, cook grand meals. She knew people had lost their maids, cooks and butlers because of the war but never quite believed this applied to the very wealthy, and Ann Tooks was *very* wealthy, two or three million. Curry had said, "It all came from her grandfather who invented something commonplace that, once invented, became indispensable in every home. Something like the seal on certain kinds of jars or bottles, maybe it was the doormat. Who cares? She had two brothers and the cash came down through their father. When he died it was split into three equal portions and bingo, rich lady."

"We're friends of Tim Weaving's," Curry said. "We know you were close to him, and it seemed the right thing to do, drop in and see you. We were in this part of London so thought we'd come."

"But, if it's inconvenient..." Suzie began, just as they'd rehearsed it.

"No...No, please come in," Her face said she didn't really want to see them, and her manner, gestures, body language said go away, but they took no notice, went in just the same.

"Can I get you anything? Cup of tea? Coffee? Though I've not got any decent coffee..."

"We're fine Miss Tooks," and as he said it realised that her name allowed for some of his quirky humour: Miss Tooks. *The greatest mistook of my life, was saying goodbye to you.* He laughed inside, solemn look outside.

"My friends call me Annie."

"Annie," Curry tried it on for size.

"Then how are you, Annie?" Suzie asked as they entered

the drawing room. Very nice, she thought. Good furniture, modern, deep leather chairs and a long matching buttoned Chesterfield; predominantly green décor, green leather on the chairs and the Chesterfield. The walls papered in an exquisite light green paper with a discrete contrasting design, two shades of green, blending well. Some jade on the mantelpiece, and a couple of large green glass ashtrays on the side tables. Good pictures, four of them, though Suzie couldn't have named the artists. Though she did note they were chosen for subject, impressions of woods and wide meadows, hint of a windmill on the skyline: Norfolk, she thought.

It wasn't until they were actually in the room that Curry started to introduce himself and Suzie. They shook hands and Annie Tooks said how nice it was of them to come, she was grateful. She was lying, that was plain by her manner, the way she spoke and the fact that she was holding her hands crossed in front of her, over her breasts, classic defensive movement.

Then she came clean.

"I think I should tell you that I fell out with Tim. Much earlier this year. In the spring. Irreparable. I'm still upset by the news of course, naturally, though I hadn't even seen him or spoken to him since March, the bastard. He was a bit of a rat with the ladies. Though I wouldn't have wished his kind of death on a rat."

"How did he end? How was he killed?" Suzie asked, waiting. "We haven't been able to find out." A cop's question she had learned from a sergeant when she was on the beat. They had gone one day to break the news of a close relative's death to a well-known local man and the sergeant had told her she was the one who had to do it. She had obviously been nervous and hesitant, so when she told the man to sit down he immediately said, "It's alright. I know you've come to tell me that my aunt has died."

Without a pause the sergeant had said, "How do you know

that?" concerned that this may not be a natural death. As it happened, a friend of his aunt had just telephoned him with the news, but Suzie had never forgotten the speed with which the sergeant had asked the question and she had learned from it.

Now in the Hands Place flat, Annie Tooks said, "Oh, I don't know the details, but he was murdered. That's enough isn't it? Murdered with a woman. I should imagine some jealous husband...Didn't the papers say she was married to someone who'd been awarded the Victoria Cross?"

"Yes, but..." Suzie began.

Curry cut in, "Look, if there's anything we can do..."

Annie Tooks lifted her head and it was clear she was beginning to cry, not weeping with sorrow, angry tears now brimming in her eyes. "No, really..."

"I mean, his parents. We're in touch with his parents."

"I never met his parents," she said coldly, all but spat, the anger showing now in flushed patches on her cheeks and tears starting to run down, little deltas forming on her skin. "I was supposed to meet them. Several times. We were to announce our engagement...." Gulping air now. "But it never happened. He never got around to it. It was always just over the horizon..."

"I'm sorry," Curry flapped his arms as though saying, 'what could I do' and Suzie moved over and put an arm around the woman. One way or another she'd had a lot of practise comforting people.

Now, close to Annie Tooks, Suzie saw that the corduroy skirt she wore was an expensive garment, tailored, the material a crushed raspberry colour, the twin-set of a similar shade, yet the clothes looked dowdy on her and Suzie realised they were uncared for, creased, dirty, stained. She also wore no make-up and her hair needed attention, possibly some more of whatever she used to turn it into the light golden colour. Clothes were difficult enough these days with rationing, 'to provide a fair distribution of available supplies' though most women she knew tried to keep what they already had, mainly pre-war garments, in good, and smart, condition. Suzie remembered when clothes rationing had come in, over the Whit weekend of 1941. The plan had been kept so secret – to avoid panic buying – that, when the ration was announced as sixty-six coupons worth a year, there were no coupons available and clothes shops initially took margarine coupons instead.

Harrods advertised that now clothes were on the ration a sewing machine was almost as good a weapon as a spade. But by now, Christmas 1943, it had become increasingly difficult to look bandbox smart. Most people were either in uniform or shabbily dressed. Annie was more than shabby and Suzie remembered her mother saying of a woman who'd started to look down at heel, 'that woman's letting herself go'. At the time she'd thought that a strange expression. Now looking at Annie Tooks she saw how apt it was.

Annie wept at full bore now, while Curry was trying to talk her down from fast approaching hysteria.

"Annie, listen to me," Curry managing the paradox of firm and gentle. "We've only just met. You need to talk, Annie. Talk to us. Come on now, it'll do you good…"

"Problem shared…" Suzie added.

Slowly the raging fury subsided and was reduced to quiet sobs. "I'm…I'm crying…for him…" she managed. "I loved him so much."

Oh Lord, Suzie thought, how melodramatic are we going to get?

"He let you down?" Curry asked, bringing about a fresh tide of howling tears.

You can discover much by guile, Elsie had counselled.

"Talk about it," Suzie added. "Spill it out, Annie." *Oh God, I feel like someone in a bad film*, 'Spill it out, Annie'. In her head she heard it with an American accent.

But Annie did. Spilled it out: how Tim Weaving had made

the sun shine every day, how he'd asked her to marry him and she, trusting, had felt that the offer having been accepted, immediately opened the bedroom door.

"I gave him everything...Did everything he wanted...Made myself available in every possible way." The tears again drizzled, a rallentando of sobs, degenerating to lento.

Bloody hell, Suzie said silently, *is this going to get even more melodramatic?* Her eyes caught Curry's and she had to look away.

"Let it all out, Annie," Suzie muttered, still with her arm around the woman, fingers clawed about her shoulder. "Tell it all."

"I suppose I fall in love too easily," she said.

Jeeroosaalem. How old is this woman? I fall in love too easily. Crikey.

"I met Tim Weaving at the house of a friend: Sylvia Picket, girl I was at school with; you can imagine the nicknames. She was in the middle of a little run around with one of Tim's officers."

"Which one?" Curry asked, as though it didn't matter a damn to him.

"Wilson Sharp. Captain Sharp."

"Sure," Curry smiled.

The saturnine young captain. Suzie kicked it around in her head. Countryman, walked loosely, behaved as he would strolling down a village street. She thought of him as tough, as though he had confidence enough for the whole regiment. He was tall, tanned face, dark-hair, floppy dark hair. Sharp had given Tommy a hard time about the morals of men and of war.

"Wilson Sharp," she said aloud. "Wouldn't like to get on the wrong side of old Wilson Sharp on a dark night."

Annie stopped crying, took a long sniff of air through her nose. "No. No you wouldn't. Some civvies tried to pick up Sylvia in a pub, Lord Nelson out near Wantage. Young civilian chaps, working locally I think. Wilson Sharp saw them off. Went for them like a bloody bulldog. Sylvia told me they turned and fled. Wouldn't have minded Wilson for myself really."

"But you had Tim, Colonel Tim Weaving."

"For a while. 'Till he found someone else and didn't even tell me... Julia... Sylvia and Wilson are engaged and I hear it's serious. Wants to marry her quickly it seems."

"Richardson," Suzie added. "Julia Richardson."

"That's the girl." Pause. Could have heard a bomb drop in the silence, or a pin for that matter. "I'm sorry." She relaxed, body sagging, then another intake of air through the nose, the back of her hand across her eyes, getting rid of the tears. "I'm so sorry...I think I've had a stupid bit of the hystericals..."

"He treated you badly," Curry told her.

Suzie said, "You're entitled to the Harry hysteriers." Everyone had started to use the military affectation of Harry in front of words and 'ers on the subject – Harry crashers, Harry brokers. Her widowed brother-in-law, Vernon Fox now a Royal Marine Commando Lieutenant had told her that when he was at Deal they had an imaginary Marine Harry Flakers because they were all tired out at the end of a strenuous day.

"Let me get us some tea," Annie stood up, eyes red-ringed and cheeks stained; but now she was invested with a terrible calm. They followed her through the hall into her small kitchen knowing that sudden calm in people prone to severe emotional fits was not a good sign. Sometimes an unusually tranquil mood following high drama signified deeper problems.

She filled the kettle and put it on a gas hob, slipping the whistler onto the spout. She was collecting cups from the small Welsh dresser that took up almost an entire wall when Suzie saw her lean forward grasping at the edge of the dresser, her knuckles showing white.

"You okay?" Suzie beside her, ready to hold on if she

seemed about to collapse.

The girl nodded, teeth clenched. "The bastard," she muttered again, then got control of herself, straightened and continued preparing the cups, asking who wanted sugar, pouring the milk.

"It really is amazing," she finally said as she was warming the pot with water from the almost boiling kettle. "Amazing how one man can wreak such devastation on a woman. I thought I was almost over him, but I'm not nearly in the clear yet."

"What actually happened?" Curry asked. He was good at making questions sound casual and lacking in importance.

"More or less what I told you. We were ridiculously happy – I was anyway, and I thought he was. Making plans for the future, though he wasn't happy about getting married before the end of the war. I wanted a quick wedding. Soon. He wanted to wait, said once we made a move into Europe it'd be over quite quickly." She made the tea, pouring the boiling water into the pot, stirring as she did so, her hand steady as her voice. "I must say I wondered about that. Other people I knew, quite senior people, would tell me that it certainly wasn't all over once the second front began, and I knew that. I know the Germans have a great well-trained army. They're good and fanatical fighters. Am I right?"

Suzie looked at Curry who said that she was certainly right. "If, and it's a pretty big if, we do open a second front in Occupied Europe it'll be a hard battle and I wouldn't like to put money on the outcome. If we get a toehold somewhere on the continent it could take months to fight our way through. On the other hand a lot of people believe that the round-the-clock bombing's killing the Nazis will to go on; knocking out their armament industry, smashing their lines of supply, certainly demoralising their civilians."

Annie had put the cups on a tray and they followed her

back into the drawing room. Setting the tray down she made a little tutting noise, said she looked a fright. "I'll just go and splash some water on my face."

Suzie was back on her feet. "I'll do the same if you don't mind."

Annie gave a gentle laugh. "Don't worry, I'm not going to do myself an injury. You're welcome to come with me. I'm a bit flattered." And she strode off quite briskly.

Back downstairs again, five minutes later, Annie, now clean of the traces of tears, leaned back in one of the comfortable armchairs, looked at Curry, then Suzie and back to Curry again. "You're the police, aren't you?" Stating rather than asking.

Curry calmly told her no. "We're not the law, Annie, but we are investigating Tim's death. Was it so obvious?"

"It was Miss Mountford being so attentive. Just an idea. I said to myself, these people're too good to be just ordinary friends."

"It's not desperate. Tim was a good man, a fine soldier. We're just tying up some frayed ends."

"May have been a fine soldier but he wasn't a good man. Good men don't play fast and loose with women's emotions."

"You were telling us what actually happened..." Curry prompted.

She eyed them both; more coldly this time. "Yes I was. Where had we got to?"

"You were very happy," Suzie told her. "And you thought he was. But he wanted to wait until this unpleasantness was over."

"Yes. Well, I was deeply in love with him – I expect that makes me sound like a sixteen-year-old girl instead of a woman of twenty-six..."

"Not at all," Curry said, and Suzie shook her head.

"I saw him every weekend, and sometimes during the week

if he could get up to town. In the beginning he showed incredible respect. I suppose I offered everything to him on a plate, but he refused: said he wanted to wait. But...well...we didn't wait of course, and I felt it was terribly daring and very wonderful. Two people becoming one *is* wonderful: Christmas morning every day." She said nothing for a few moments. Then, "Isn't it? Or am I being a stupid inexperienced girl?"

"Love can be incredible," said Suzie without much conviction.

"You regarded yourselves as being engaged?" Curry asked.

"Of course. I was supposed to meet his parents and have a big engagement party, but it never materialised."

"Then?"

"Then one weekend he went back to Brize and said, 'I'll see you next week my darling. Love you.' And that was it. Never saw him again. Next thing I knew he was announcing his engagement to Julia Meg Richardson. In the *Times* and the *Telegraph*. They had a little story about him in the *Daily Mail* as well. Bastard. I could have killed him. Still could actually, if he wasn't already dead."

"Come on Annie," Suzie began. "We all say that when someone really..."

"No, I mean it. I absolutely mean it. One of my brothers also wanted to do him over. The one who came and saw me, dropped in the day I saw the announcement and had tried to ring him at Brize, got turned away." She put on a hoity-toity voice, "'I'm sorry, ma'am, the Colonel's flying at the moment, won't be in the office for some days.'"

Curry asked her for the name and address of the brother and she refused it with a shake of the head. "Any policemen been to see you yet?" he enquired.

"Are they likely to?"

"I think highly likely." Suzie raised her eyebrows. "There should be a smooth old bugger called Livermore. How about him? Tommy Livermore? He'll be round."

"Anyone else you can suggest?" Curry asked. "Anyone else didn't like him?"

"Yes, of course. Husbands of girls who've gone off into the haystacks with Tim. Husbands and boyfriends. I should imagine they litter the Home Counties. I also know at least one of his officers that Tim was scared of."

"Which one?"

"Well, two actually. Major Hutt and old Bomber Puxley."

"One more and he'll have a full house." Suzie said inaccurately.

"Bomber Puxley's a bit of a card, actually. Squeezed my bum as we went into the mess."

"Thought Tim Weaving was an officer and a gentleman," Curry said almost to himself.

"Thought they'd follow him into the jaws of hell, such a good officer." Suzie slid back into her chair. "What Wilson Sharp told us, anyway."

"Nobody's criticising his behaviour as an officer." Annie flushed again, but no tears. "It's the gentleman bit that doesn't quite work."

Curry looked at Suzie with just the trace of a smile; his face saying, *we're on the right track it's one of three people.* Out loud he said, "Hutt, Puxley and Sharp. Are you saying one of those officers could have...?"

"Killed him? Certainly." Annie Tooks, perky now and assured, but with the anger still sizzling away.

"You ever met the new CO? Colonel Belcher?"

"Barney Belcher?" Annie looked surprised.

"That's the one."

"He had cause. Just cause. Tim pinched his wife. Couple of years ago when they were at Ringway. They had a real set-to the pair of them, outside the mess. It's an old story and I think it was Wilson Sharp who told me."

"Where is Mrs Belcher now?"

Annie shrugged, "Not a clue. They split up last year. Tim used to say she was a bit of a bicycle. Unfaithful to Barney only once – with the Glider Pilot Regiment. That was Tim's kind of humour."

"I thought you had names to give me," Curry smiled at her, trying his charm.

"I couldn't possibly remember all the names," Annie smiled back. "No names no pack drill, eh?"

Later as they were driving towards Curzon Street, on the way to see Julia Richardson, Curry said he thought Annie talked a lot of tosh. "Bitter woman ruled by jealousy, that girl. Case of give a dog a bad name, I'd say. Don't believe half of it about Colonel Weaving."

"You're terribly good at the interrogation, aren't you? Tommy says that anyone who could do it and make it seem like an ordinary conversation was brilliant. That's you alright."

"Tell you what," Curry's knuckles whitened on the steering wheel. "I really don't give a fuck what Tommy says about anything, so be an angel and don't quote him again." About half a minute later he added, "Heart". Tommy Livermore's favourite endearment, used by Curry now to let her know he wasn't really angry with her. Well, not much.

Chapter Fifteen

ONE CHRISTMAS, WHEN he was ten years old, an uncle took Sadler to the pantomime in London and he could still conjure up the memory, the gilt and the red plush under his hand, the taste of the chocolates. And best of all the most wonderful scene when Aladdin, the principal boy who was really a girl, said the magic words, 'Open Sesame,' rubbed the lamp, so that the stone rolled away allowing him entrance to Abanazar's cave. The scene seemed to dissolve there and then, before Sadler's very eyes, revealing a vast treasure chamber.

There were chests brimming over with silver and gold ingots, open caskets full of jewels, rubies, diamonds, emeralds, carbuncles; crates out of which spilled golden goblets and boxes of silver inlaid with precious stones; gold doubloons, pieces of eight, Napoleons. The sight dazzled his eyes and sent his brain reeling. And that was how he felt now as General Frederick Morgan, Chief of Staff to the Supreme Allied Commander, went over the outline plans for Operation *Overlord*: the programme that he and his staff, together with Colonel John Bevan's staff from the Central War Rooms at the War Office, had carefully assembled over the previous eight months, a job made twice as difficult because they were forced to work on the scheme for the greatest single operation in history without benefit of a Supreme Allied Commander.

Sadler felt his stomach churn, fluttering with excitement. He had found the Holy Grail, the lost chord and the secret of the universe, a totally enthralling prospect for it would lead inexorably to the rout and defeat of the Allied armies. At its best it was the greatest secret of World War II; the most arcane knowledge concerning the actual landing area for the invasion; the fact that it was not the assumed territory between Calais and Dieppe, the Pas de Calais – the short and easy route into Occupied Europe – but the stretch of coast containing the beaches of Normandy and Brittany: the place least well-defended by the German armies under Field Marshal Erwin Rommel. To the west was the Contentin peninsula with the important port of Cherbourg on its most westerly side, yet the bulk of the peninsula was an unsuitable battlefield for heavy armour. The marshy, waterlogged stretches of the Contentin was not only inappropriate for the tanks and other armoured vehicles, but also the locale gave advantages to the enemy who, it was reckoned, might easily bottle up the invasion forces within the confines of the peninsula for a considerable time.

Sadler immediately recognised that this information alone – that the landings were planned for Brittany and Normandy – would be stunning news when he got it to France. This was the crux, the very hinge of fate. The future governance of Europe, maybe the entire world, depended upon this knowledge alone.

"Sir, has anyone addressed the fact that our major spearhead may well require a wider front than the one we're going to use in this scenario?" A redheaded US Army Colonel asked, and General Morgan said he understood this was a point that General Eisenhower had already queried. "We're looking at the possibility of adding another beach landing further west," Morgan told them. "But, as you can see, this would bring certain dangers upon us," tapping the large map set up on a blackboard easel, referring to the difficulties presented by the Contentin. "The priority of the invading force must be surprise, then the capture of Caen, Bayeux and the road to Saint Lô." Tap, tap, tap, with his pointer on the map. "Before that the two major problems will be the size of the front when we get off the beaches. Much depends on *Fortitude.*"

There was a grave nodding of heads and muttered agreement. For the fraction of a second Sadler paused wondering about the code reference, *Fortitude*. Most likely this was some deception operation but, if it did not come out naturally in the General's briefing, there would be difficulties in filching the details of *Fortitude*. He thought about it for less than fifteen seconds now, coming to the conclusion that it was a side issue. He had the most vital intelligence: that sometime in the late spring or early summer, at a time when the tides were right for it, the Allies would fling huge numbers of troops onto the long beaches of Brittany and Normandy. With support from their large and heavily armed navy these troops would spring from the sea and fight their way off the beaches. At the same time other troops would leap forward inland, large numbers of men arriving by air, by parachute and glider.

This was the essential information he had been sent to steal and, by his own account, he had done so brilliantly. It was, he considered, enough for any man. To get this back to his masters in France and Germany would surely be enough. This information – the battle order of the Allied Armies and the exact location of the landing areas in Normandy – would checkmate the Allies on the battlefield and bring a decisive victory to the Führer's glorious armies.

The conference went on for three more hours and while *Fortitude* was mentioned several times nobody went into details.

As they were leaving, late in the afternoon, Sadler, bumping against an American infantry Colonel, muttered his apologies and then said, "I missed some of the earlier briefings, tell me about *Fortitude*."

The American shrugged and chuckled, "Better get your own people to talk about that," he growled. "*Fortitude*'s supposed to be our ace in the hole, but we don't set much store by it."[1] Sadler's own people, however, seemed desperate to get away on leave. "Talk about it after Christmas," one of his comrades told him gruffly. "I want to get the six-fifteen to Reading, where there should be a little golden-haired popsie waiting for me." The sentence ended with a lecherous wink.

Sadler, blessed with a large portion of hindsight, knew that he might well be missing after Christmas, possibly lost believed drowned, or dead from some other kind of accident. Deep in his mind he continued to work out his next move.

So Sadler went away, for now, and checked into a hotel near Marble Arch where he spent the evening writing a minutely detailed report of what he had learned from the briefing at Norfolk House: of the beaches where the men would land, of the possible LZs for the parachute and glider troops; of the minutiae concerning the naval and air forces that would support the hundreds and thousands of men and their deadly machinery which would crash into Northern France as soon as the signal was given.

When the work was half completed, he went down to the hotel's restaurant around eight in the evening, incredibly crowded this Saturday night, and had dinner: a chestnut soup, herrings in tomato sauce with duchesse potatoes and cabbage a Londres. For desert, a so-called figgy pudding.

Printed at the top of the menu was the Ministry of Food New Meals Order 1942.

> (a) No more than one main dish and one subsidiary dish
> can be served. (b) Any main dish containing more than one
> specific food can be served. (c) No more than two subsidiary
> dishes, can be served. (d) No more than three dishes can be
> served. And at the bottom of the wine list – he had ordered a
> bottle of 1934 Beaune costing 65 shillings[2] – were the death-
> less words, OWING TO THE AIR RAIDS IT IS PREFERABLE
> FOR THE RED WINE TO BE DECANTED.

Once more Sadler allowed the word *Fortitude* to slink through his mind. Maybe he should try again in the New Year: try to find out about *Fortitude*. But by the time he had finished the wine it did not seem to be so urgent. For the umpteenth time he thought about the enormous amount of intelligence he had gathered in a matter of five hours. He could leave *Fortitude* to take care of itself and later, when he'd completed the report and put it into cipher, he would make contact with Julia.

Before he went to his room Sadler picked up a copy of tonight's *Evening News*. Leafing through it, he noticed, among the advertisements a section on church services. One in particular caught his eye: St Paul's Cathedral, Saturday 18th December, 1943 at 6.30 pm Evensong will be a full Choral Carol Service.

FORTITUDE WAS QUITE capable of taking care of itself, for this was the great hurricane upon which *Overlord* pivoted. The first concept of *Overlord* was surprise, the hundreds of ships and landing craft coming suddenly upon the beaches, Men hurtling through the air, landing where nobody thought possible: coming out of the night into the dawn with massive firepower to blast through the enemy defences, crying havoc as the dogs of war were unleashed. What was required to perform this great trick was an act of strategic misdirection.

To achieve the necessary surprise they had built a complex deception plan, a sleight of war that would lead the German armies sitting across the Channel to clearly see preparations for an undoubted attack in the Pas de Calais and nowhere else.

To attain this, General Patton appeared to command a fictitious 1st US Army Group (even larger than the huge real 21st Army Group) with dummy camps, tanks, vehicles, landing craft and supported by real wireless communications, hundreds of dummy aircraft and a wonderfully massive construction near Dover, claiming, by rumour, to be a tank from which fuel could be pumped across the Channel to service the tanks and armoured vehicles once they had made the journey and were fighting around Calais and Dieppe.

The 'landing craft' were made from tubular scaffolding bolted to oil drums and covered with canvas. These craft were sent nosing down to the Dover area then taken back again, dismantled overnight and reassembled to provide another flotilla so that enemy reconnaissance would detect movement. This was also maintained among the dummy vehicles, some of which were so light that they could be lifted and moved *en masse* by a few men and women.

There was a further fantasy British 4th Army in Scotland, complete with wireless traffic, the army posing a threat to Norway. But the largest part of the operation was the mythical 1st Army Group that made preparations in *en Claire* radio traffic over several months, making no secret of its fairy-tale aims.

To plunge home and reinforce the illusion of a landing in the Pas de Calais the twenty or so captured and turned German agents now controlled by the XX Committee would sent radio messages to their case officers in France, Germany and Portugal, or communicate by secret writing. All their information would concern the details of the fictitious invasion force and its objectives.

The final masterstroke planned for *Fortitude* was that during the hours of darkness in the early morning of D-Day, while the colossal fleet made their way towards the Normandy coast, a number of bomber aircraft would circle the Channel, off the Pas de Calais, and drop *Window*, the metallic strips used to confuse radar, thus giving the impression of an advancing invasion fleet.

So, at the given time, the components of *Fortitude* would come together, combined with an aerial bombardment throwing both the strategic and tactical leaders of the Wehrmacht, Panzergrenadiers and Luftwaffe into disarray and uncertainty and so be responsible for the Germans looking the wrong way when the balloon went up.

And Sadler knew nothing of this, except for the word *Fortitude.*

WHILE SADLER WAS still in Norfolk House listening to General Morgan's briefing so Curry Shepherd and Suzie Mountford drove in Curry's Vauxhall Ten towards Curzon Street, where they would park and go on foot to Shepherd Street.

Curry was deafeningly silent behind the wheel and Suzie finally asked him if he was okay.

"Just thinking things over, and coming to the conclusion we're running out of time," He told her. "If Elsie's really put it all together none of us has many days left."

"Hutt, Sharp or Puxley?" Suzie mused.

"Or Bart Belcher," Curry negotiated Hyde Park Corner and into Piccadilly as two Bren gun carriers and a 15 cwt truck pulled in ahead of him, the men in the carriers muffled against the cold.

"Then we have to stop them bloody sharpish."

"Quick as the Aztec Two-Step."

"What's that? Aztec Two-Step?" She wrinkled her face into a puzzled innocence.

"Quick as Montezuma's revenge. The runs, old Suzie. That's it."

She made an exasperated sound. All men, she thought, they're all the same, knee-deep in crudities. Foul-mouthed and vulgar.

Curry leaned over and patted her knee, which was a bit of an advance on things so far. "You think you know how to get into our Julia's good graces?" he asked, giving the knee a squeeze.

"Only how Elsie suggested. Play the wide-eyed innocent. I'm not much of an actress."

"You don't have to be much of an actress. Just be your own sweet self."

She didn't feel like her own sweet self: after all they really had nothing tangible to go on. It was like trying to bottle smoke. Elsie had told them he'd struck gold when the lads in MI5 had been concerned about Tim Weaving and the girl Richardson.

It began with a standard vetting because they were inordinately concerned about the officers attending the COSSAC planning meetings. The CIGS in particular was paranoid about the security surrounding *Overlord*[3]. So, when Colonel Tim Weaving announced his engagement to Julia Richardson they had done a superficial background check. Almost as an afterthought the Watchers began to have a look-see at Julia's house in Shepherd Street. The brief was to peep at the comings and goings over forty-eight hours in teams of three. One of each trio detailed to follow when necessary.

What was it Elsie had said? *Julia Richardson, lives in Shepherd Street. Amazing area that. Ladies of the night, frail sisterhood, girls' boarding houses, proper slice of sin round there. Damned difficult place to put watchers they tell me. Fellows standing about casually get accosted every few minutes. Some tart comes stooging up, 'Want to come home with me?'*

When L C Partridge, the ginger man, talked to them about Julia Richardson Suzie felt it was for her benefit alone because Curry appeared to know everything already. Almost immediately, the Watchers had produced one large piece of information causing the brief to be extended until further notice.

"Thing is," Elsie told them, "Thing jolly is that our Julia gets herself engaged to Tim Weaving but has another pretty close male friend, fellow in the Swedish Embassy name of Lars Henderson. Very tight they are."

So tight that they're doing it on a regular basis, "The horizontal jig, beast with two backs sort of thing," as Elsie put it.

Not just once but five times, the Watchers counted in that first forty-eight hours. "Not really suitable wife material for someone as precariously placed as Colonel Weaving," Elsie had sighed.

Now, in the Vauxhall, Suzie said it was really all conjecture wasn't it? Elsie was jumping to conclusions and Curry snorted. "Believe me, Elsie doesn't jump. Like God he moves in a mysterious way. Our chum the spy is deeper than the deepest ocean. Elsie's narrowed it down to someone close to Tim Weaving. If he's done that you can bet your knickers he's right. This bloke, let's give him a crypto, call him Cyclops – one-eyed giant. Cyclops, according to Elsie, will hang himself by his own tradecraft."

Elsie had used the word tradecraft which Suzie had never heard before, and didn't understand, so Curry explained. "Security and intelligence world's equivalent of military field-craft: technique of going undetected, rules for contact, signals, living, all that stuff."

According to Elsie, Cyclops was obsessed by the secret routines. "He'd been seeing young Julia regularly but couldn't just hand over stuff to her, sort of face to face. Has to go through an intermediary, a cut-out, because that's what the tradecraft demands. It'll be the death of him." Count of three. "With any luck."

"And Elsie just pulls all this out of the air?" Suzie asked as the car turned into Curzon Street.

"I told you, Suzie. Elsie moves in a mysterious way, like God, his wonders to perform. We are visible servants but he has many more, people who can't be seen..."

Like Big Peter and Little Trevor? And his minder, Eddie?"

Curry shook his head. "They're all pretty visible, love. It's the invisible ones you have to look out for: his footpads, creepers and fingermen; his poppets and pinchers, forgers and fiddlers. Old Elsie has an army living out of sight. The people in Baker Street at Special Operations Executive working with the resistance people, and the boys and girls with MI5 and 6 are sometimes jealous of him. And you have to watch his lads on the kippers."

"Kippers?"

"Kippers and bloaters. Motors. I made them up."

But Suzie knew Curry was no fool and while it all sounded far-fetched to her she could see that Curry believed most of it, so why should she doubt him?

"Let me see if I've got it straight," she said as Curry parked the car and sat back to hear her out. "Elsie seems to think they've got a dodgy bloke in the Swedish Embassy, a fellow who slips stuff in on the QT, then sends it over – over in the diplomatic bag – to Sweden, to Stockholm where there's probably another dodgy bloke who lifts whatever it is out of the bag and passes it to the German Embassy. Once there it can be sent straight to Berlin, or wherever."

"That's Elsie's construction of it and I shouldn't be surprised if he believes Julia Richardson imagines she's only giving a harmless hand to the neutral Swedes."

"So, our Cyclops is getting someone to pass intelligence to Julia who passes it to the Swede, Henderson did you say?"

"Lars Henderson, yes. Elsie wants him made *persona non grata*."

"And Lars gets it to Stockholm in the diplomatic bag where another iffy Swede nips over to the German Embassy with it."

Curry gave an affirmative nod. "Sounds complicated doesn't it? Like one of those convoluted detective stories you hear on the wireless." He put on a breathless urgent voice – "Mrs Carstairs couldn't have seen the vicar in the churchyard at three o'clock because the Colonel was talking to Bob the gardener at five past three while old John over at the Bull & Cow could never have read Bert's letter...and so on *ad nauseam*." It was a reasonable imitation of some of the tortuously plotted intricate radio plays with which the BBC bulked out its schedules.

Suzie laughed, then went quiet. "It's bloody serious, isn't it?" realising as she said it that this was a huge and somewhat dim *précis* of the situation.

"If Elsie's right they could have the details of *Overlord* in Berlin by the end of the week." The statement was lit with melodrama. Curry paused, shook his head, then said, "Christ."

As they walked through Shepherd Market into Shepherd Street Suzie asked how in heaven's name they could muscle in on the business of becoming a go-between getting from Cyclops and Julia.

"You can but offer, Suzie. Just keep your bowels open and your powder dry."

Too much, she thought, This is really just too much.

Curry pressed the bell-push. Far away inside the house they heard the electric buzz of the bell and a cut glass voice saying, "Just coming. Hold your horses."

Chapter Sixteen

AN ELABORATE LADY – late twenties – opened the door to them, only a crack, less than twelve inches, peering out, eyes going straight past their shoulders and down the three steps, searching the pavement beyond, worried that they could have arrived with people she didn't want to see.

"Yes?" Voice like a cello, very posh and rather grand, at times swooping.

"Julia Richardson?" Curry asked and Suzie saw the woman trying to make up her mind whether she should own to it or not.

"Yes," coming down on the side of truth and pulling the door open another six inches. "What can I...?"

And Curry went into his routine about being friends of Tim Weaving and had spoken with him only a couple of days before he'd been killed, "He mentioned you, said where you lived. We came to offer our condolences." The same spiel they'd agreed, and the woman smiled saying it was good to know that Tim still had his sense of humour before he died.

She wore what women were calling a housecoat these days, a long dressing gown in red and blue, buttoned down the front with a bit of a waist to it and the big skirt trailing on the floor, heavy on clothing coupons – kind of thing you saw Beau Brummel wearing in movies about the Prince Regent and his pals.

Suzie thought the hair was good, sleek, black, falling to the shoulders, nicely done, in good condition, two hundred brush strokes a night she guessed. Nice oval face, snub nose, dark eyes and colour in her cheeks. From what Suzie could see she carried no extra weight.

She pulled the door open and as she did so seemed to relax, as though she was on familiar ground. She's accepted us, Suzie felt as they passed through into a wide hall decorated with heavy wallpaper, a dark blue sprinkled with small gold fleurde-lis; there was a thick blue carpet under foot and the walls were decorated with eighteenth-century maps in Hogarth frames, tasteful, Berkshire, Hampshire, Dorset and Cornwall; a small oak table and chair to their right, with a telephone and message pad; doors to left and right and the wide, curving staircase straight ahead.

Julia Richardson led them through the door on the left, into a sitting room. "Excuse my disarray," she said running her right hand, palm outwards from neck to waist, indicating both her body and state of undress.

Excuse my disarray, did anyone really speak like that? Suzie wondered.

"James Shepherd," Curry introduced himself, "and my friend, Susan Mountford." He stuck his hand out and the woman took it with thumb and two fingers, then did the same to Suzie, a limp gesture. Tommy used to say you should never trust anyone with a limp handshake, so she decided not to trust Julia Richardson.

The room was cluttered, little side tables here and there, arranged almost haphazardly: a three-piece suite covered in a floral pattern, huge red roses with green stems and thorns visible against a creamy background, the furniture placed in an almost geometric pattern, the settee pushed a shade too close to the fireplace – a log fire burning merrily – and the two chairs as near as they could get. There was a sideboard against one of the three walls, a nice mahogany with some polished silver pieces on display.

Two windows looked out onto the street, between them a strange picture of an inn interior, meant to be early nineteenth century but too good to be true, a man in a crimson waistcoat ('weskit' she presumed from the period novels she'd consumed as a young adult), sporting a long-stemmed clay pipe, showing off a boy to two equally flush and coloured waistcoated men seated close to the fire. There were tankards of ale around, and some men sitting in close conversation at tables near the wall, the odd serving wench wandering around in the background. Could have been Squire Trelawney and Dr Livesey introducing young Jim Hawkins to Captain Smollet in a cheap edition of *Treasure Island*, ideal for a chocolate box – if you could get chocolates – or the subject of a jigsaw. Here it was as out of place as an erotic painting in a nunnery. The picture almost mesmerized Suzie it was so out of place. There was a looking glass in an ornate gilt frame over the fireplace and too much tat on the marble mantelpiece, a little green bowl decorated with gold dragons, a dark wooden crucifix with inlaid mother-of-pearl, an African bowl and – once more an incongruity – a model Spitfire on a curved stand.

Julia Richardson dropped her voice to a loud whisper, indicated the settee silently asking them to sit while she said to Suzie, "A former boyfriend," having seen her looking at the Spitfire. "January '41 over the Channel. Sad, I was at school with him. James. James Simmnel."

"One L like Lambert, the Pretender chappie, Simmnel," Suzie muttered.

"Good God," Julia Richardson sounded as if the breath had been knocked from her body. "You knew James?"

"I met him, Jamie Simmnel? Yes?" Suzie nodded, remembering the time and place she met him, a perilously young flight lieutenant, at a flight dispersal towards the end of 1940, there at Middle Wallop when she had to question his flight commander, Fordham O'Dell. Christmas Eve, 1940. That dreadful year that still haunted Suzie. The Christmas she was sent to talk with Squadron Leader O'Dell, fitting it in with her Christmas visit to Charlotte in Overchurch, and all that went on at that time. Jamie Simmnel – *M'father says we're descended from scullions and dairymaids* was what he'd said and Fordy O'Dell had asked her if Jamie had been looking after her, *Can't cook and has difficulty putting milk on his cornflakes,*

Fordy had said.

"Extraordinary," Julia said. "How on earth...?"

"Oh, some squadron party at Middle Wallop," she lied rather too quickly. "My sister used to live quite close. We were there all the time, or in the local..." and she knew that was a mistake because she couldn't remember the name of the local pub used by the pilots.

They went into a little sidetrack about how small the world was and all that, and Suzie again said how sorry she was about Jamie Simmnel.

Julia said, quite coldly and suddenly, "You're police aren't you?"

"What?" Curry with an upward sweep of his voice and quite convincingly.

"You're police and you're on the murder investigation – Tim's murder I mean."

"My name's James Shepherd and I work for the Ministry of Agriculture and Fisheries. Suzie would have bet that he had a visiting card – which he did and drew it from his wallet now, handing it to her – complete with a fake telephone number where it would be answered by some girl who'd say, "Mr Shepherd's out at the moment," or "Mr Shepherd's away for a few days. Can I get him to telephone you back?"

They had arranged all this and Suzie provided her story now, she worked for the House of Commons, wanted to join the WAAF but they wouldn't take her because of some medical problem. It was "Pretty dull working in the House, and they hardly paid a living wage. Scandalous."

Curry had taken her through it all, his cover story, then her's – called it a Legend, very calm and ordinary. "I'm a close friend of James' and we've known Tim for ages, In fact James was at school with Tim."

So they began to go through their phoney backgrounds, quietly digging into Julia's past, present, and possibly her future.

"We are terribly sorry," Curry leaning forward, full of sincerity.

Julia Richardson started to giggle. "I think you should know that Tim Weaving and I were never really engaged..."

"But I saw the announcement in the *Times*..."

"He told us..." Suzie added.

"No," Curry kept a straight face, eyes wandering and uncertain. "You weren't really engaged?" Waiting, trying to will himself to appear shocked.

"But we talked to people," Suzie frowned. "Talked to people who met you with him. Tim, you were with him at Brize Norton. They had a party for you in the mess. We know about it." She counted to fifteen then added, "But his parents, both of them, they said...talked about the engagement..."

"Probably said they were surprised, and as for the party...You knew Tim, any excuse." Julia Richardson was quite calm but quiet.

"Surprised?" Curry putting a great deal of query in his voice.

"He had his reasons," Julia told them, signalling them to keep quiet and let her do the talking. "He was in a bit of a fix..."

"A fix indeed?" Curry waited, straight-faced. Solemn.

"...Yes, a bit of a fix. Tim Weaving was an idiot sometimes...With women, I mean. He had got into a bit of a state with a girl called Annie Tooks. Bit of an hysteric he told me. Wouldn't take no for an answer. Only way to do it was fuck off out of it," she pronounced it 'orf'. *Fuck orf out of it.* "Show her a clean pair of heels, so to speak. Well, a clean something or other."

Suzie said that sounded rather ruthless.

"Timothy was ruthless. I've known that for years." Very matter-of-fact, Miss Richardson.

"Doesn't sound like the Colonel Tim Weaving we knew,"

Suzie sounded saddened by this revelation, and not a little shocked by Julia Richardson's language, as if she was not one of the girls and didn't approve of the girls all that much.

"So you just agreed...agreed to go along with the story?" Curry asked and she tilted her head in acknowledgement, yes, that was about the top-and-bottom of it. "I was very fond of Tim. He couldn't hurt me though. A shit like that could never hurt me," said the forthright Miss Richardson.

"Well," Curry sounded angry, trying to keep rage battened down below the hatches. "Well, I see," meaning he didn't actually see it at all. "You feel nothing then, Miss Richardson? About Tim's death?" He flapped his arms, and did a penguin gesture.

A short silence seemed to lengthen the distance between them.

"No. No, I wouldn't say that," Julia looked away, not meeting their eyes. "No, I felt immense bloody sadness. I mean we're losing people, friends hand over fist, losing them to the bloody Nazis. But you don't really expect your chums to go down to some common little murderer."

Suzie said no you didn't, and Curry asked to be excused, as they used to say at school. "Sorry, but can I use your bathroom?" was what he said and Julia said, of course, "Straight up the stairs and it's on the right, three stairs up to a white door."

It was what they had agreed. Curry said he'd be away for about four to five minutes so she went into it straight off.

"James wouldn't like it, me mentioning this..." Suzie started.

"Mentioning what?"

"Tim knew that...Well, that I really hardly make enough at the House of Commons. He said if I was ever in the area I should look you up. Said that you had helped some of his pals. Work, he said you sometimes were able to get work for friends. I just wondered...?"

"Work?" sounding puzzled, then, "Oh, yes. The bits of

courier work. Things I do for the Swedish Embassy? Would that be it?"

"He mentioned the Swedes, yes."

"It's very little. About a fiver a pop. All a bit cloak and dagger, but yes, give me your phone number."

She didn't sound enthusiastic, but Suzie rattled off the special number that the little ginger man, Elsie Partridge, had provided.

"I'll give you a tinkle if there's anything. You know, any friend of Tim's."

They walked back to the car parked in Curzon Street. Walked in silence until Curry said, "What a little darling."

"The longer we go on with this the more I dislike Tim Weaving." She sounded as though she wanted to spit. "Unpleasant bugger."

"He wasn't exactly nice either," Curry said with a grin and Suzie gave a little laugh. "You gave her the bait?" he asked.

"Of course, and I think she took it."

"I wonder," he started the car put it into first, pulled out and began to retrace their route back to Ivor Place. "You really think you popped the idea into her head? Seemed a bit of a long shot to me."

"And me, but I suppose Elsie knows best."

Suzie leaned back and began to think about the identity of Cyclops. Did it particularly matter to her? Surprisingly it did, not so much because he had been behind Tim Weaving's death but because whoever he was had become a traitor.

Hutt? Major Shed Hutt. Cyclops? Shed Hutt was from the landed classes with people, not a father and mother, but 'people'. There was an estate in Scotland, a castle and probably a house or flat in town. She wondered if he had been mixed up with that knot of supposed intellectual upper class wafflers who wanted to back Hitler and the Nazis. What were they called, the Clivedon set? Approving of Hitler's selective breeding. Oh, Yah, yah.

Wilson Sharp? Cyclops? The village-born, plough-following, confident young officer Wilson Sharp, tall, tough, bronzed and dark-haired. Maybe, he was certainly single-minded enough.

Puxley? Cyclops? Certainly possible. Accused of being treacherous in the RAF, another one who was single-minded. Puxley had simply swapped one job for the next.

Or perhaps Colonel Bartholomew Belcher. Could Belcher be the profound liar and thief they thought of as Cyclops? On the surface he appeared to be a pompous, empty-headed man who in spite of his lack of imagination had been able to master parachuting and flying a glider. Perhaps that should read *because* of having no imagination. Certainly their Cyclops had shown no imagination when he had tried to have them killed. Just bloody stupidity trying that on the spot, at Brize Norton. Someone had once said to her that the bravest men were often men who had no sense of creativity and could never imagine the worst that might happen if they took the bravest course. She didn't know if this was true or not, but if it was then Bart Belcher could be the bravest man who ever walked the earth. He would certainly be the thickest.

Yes it mattered. Suzie allowed the thought to drain through her mind. One treacherous bastard, she thought. One who could reach out and scoop up the details of the forthcoming invasion. Yes. She thought of the dead, who in the last war, the Great War, the war to end all wars were called the Glorious Dead. If the Allies planned to barge across the Channel and smash their way over the beaches of France, she thought of the dead who'd lie three or four deep in the sand, their blood soaking several feet deep, and that would, in the end, be down to one man. Cyclops selling his country out.

Chapter Seventeen

THE TELEPHONE RANG in Julia's Shepherd Street house around ten-thirty-five, and she let it go on for at least four rings. She never gave the number when she answered, like most people did. They'd say, Flaxman 46789 bold as brass, but a policeman had told her, "Never do that. Never give your number because unscrupulous people will call you at random, check the number, ask for your address then use it to your disadvantage." Julia didn't really understand how they'd use it but at the time she'd trusted the cop. Wrongly as it turned out, but that's another story.

Sadler was in a telephone booth downstairs on the ground floor of the hotel, close to the big reception area and near the restaurant where he had eaten earlier. He still had a few hours work to do on his report, but there was plenty of time for him to finish it.

"Mopsy?" he said when Julia answered.

"Who do you want?" she said, recognising his voice.

"I want Mopsy Flanders. Oh, lord I think I've got a wrong number."

"Yes, I think you have, there's no Mopsy here, and no Flopsy either."

He apologised, half-heartedly, and hung up." Now he would wait for six or seven minutes while Julia got herself into a coat, put on some sensible shoes, found her torch, then headed out to the phone box on the corner of Market Mews.

One day, Sadler considered, the General Post Office would put an end to telephone boxes that were able to receive calls; too many people could use them for nefarious acts; they were a godsend to whores and their pimps, also for illegal gambling and villains who had no access to a private telephone and regarded certain numbers in call boxes as their own: as indeed Sadler and Julia always used the box on the corner of Market

Mews when they did not wish to use Julia's telephone, easy prey to the official Watchers and Listeners belonging to the police or MI5, the Security Service: only Sadler didn't tell that bit to Julia. Sadler simply stuck to his elaborate lies and Julia, a foolish girl, swallowed them whole.

After almost ten minutes, Sadler dropped coins into the box and dialled the number in Market Mews. Julia picked up on the second ring and Sadler pressed Button A.

"Good," He said after making certain that it was Julia at the distant end. "Tomorrow," he told her. "Tomorrow. Nice and public. St Paul's Cathedral. Carol Service at 6.30 pm."

"A bit quick," she sounded doubtful, adding, "but we'll manage."

"We'd better. This is very important."

"I said we'll manage," she snapped, then asked if there were any special orders. Sadler went through what he called the dress of the day. Red hat and a dark scarf visible at the neck. Also visible a copy of the *News of the World.* "Sticking out of her bag, or she could be carrying it."

He said she could sit where she liked, though preferably towards the rear of the church. "Okay?" he said. "Tell her I'll find her."

"That all?"

"No, we have to exchange passwords."

"What d'you suggest, then?"

Sadler had chosen something from the Bible. From the Book of Proverbs. He would say, *the length of days is in her right hand.* The girl would reply, *and in her left hand riches and honour.*

"It's enough," he said. "She should get to the service early. It'll be a full house."

"Will do."

Sadler closed the line and Julia walked slowly back through the black streets to her house.

Inside she poured herself a large brandy from the bottle she'd managed to get for Christmas, and sat down to make what turned out to be the first of a number of telephone calls.

She started by telephoning Daphne, who was a nice girl; as the tired joke said, she had a lot of friends, never did it with enemies. She was not a whore, never worked the streets or anything like that, but, if pressed, would have to admit that her means of support came from gentlemen who found her amusing and attractive. The gentlemen concerned were mainly officers of the USAAF and they valued Daphne when on leave between their bombing missions in B17s – Flying Fortresses – and B24s – Liberators. Daphne liked to think she was concerned with valuable war work, giving succour to members of the forces. But the truth of the matter was that while she was not a whore she could easily be classified as an enthusiastic amateur.

"Daphne, dear. Would you like to earn a few quid?"

"Sweetie," Daphne all but sang. "What's going on? When can I earn some poppy?"

"Tomorrow evening. About an hour's work is all."

"Oh, sweetheart I can't do it, not tomorrow, I'm all booked up tomorrow. My friend Wilbur's coming down for three days, and..."

"What a blow. It's such a simple business, only take you an hour, hour and a half, and you can stay dressed. Piece of cake."

"I just can't Jules. No way. I can't let Wilbur down." She giggled, "Not that he'll let up. Arrives in the morning and if I know Wilbur he'll keep me occupied until very late at night. Doubt if I'll stir outside all day. Mmmmm."

"Well, if you can't you can't dear."

"Some other time then Jules, okay?"

"TTFN, Daph."

TTFN stood for Ta Ta For Now. Another of the interminable catch phrases from Tommy Handley's show, ITMA –

It's That Man Again.

She rang Sybil who worked at Boots The Chemist in Oxford Street, but Sybil's Dad was ill in Romsey and she'd had to give up her job and go to look after him.

Beryl and Betty were both otherwise engaged, going off somewhere over the weekend, then with their families over Christmas.

Julia was stymied. She drew a blank with Unity, a posh girl who lived in Mayfair and would usually do anything for anybody, but she had relations visiting and couldn't get away, "Not even for a minute, Julia. Sorry."

As for Irene, her husband answered the telephone and when Julia asked for her he said, "She's gone to her bloody mother's and I'm only on five days leave bugger it."

Julia was in baulk, didn't know what to do. Then she remembered the young woman who'd come with the handsome man that afternoon and she scrabbled around to find the paper on which she'd written her name and telephone number. Suzie, that was the name, didn't seem to have a surname, but Suzie would do.

She lunged for the telephone.

Ruth, the redhaired maid-of-all-work at the WOIL offices in Ivor Place was still on duty, tucked up reading Eric Ambler's *The Mask of Demetrius* in a camp bed close to four telephones. She struggled out and picked up after six rings and gave the number. The caller, with a voice like a cello, asked if Suzie was there. No surname, just Suzie, and Ruth told her Suzie was out, "At a party," she said, adding she should be in any time if it was urgent. The caller said she was Julia Richardson and could Suzie call her when she came in because it was rather important. What she had actually said was, "She could learn something to her advantage." Julia was a sucker for that kind of flowery language.

Ruth said she'd tell her as soon as she got back and Julia

Richardson gave her the number. Ruth repeated it, then repeated it again as though she was reading what she'd just written down. "And it was Julia Richards was it?" she asked.

"Julia Richardson," Julia said, stressing the *son*. "It doesn't matter what time she gets in. Could she ring me anyway, whatever time. Tonight? Right?"

"Hooked," Curry Shepherd said from Elsie's office door. He had obviously been listening in on an extension.

"Curry, you'll get me shot. How long have you been here?" Ruth asked in a flirty voice.

"Long enough to see you getting ready for bed. Quite like old times."

"You're a Peeping Tom, Curry Shepherd."

"Ah, I thought I was a Curry Shepherd. You'd best ring Suzie. Tried every trick in the book to get me to stay at her place tonight. In the guest room of course."

"Naturally," Ruth looked up from under her eyelids in what was supposed to be a seductive sort of way as she started to dial Suzie's number.

"But I knew you'd be here, ready and waiting." Curry continued, the leer turning to a melting smile as Ruth put her hand over the receiver rests, then picked up the phone again, preparing to redial. "There's not really room in this camp bed." Curry thought what a dazzling smile she had. "Not the same as in the flat." Ruth added.

Curry started to remove his jacket. "We've managed before." He said. "What about the telephone, sweetheart?"

SUZIE WAS STILL getting ready for bed and wondering if she had lost her allure when the telephone rang. For a second she wondered if it was Curry. Had he changed his mind? Later she thought the disappointment must have been obvious as she answered too eagerly.

Ruth told her what was going on and what to do, mothered

her a bit, asking if she could manage this relatively simple phone call. "Just listen, make notes, that's very important: be meticulous about the notes. Try to sound interested without being inquisitive. Remember the money fascinates you. Cash is your motivation…Oh, yes, and remember you've just come in from a party. Be bubbly, if you know how to be bubbly."

"I think I can manage, thank you. And I know how to be bubbly in all senses of the word." Suzie told her, acidly, over the telephone. She really didn't like Ruth but if she had been asked why she couldn't have given a reason. Then, in a matter of minutes she was talking to Julia Richardson in the house where she lived in Shepherd Street.

"Darling," Julia gushed, "Thank you so much for ringing back. You *did* ask me if there was a job going – pin money, remember?"

"'Course I remember. You've got something I can do?"

"I think so, but I'll have to explain because it always sounds a bit iffy…"

"How much?" Suzie asked, trying to get into the role as Ruth had explained to her.

"Five quid and you have to go to church for an hour or so."

"I don't mind that. I'll do anything."

"I'll tell you what it's about. Put you in the picture."

"Please."

"Friend of mine supplies non-military information to the neutral Swedish embassy – stuff about costs of food, clothes, that sort of thing. And digests from the War Office official briefings to the Press. This fellow also helps in training some of our own security people, so he arranges these exchanges of information as clandestine exercises. Trainees are told a time and place where the information is to be handed over. They're also given a description of the person who is to receive the information. It's usually a thick envelope that's passed to you in a public place. Right?"

"Right," Suzie agreed,

"All you have to do is be at the designated place, wearing the identifiable clothes or whatever I tell you. Then someone will contact you and pass you the envelope which you bring straight to me."

"What does designated mean?" Suzie decided to play the dim lame brain.

"It means where I tell you to be."

"Oh, right."

"In this case it's St Paul's Cathedral. Tomorrow evening. There's a carol service there at half six. Get there early, like half-five, a quarter-to-six. Understand?"

"Yea, 'course."

Julia gave her all the details, red hat, dark scarf, copy of tomorrow's *News of the World* – "You'd better carry that, but make sure it's visible to others."

"Won't feel right carrying that paper into a church." Suzie turned down the corners of her mouth, acting the part. At that time the *News of the World* specialised in the sexual pro-clivities of choirmasters, scoutmasters and clergymen, ped-erasty was one thing, but simply being homosexual was a crime in those days and they'd bang you up even if you were a consenting adult.

"Don't worry about that. Now there's a kind of password. It's from the Bible. Ready, 'coz you'd better learn this by heart." She repeated *The length of days is in her right hand, and in her left hand riches and honour,* made Suzie write it down and go through it again and again until she had it off pat. Only when she was certain everything was covered did Julia break the connection.

Suzie leaned back and digested the situation which seemed perfectly simple. The hat was no problem, burgundy would pass as red, the one with the divided crown, like a man's tril-by but lower and with a wider snap-down brim at the front, perfect match with her favourite coat, the one with the D-rings and a belt like a trench coat, with buttoned flaps across the chest, fitted at the waist and long military skirts: the coat her mum had bought for her at Fenwicks before clothes rationing came in.

She had plenty of dark scarves, and —

The telephone rang again.

Curry said, "Suzie, the office has just been on. I gather we've got a nibble. Good show, eh?"

"Yes, I suppose it is." She sounded less than happy and wondered afterwards if she was trying to tempt Curry to come down and hold her hand.

"You don't sound thrilled."

"I've been a stalking horse before, and it was not the most pleasant time of my life."

"I thought that was being a tethered goat."

Clever bugger, she thought. "Same difference, Curry. I go out there and wait for the guy who killed Colonel Weaving to creep up on me. There'll be a lot of people in St Paul's Ruth tells me, so how are we going to be sure...?"

"How're we going to be sure you're safe? That'll be a piece of cake, Suzie. A doddle. Don't worry about it, we'll have all exits covered, our people will be on you all the time. Nothing's going to happen to you, Suzie. We're much to careful and professional."

She reflected that she'd heard that before.

"Come down to Ivor Place in the morning. Nine o'clock. Elsie and some of the boys'll be there. You'll be fine."

Suzie got undressed, had a bath, stuck to the current rule of five inches of water in the bath and thought to herself that she was a bit of a prig. Obeying the five inch rule made her feel good and she thought that was a bit much, feeling happy about keeping to a restriction nobody could really enforce. She fiddled with her toes on the hot tap and let another inch of water flood into the bath.

She felt guilty about that and when she was out, dried, powdered and in her night clothes she sat on the bed sipping a cup of milky cocoa. She really had thought Curry was interested in her. If he had been he certainly didn't seem to be interested any more. When he had told her about Tommy's questionable dealings over her commendation and the offer of a George Medal, she'd have sworn he'd been exceptionally interested, but now she wondered. She recalled that when she was at her first posting to CID at Camford Hill, Shirley Cox had told her that one of the other officers had said he thought she – Suzie Mountford – was a flibbertigibbet: frivolous and a bit of a teaser. At the time she had been outraged but now she wondered. Had this been how Curry Shepherd had seen her, easy and flippant? If so he really hadn't wanted to have all that much to do with her. By the time she had the light off and was cuddling her hot water bottle, snug inside its Peter Rabbit cover, she started to wonder about the way other people saw her.

> *O wad some Pow'r the giftie gie us*
> *To see oursels as others see us.*

She remained awake for some time wondering about the reality of her way of life and the manner in which she behaved towards others. By the Church's rules she supposed that she'd been a touch frivolous, and had certainly indulged herself with regard to the so-called sins of the flesh, but she had salved her conscience by focusing on the fact that – apart from that one night with Wing Commander Fordham O'Dell – her acts of fornication had been with the man she had intended to marry which, she felt, cancelled out much of the guilt. An elderly priest had once told her that the sins of the flesh always seem exceptionally bad to us because they are so personal, and he had gone on to say that he felt they were probably very small sins in the eyes of God, but enlarged initially by the celibate nature of those who deciphered God's codes, and the laws made in those early days possibly did not have the same impact now, in time of war, when each day brought a new challenge and death hovered everywhere.

She thought much about the choices she had made in life, in particular the dreadful rift that had taken place when her father was killed and the numbing shock of her mother's second marriage to the sometimes loathsome 'Galloping Major'. Then of her time with Tommy Livermore, her career advanced much sooner that she could possibly have hoped when she was put on a clear track as one who would be especially needed in the Force once the war was done. But it was her relationships with those she was called to work with that caused her the most confusion now.

Eventually she dropped into sleep, her mind in chaos, the slumber proving to be fitful and restless, her sleep, heckled by vivid dreams in which she was chased across shifting sands by faceless men who eventually caught up with her, reaching for her neck with clammy hands that finally woke her to the Sunday morning. It was a Sunday last time, she reflected, Sunday 29th December 1940, the night of the second great fire of London, the night when Tommy Livermore baited a trap with her. And now, three years later, Suzie knew that she would again put her life on the line out of a sense of duty and loyalty to her king and country.

Chapter Eighteen

"YOU KNOW YOU don't have to do this, Suzie," Elsie Partridge looking straight into her eyes, smoothing a hand across his bald pate. "Nobody's going to think badly of you if you pull out now." But looking around the room, at Curry Shepherd, and the two men she had just met – Big Peter Hammill and Little Trevor Haines – she knew their eyes were saying the opposite. If she pulled out now they'd always have a mark against her name, if not on paper then certainly in their long memories.

Suzie was glad that Big Peter and Little Trevor were on her side. She wouldn't have wanted them as enemies with the likelihood of running into them alone on a dark night. The only thing humorous about Peter and Trevor was that Big Peter was a short, wiry man while Little Trevor was built like the proverbial brick washhouse, and tall with it. It was clear that they knew their job, which she suspected was to pulverise people, with maximum force. They spoke in grunts and nods, and the pair of them showed a great deal of care for her and were now given to patting her on the arm, followed by a head-rolling wink coupled with the words, "Suzie? Okay, girl?" or just "Suzie," with the exaggerated wink.

Curry was already there when she arrived just before nine o'clock, having taken a taxi to Baker Street, then walking down to Ivor Place. Ruth was also in the office and the pair of them looked slightly blurred around the edges, dishevelled and not as razor sharp as they might have been. Suzie's mind turned quickly to thoughts of how they may have spent the night, and she again cursed herself for the silly imaginings that had led her to think any attractive male would automatically find her equally tempting. The plain truth of the matter was she wanted a change and fancied Curry Shepherd rotten. Not an edifying state of affairs.

Elsie came in muttering something about needing coffee and hearing news that Winston was much better. There was a ensuing conversation in which Suzie, earwigging madly, to use Tommy's expression for listening in to other people's conversations, gathered that the PM was abroad again on one of his jaunts to meet President Roosevelt and others in Cairo, she thought, where he had been taken seriously ill.

Peter and Trevor came in soon after nine-thirty and they sat around for a couple of hours talking about how things should be arranged later in the day. They discussed the options they could use inside the huge cathedral, or how they could cover the steps and the doorways outside. They also debated how to prevent things from going wrong and Suzie felt moderately cheerful by the time Elsie made his speech about her not having to do what it was obvious they all wanted her to do: set herself up so they could nail Cyclops as they all now called him.

Elsie Partridge had a good deal to say about the disposition of his people outside the building and the crowding there would be during the arrival and departure of some of the congregation. "A number of important people're going to be there," he told them. "Military, Royal Air Force and Naval staff officers will arrive and leave by car, as will whoever's going to represent the PM – I gather that'll be Mrs Churchill, with Anthony Eden[4] in tow. So there'll be the usual jumble outside, crowding and delays: though there'll be a couple of brace of military police sergeants marshalling the traffic, which will help." He told Suzie to keep an eye out for them, "If something goes wrong, head for them, otherwise keep away. We don't want anybody really close because we've got to give Cyclops air, a clear run."

He said he didn't think they'd have to worry about leaving, at the end when the service was over. "Chummy'll almost certainly make his move quickly, at the start of things. After all he asked for his contact to be in the cathedral early."

There was a lot of, "Don't worry, we'll be on you like leeches" talk, and around midday Ruth and Curry happily volunteered to go out for food from the mess over in Baker Street. They returned with unappetising sausages ('Ah sweet mystery of life at last I've found you,' Big Peter sang in a cracked, gravel voice), a large pile of chips, almost cold, and some bread which looked as though it had been sliced by the giant at the top of the beanstalk.

Ruth made some surprisingly reasonable coffee and as they sipped it three strong-arm boys came over from the Branch, two DCs and a DI Suzie knew by sight but not by name. They eyed her up as though they were calculating her weight at a country fête, and the DI introduced himself as Bob Lambourne. "We're just taking a look-see," he told her. "So we'll know you in the cathedral." He paused, licked his lips and said, "Actually, I'd know you anywhere." Which Suzie thought was meant to be a compliment, though she didn't dare say that she found it offensive.

Three other tough guy types came in later and did not introduce themselves so she presumed they were from 'Five' as Elsie referred to the Security Service. They were all on nodding terms with Elsie and Curry and they also seemed to be carrying out a minute and detailed examination of her form and figure.

Just after they left, Tommy Livermore came in with his new WDS Cathy Wimereux. Nobody had warned Suzie that he was coming so she suddenly found herself looking straight into his face and giving him a weak smile. He nodded in return then spoke quietly to Elsie who appeared to have been expecting him and said loudly, "That's a pity," then addressed everybody. "DCS Livermore has done as I asked him and felt the Richardson girl's collar. But so far I'm afraid he's drawn a blank." He turned directly to Suzie, "We had hoped it might save putting you out in St Paul's Suzie, but that's gone for a burton."

Tommy took up the story, saying that he'd arrested Julia Richardson at the Shepherd Street house at seven that morning. "Before we went in we gave the place a good looking over from outside," he continued. "Nobody appeared to be watching it, or keeping a look-out." Turning to Elsie he said they had been most discreet. "I've left a couple of people there with their heads well down just in case you miss chummy and he goes back there for want of anywhere else to run."

"Unlikely," Curry sneered.

"You never know," Tommy squashed him, then said he'd got the Richardson girl at the Yard. "We've had a long talk," he went on, "and she seems genuinely shocked about the Swede, Henderson, and she says she's no idea who our man is; says their business has always been done over the phone. I don't believe it for a minute, but she's playing at being a Dumb Dora, as our Allies would say. In other words she's staying schtum. Personally I think she knows alright, but it'll take time once you've pulled him in."

As Tommy was leaving, heading back to Scotland Yard, he smiled at Suzie and wished her good luck. She looked away and felt herself blush. After that she found that she couldn't look any of the other men in the eye. Later she thought that Cathy Wimereux had seemed somewhat cowed and didn't have much to say.

When Tommy's people had gone, Curry said something about her being really well cared for tonight.

"Think we'd better let you go home," Elsie said. "Have a bit of a rest before you get all dressed up for church. I'll get Roy to come and take you to the car." And Curry made some tasteless remark about her having to wear a red hat, "...know what that means, Suzie? Red hat?"

"Yes, Curry," she said as though showing great patience to a four-year-old. "I know all about red hats meaning no drawers, and that's about as accurate as the one Tommy told me was rife at his prep school, that girls wearing ankle chains indicated they had the curse."

This was going a bit far; Elsie looked shocked, and Curry shut up, looking uncomfortable. Nobody laughed.

Then Roy arrived and she was surprised to see that his face was familiar.

That morning when she'd left her flat and taken a taxi to Baker Street, she had kept her eyes open as Curry had advised and quickly noticed a grey Vauxhall behind them, then overtaking when the cab pulled over to drop her. As she walked on to Ivor Place she saw the car again, first coming towards her, then, a few minutes later driving past in the other direction. There was a tall, greying, somewhat nondescript man at the wheel. So she took the registration number and reported it to Curry as soon as she arrived at the Ivor Place house. He had simply nodded and told her she'd done well to keep her eyes open.

Now, Roy was ushered in, the same grey man who had been trailing her car this morning – another member of the WOIL team, their best driver who would be taking her down to St Paul's tonight. A taciturn man with a nice smile that lit up his face and eyes when he used it. I'll be safe with him, she thought, because he was the kind of quiet man who exuded confidence.

Roy told her he would pick her up in Upper St Martin's Lane spot on five-thirty. "I'd like to get the car into a good parking place near St Paul's so that I can scoop you up once the fireworks are over," he said, and Suzie remarked that she wasn't expecting any fireworks.

"That's the thing in this game," he said. "It's when you're not expecting them that they do the most damage," a remark said so seriously that it made her twitchy.

* * *

IT WAS STILL light when she left her building, at the top of Upper St Martin's Lane at just gone five-twenty and started to walk towards the Strand and Charing Cross, wearing her burgundy coat with the collar high around her neck, the matching hat with the brim cocked over her right eye, and a wine red scarf, knotted neatly in the way Americans called an Ascot. She carried her best square leather handbag with a copy of the *News of the World* protruding from the top.

It would be light for some time yet, with British Summertime in effect all year round now – Double British Summertime in the late spring until late autumn, to help the farmers. There was a heavy gun-metal sky; complete cloud cover and occasional gusts of a bitter wind coming up from the river.

The grey Vauxhall pulled up just as she reached the intersection with the Strand, Roy pushing the passenger side door open and Suzie making a fuss as she got in, thanking him and nodding, just in case, though she knew it was unlikely anyone – apart from the people attached to WOIL – would be watching. They already knew Cyclops was more concerned with the obvious affairs close to him than anything at a distance. He certainly didn't have the necessary manpower, and anyway probably wouldn't trust anyone but himself to do the job thoroughly.

All the official cars were fitted with a mirror on the passenger side as well as the one for the driver, and Suzie adjusted it now, keeping her eyes moving from road to mirror, guardedly watching for surveillance.

She wondered briefly if it had been wise to arrest Julia Richardson at this early stage as she could well be the one person in his small network whom he may just try and contact before the carol service

They hardly spoke during the journey towards the square mile of the City of London where St Paul's, with its great familiar dome, stood out from the rubble and devastation which had visited the area in December 1940. During that night of holocaust over 30,000 incendiary bombs were dropped into the City, gutting almost all the buildings, including the Guildhall and eight churches, it was amazing to think that Christopher Wren's great masterpiece had been left almost unscathed.

As she looked around her during the journey, down Fleet Street and onto Ludgate Hill, Suzie thought how drab the buildings appeared, sooty and sombre, as tired as the British people were with the war, drained and depleted by the constant strain, the ever-present worry, news of deaths and concern for the future. There also appeared to be a thin, tangible mist hanging in the old streets at this time of the year, as though some grim life fluid was seeping from the roads and stone of the structures and ruins that now punctuated these environs.

Suzie moved in the front seat, craning upwards to see the Dome of St Paul's rising to over 300 feet above the pavement and she realised that she felt more than anxiety. Her tummy turned over in a flutter and she could sense the fear deep within her as Roy brought the car to a halt at the bottom of the long steps leading up to the west façade. He slipped from the driving seat and trotted round to the pavement, reaching for Suzie's door as she opened it. A military police sergeant seemed to appear out of the pavement and Roy nodded to him, slipping an official-looking card to him. The redcap nodded, said something and pointed to his far right.

Roy smiled and turned to face Suzie, looking up towards the church, as Suzie faced away from it. "I'm going to park somewhere over there," he raised his left arm, pointing to what was Suzie's right. "I'll pick you up here, bottom of the steps as soon as I can get to you when you come out. You'll be easy enough to spot with that cheeky red hat."

Suzie nodded and smiled a thank you, grateful that he had not gone on with the old adage about red hats. Then she slowly turned and began the walk up those long wide steps towards the west door wondering what the next hour or so would bring.

It crossed her mind that she had always loved and treasured the run up towards Christmas.

Chapter Nineteen

SHE HADN'T BEEN inside St Paul's since 1939 when she had been briefly attached to the Vine Street 'nick', and so had forgotten how its size hit you in the face, opened your eyes and gave you a sense of wonderment. The vastness of the interior, with the great pillars and the dome reaching up above the transept, made one feel puny and brought to mind the colossal disposition of God's creation when set against the infinitesimal nature of mankind.

From a sidesman she took a leaflet containing the order of service, then settled in a place at the end of a row, some six seats from the back, the cathedral already starting to fill up.

Most of the congregation were in uniform and there was a buzz of expectation throughout, memories of peacetime Christmases flooding back, friends smiling and nodding to one another across the chairs, people arriving, senior military officers with their ADCs, many from the women's services crowding in, ATS, WAAFs and WRENS looking smart and spry, faces shining some like children, some 'other ranks' girls being squired by officers. Civilians were in the minority and mainly middle aged or elderly. Since 1939 regular congregations at churches and chapels had grown: in times such as this people turned back to God as a rock in their lives, an anchor, an eternal hope.

The ARP, Fire Service, Police and Ambulance Services were also well represented, a whole cross section of life, she thought. When the war finally ended they would probably lose this feeling of a universal cause where all were, to use Shakespeare's phrase, *truly a band of brothers* dedicated to defence and defeating the Nazi might. Suzie felt an extraordinary pang of sadness at the thought of this sense of common purpose filtering away, the world she knew returning to the daily round and common task of a peacetime existence. Immediately, of course, she felt guilty at not wanting to lose this *esprit de corps* that was inevitably welded to war. Did it mean that she didn't really want the war to end? Even with all its attendant horrors. She looked around, with a shy smile on her face, as though to misdirect anyone who might read her mind.

There were two big Christmas trees standing near the chancel, candles were lighted and flowers decorated everywhere: holly, ivy, Christmas roses, even the pagan mistletoe. The whole church took on a paradoxical sense of normality, as though the war was a thing apart and nothing to do with the congregation or what they were about to celebrate here.

Suzie tried not to be furtive as she looked about her, glancing down at the Order of Service and then up again, each time in a different direction, trying to see if there was anyone she recognised. She thought she had glimpsed the bulky figure of Little Trevor Haines over to her right, but when she looked again he was gone. She saw no signs of Curry or the men from 'Five' or the Branch which she knew was good, for it meant they were skilfully hidden among the congregation. She searched among the backs of peoples' heads to see if she could recognise anybody from the recent past, but the only familiar face was a girl she had been at school with, Janet 'Eggy' Eggmore, now a dark beauty in a WAAF officer's uniform, unbelievably poised. Fancy, she thought, old Eggy grown up and confident with a Flight Lieutenant glancing at her adoringly.

As though spotting an old school mate wasn't bad enough the organist now started to play 'Jesu Joy of Man's Desiring' which was their favourite voluntary music back in the chapel with the good Anglican nuns at St Helen's. So, in her head she slid away from the present back into the childhood past of schooldays when life was reasonably safe, Daddy and Charlotte were still alive and the centre of her world was warmed by happiness.

The organist moved smoothly into 'Sheep may safely

graze', another piece of magic, holy music from the past, but suddenly someone stood beside her chair. Her stomach turned over, dragging her back into the present as she looked up to see a tall, RAF officer, a Squadron Leader with pilot's wings on his left breast above a strip of medals, including a DFC and bar, visible through his unbuttoned open greatcoat. He smiled and indicated the chair next to her, asking quietly if it was empty. She nodded and hunched back to allow him in.

If he was Cyclops' messenger, she thought, he was nobody she'd seen before. Then she realised that he had, in fact, been in the officers' mess at Brize Norton. Not the doctor who'd been in to see them after the car explosion, but someone else. The GPR Mess at Brize, as they were leaving. She remembered him now with his corn hair and flourish of a moustache, and a basso profundo voice that gave her a tiny attack of goose pimples as she stood waiting to get into the car, after the bomb, when they were waiting to be driven up to London on their way to see Elsie Partridge. Yes, of course.

What a good choice, she thought. Cyclops may well be a bit of a clot in some directions – taking pot shots at them, trying to blast them to eternity with a car bomb – but he couldn't have picked a nicer looking fellow who now moved past her and began settling himself into the seat close to her. So close that at one point his left knee briefly touched her right knee as he was fiddling with a large and bulging brief case. No doubt, she decided, the brief case carried whatever was to be passed over to her.

It was an old and smooth leather job, like a large music case complete with straps, handles and buckles, little straps pulling the soft leather cover over and into place. He fiddled with the case on the floor, then pushed it under his chair, the top part of his body swinging round in a series of exaggerated movements. Maybe he wasn't going to get the package out yet. No, stood to reason, he'd go for it towards the end of the service.

All she had to do was wait. Piece of cake.

At that moment the organ burst into a series of fanfare chords and the procession began. She had thought it would all start with 'Once in Royal David's City' so it rather took her by surprise that the processional was the Advent hymn, 'O Come, O Come Emmanuel, to free thy captive Israel'. A tenor sang the first two lines in a rich deep brown voice and when they all joined in she was thrilled to hear the RAF officer's bass profundo voice next to her rejoicing in the Christmas words.

Led by an acolyte carrying the cathedral's processional cross, the choir, in their red cassocks and snow white surplices came swaying down the aisle, the boys singing their hearts out, all looking like little angels with the men following them, the delicious sound swallowing Suzie and again directing her towards the past and memories of life when her father still lived and life was comparatively straightforward.

The clergy followed the choir, the Dean of St Paul's and other Cathedral clerics, then, tonight, the Bishop of London and his chaplain. And it was the bishop who said the Bidding Prayer before they began to sing again, an abundance of carols pointing the way towards the meaning of Christmas. They sang 'Away in a Manger' that so reminded Suzie of the days at school when they would listen to the very small girls singing that carol and smiling at the way they bobbed at each mention of Our Lord's name; then 'In the Deep Mid-Winter' which always made her smile as it had been her favourite carol as a tiny child and she couldn't pronounce 'snow.' In later years her father had done an imitation of her rendition which, after the first verse went –

> 'No had fallen 'no on 'no. 'No on 'no
> *In the deep mid-winter, long ago.*

There was the first lesson – the lovely one from Isaiah with the hugely comforting prophecy, written hundreds of years before the birth of Christ and containing the words:

For unto us a child is born, unto us a son is given, and the government shall be upon his shoulder: and his name shall be called Wonderful, Counsellor, the mighty God, the everlasting Father, the Prince of Peace.

Suzie would freely admit that she could be an emotional woman at times, and also that this passage from the Bible with its world of hope always made her want to hug herself with the joy of it all at Yuletide. It happened every year when she heard those words, and the line in 'Hark the Herald Angels' that went...*And Christmas Comes Once More.* These were triggers of happiness and she really didn't care if anyone thought her sentimental or even silly. For her they underlined the great and eternal wheel of praise that is the Christian year. That's how she had been brought up, and she rejoiced in it.

Then they sang 'In dulce jubilo', a carol that taxed her memory and sentiment, for this was something she used to sing with her father, he doing the melody with her providing the descant. The recall of those things and the happiness that lay in her recollection brought tears to her eyes and she clung to the back of the chair in front of her in an attempt to calm herself and control her shaking body. It took a considerable act of self-discipline to bring herself back to the present and subjugate her physical reactions.

The carols continued, 'O Little town of Bethlehem', 'Silent Night' (No German sung here), 'I saw three ships a sailing by', 'Angels from the realms of glory', 'Ding Dong Merrily on High'.

The squadron leader next to her appeared oblivious to everything except the beautiful sound of his own voice which he obviously knew was magnificent.

The next lesson, the birth of Christ as told from St Luke's

Gospel, followed by 'O Come All ye Faithful', during which the bishop took up his position to read the collect for Christmas Eve (a little early of course, so she didn't know what the nuns would have thought of that).

Then the final carol, 'Hark the Herald Angels sing', the organ booming away and everybody singing louder than ever as the service drew to a close and the Bishop gave his blessing – the one taken from the Book of Numbers –

The Lord bless you, and keep you:
The Lord make his face to shine upon you, and be
gracious unto you:
The Lord lift up his countenance upon you, and give you peace.
Amen.

She expected the Squadron Leader to make his move, but he simply buttoned his greatcoat, picked up his briefcase and stood patiently as she waited, watching for a convenient moment to move into the throng, already thickening in the aisle, heading towards the big west doors. Of course they had to wait for the good and godly to go first – Mrs Churchill, smiling, several high-ranking officers looking important, then the press of people. In the aisle the crush built up, with scores of people moving slowly towards the back of the cathedral.

Twice Suzie tried to get out but nobody gave way to her and eventually she lurched forward, for a moment convinced that the RAF officer behind her had pushed and crowded her into the slow snake of people moving steadily.

As she reached the doors and felt the cold air blowing into her face, she tried to push towards the right, the further right she could get, the better position she would be in to get picked up by Roy at the bottom of the steps. But the crowd pressed against her, preventing her from going where she wished, rather she was penned in, pushed to the left. She told herself to be calm, to take it gently, soon she would be outside in the open, perhaps then she would be able to move. At the same time she was concerned about Cyclops and the hand-over, after all this was the sole purpose of what she was doing – to catch their spy in the act and bring him down.

The RAF officer was still behind her, and as they came onto the steps she felt someone else press in on her back, a woman move quite close to her left side and the RAF man move to the right. She tried to look round to the right, but the Squadron Leader was so close that she couldn't turn. Then she looked to the left, at the woman, who didn't even glance in her direction. She was nobody Suzie had ever seen before and she felt herself being directed, like a sheep handled by dogs. The hell with it, she thought, taking a deep breath and preparing to break free and face whoever was close behind her.

The light was going, and below to the right, she was aware of a phalanx of cars picking up people and easing past each other in some confusion once their passengers were on board. Three redcaps seemed to be directing the traffic and she glimpsed the grey Vauxhall hemmed in by a couple of staff cars.

They were almost at the foot of the steps now. If she pushed away, then spun right round, quickly facing the road again, she might break free to duck and weave down the remaining steps, she might stand a chance of pushing through the crowd. It would be easy to yell at the redcaps from there. In any case she was sure Curry and the others must be close behind ready to break through the crowd and pull her free.

She took in another deep breath of air, her mind prepared. Then behind her someone quietly said, "The length of days is in her right hand."

Automatically she replied, "And in her left hand riches and honour," turning as the voice said, "I have something for you."

She looked straight into Cyclops' face, and heard him gasp and grunt, "No!" as he recognised her.

There were shouts from behind them, further up the steps and she realised she was momentarily alone with him.

She heard a jeep's engine scream close behind her but she didn't see his arm move, or the fist that slammed into her face, sending her spinning, shocked, with a galaxy of stars circling the blackness, a violent throbbing pain in her cheek and jaw, then darkness as she went backwards and he caught her, thrusting her into the front of the jeep as the driver pulled it out at speed and shot away, sashaying the agile little vehicle through people and other cars.

Above, some five steps away, Curry Shepherd and two of the men from the Branch were still hurtling towards the point where Suzie had been taken. They had seen the whole thing as they gently closed in, purposely staying back to let their quarry take the bait: but they had not counted on the size of the crowd on the steps. They saw people to Suzie's left and right – a woman and an RAF officer - move away naturally, and the tall officer in khaki, wearing the red beret of the Airborne Forces, hard behind her. They saw her turn and then witnessed the man's quick reaction, his fist coming back to pound a hard straight right into Suzie's face. At the same moment, with expert timing a jeep hurtled from among the cars gathered to the right, screeching up to the pavement as Captain 'Bomber' Puxley hurled Suzie's rag doll crumpled body into the jeep and leaped in after her, wedging her between himself and the driver.

Curry shouted towards the redcaps below him. But the jeep was by now burning rubber some fifty yards away.

Chapter Twenty

THERE WAS SILENCE around her, the smell of burned wood, petrol and the throb of an engine. She shook her head and realised that she was being held around her upper arms and something seemed to be wrong with her lower jaw, sharp pain creasing the side of her face and down the jawbone, so severe that when she tried to move her hands up to feel the flesh and bone, her wrists seemed to be manacled together.

"Turn it off," she heard Puxley say. "Turn the engine off."

The driver moved and the engine died. "Good job you made alternative arrangements, sir. Bloody good job."

She knew the driver's voice, and closed her eyes, trying to put the face to the voice.

"What do we do now, then, Cap'n Puxley?"

She knew it now. The ultimate treachery. Monkey Gibbon, Colonel Weaving's sergeant. On the night Weaving died he must have left the Colonel at Portway House and gone straight over to collect Puxley. Together they would have decided to interrogate the Colonel and Mrs Emily Bascombe – 'Bunny' Bascombe.'

For a moment Suzie wondered if the manacles, handcuffs she presumed, were used on Tim Weaving during his terrible final hours in the cellars of Portway House.

"What do we do now?" Puxley said, as though talking to himself. He gave a short mirthless laugh. "Indeed, what do we do? Well, we have the Humber staff car. This place is close to where the Guildhall used to be. We're not far from the edge of the City. We can get to Ludgate Hill and back through Fleet Street."

"Good job you decided to have an alternative plan..."

"I always work on the presumption that if anything *can* go wrong it *will* go wrong. Now, we've enough petrol to get us to where we're going..."

"And where would that be, then? Your place up in Norfolk?"

Suzie remembered what Branwell Puxley had said – *A nice little cottage close to Cromer…A hamlet, few houses, a pub, not even a church. Thorpe Market; south of Cromer. Dot on the map.*

"Almost. Not quite. I've no way of getting this stuff to France now," he patted his pocket. "…unless I take it myself. So, you'd better come with me, we're blown here, Monkey."

"Yes, Captain Puxley. Blown and buggered." He laughed. A cruel and sardonic laugh, Suzie thought, realising that she was being melodramatic – and why not, cramped and uncomfortable squeezed between the two men. How in God's holy name had Curry, Elsie's people, the watchers from five and the Branch let this chubby, red-faced endlessly smiling idiot spirit her away? It made no sense.

Monkey said, "How, sir? How we going to get over there? France?"

"I never thought I'd have to use it, but I've got a motor launch, in a boathouse just south of Cromer. Forty footer, single-engined."

"Fuel?"

"Enough petrol to get us to Ostend. That'll do us. They'll soon pass me on to my old Abwehr chums in France. Germany even."

"And you can navigate us?"

"Piece of cake, Monkey. I was a pilot, remember?"

"Of course."

"We'd best get cracking, then." He moved and Suzie inadvertently groaned. Puxley tightened his grip.

"What about her?" Monkey Gibbon asked. "We going to do it here? Leave her?"

"Oh, no. I want to take her with us. Insurance. I'm sure she'll come in useful. Fill in the gaps if necessary. We'll be heroes, Gibbon. They'll give you a medal. Already given me one." Pause. Then. "Come on, help me to get her in the Humber."

He moved and Suzie cried out in spite of herself, the pain

hurtling through her head, down the side of her jaw.

Puxley bent over her. "Keep quiet or I'll use this now," he said, and she felt what was unmistakably a pistol barrel against her temple. "Be a good girl, Detective Inspector Mountford, and you may even live."

Deep inside herself, Suzie knew it was unlikely she would survive. Her face and jaw gave her unimaginable pain, her head ached and already her arms and wrists felt cold and cramped. If they were driving all the way up to Cromer she couldn't envisage the condition she'd be in when they got there.

Gibbon helped Puxley lift her from the jeep, carrying her and getting her into the back of another vehicle, the Humber she presumed. A staff car, probably an RAF one filched from Brize Norton; it was too dark to make out any detail. She could feel though and knew they were binding her ankles with what felt like a harsh rope, tying them tightly. Oh, good, she thought, that'll work a treat on my circulation.

Finally they laid her on the floor in the back of the car, and Puxley said he would stay there with her. "The papers are in the map pocket at the front," he told Gibbon. "There's a torch in there as well. Only the date needs filling in on the papers. I've got corresponding ones. All I'll have to do is promote myself to full Colonel." He was fiddling with his greatcoat. Playing around with the gold-coloured metal badges of rank on the shoulders, she thought.

"Better leave off the red beret," he muttered. "And you, my lady, should keep quiet. We'll make you as comfortable as possible. I'll not gag you." He scrabbled around in the back and finally dropped an old blanket over her, and the Humber's engine sparked into life as they backed out into the road, Puxley talking quietly all the time, soothing and waiting for them to get clear and head up through Ludgate Circus, then on through Fleet Street.

Suzie tried to calculate how long it would take to drive to

Cromer. In the dark it would probably take around five or six hours. Not easy. Maybe longer.

Puxley, she thought. Of course. From the beginning it had to be Branwell Puxley. Even his Christian name, Branwell, was stacked against him. Branwell, named after the black sheep brother of the Brontës (even though some scholars seemed to have come to his defence). Branwell Brontë, wine-bibber and ne'rdowell. Branwell Puxley, traitor. She must have known from the beginning, as she suspected Tommy, and possibly Curry, had known as well.

Puxley was the obvious, the man asked to leave the RAF because of his admiration of the Nazi air force, the Luftwaffe. No, thrown out of the RAF. Nobody had really gone into the details of that, only listened to Puxley's version. He had even been to Germany and watched training: admitted to it. She wondered if that was when he signed up to serve the Führer. But he'd won the MC for gallantry in France during the Nazi invasion and the retreat through France. Well, that could be easily arranged. It simply bedded him down more perfectly, and he'd probably really be fêted in Germany now because he must have a large chunk of *Overlord* in his pocket.

What in heaven could she do? Trussed like a chicken, in fear for her life and likely to be taken with them to Belgium and France. Maybe even Germany. Nothing. She was helpless. So she did the only thing left to her, tried to wriggle into a comfortable position, closed her eyes under the unpleasant military blanket and tried to sleep as the car slowly moved through London then out into the countryside, heading north east towards the Norfolk coastline.

She woke twice on the journey: stiff, cramped, cold and in pain on both occasions. The second time she felt really unwell, unable to ease the cramps and sick with fear she now realised.

On the third occasion she awoke they were moving very slowly and Puxley was speaking again. "Over here, to your right," he said. "That's it. Switch off the engine and the lights. I'll go forward and make sure all's well."

"What d'you make the time?" Gibbon asked.

"About a quarter-past-six. Be getting near dawn soon, about seven."

She felt colder air on her, and smelled the sea, as one of the doors opened and the car moved: Puxley climbing out. She tried to move her head and shackled hands, shaking off the blanket, but it took time and Monkey Gibbon told her to stop moving about. "I got a pistol here, an' all." He snapped," An' I'm more likely to blow your head off than the Captain. I'd a' done it back in London, so think yourself lucky."

She could hear Puxley coming back, his boots hard on sand and gravel with the noise of the sea breaking not far away. She had started to shake with cold and the stiffness of her bound and manacled joints, felt as though she might pass out, was conscious of her head spinning. She heard the sea again and remembered how her father had this large seashell in his study: she used to hold it to her ear and listen to the sea which Daddy had told her was actually her heart pumping the blood around her body.

"Looks safe enough to me," Puxley said. "You'll have to help me drag the launch out. It's only a few feet down to the sea. We'll make it easy. Put the busy in first, eh?"

"As you like. I need a pee, and something to drink."

"I've taken care of myself, go and do the same. You'll get a drink when we're on board. I've some water bottles, and some hard tack biscuits stowed away. How is she?"

He heaved the blanket right off her and looked down, shining a torch at her face. "You're shivering," he felt her forehead. "No fever, but I've got a drop of brandy I'll give you when we get under way. Got to be quiet now. There's a Home Guard post about a mile up the coast and I wouldn't want to rouse them. They've no bloody idea. Shoot first, ask questions after.

Come on."

They crunched away leaving Suzie lying cold, in pain, stiff and aching on the hard gravel.

Slowly her eyes adjusted to the darkness. She lay by a low wooden shed-like hut, solid and long enough to hide the 40 foot launch they were now heaving down and over the stones, its sleek shape sliding through the two large doors that opened straight onto the beach. She was a rakish vessel, painted grey and without any distinguishing markings, no name or number as far as she could see.

Suzie cringed and whimpered as the wind bit up from the direction of the sea. The launch lay slightly on her port side, and the two men, hoisted her over the low hull and onto the gunwale planking just abaft the small cockpit with its wheel and engine controls.

She lay against a short metal safety rail, ill and terrified of what was to happen next. She could see for'ard that there were ropes running from each side of the prow and the two men heaved on them, pulling the craft down the short stretch of beach, to the sea. It took around ten minutes for them to get into the surf, Puxley yelling at Gibbon who seemed unable to hold on to his end of rope and manoeuvre the craft; he was constantly complaining and yelping like a child because he was forced to stand in water up to his knees, and stay upright against the waves which were considerable.

The launch was floating now and Suzie prayed to herself, completely at the mercy not just of the men but also of the sea. She had never been good on water and the craft banged around just over the surf line as Gibbon scrambled on board and Puxley ordered him to drag Suzie down into the cockpit so that she would at least get some protection from the weather.

Gibbon had pulled her down roughly, and she lay there, trembling and shaking with cold, soaking wet from the spray, sick, terrified and miserable with fear.

Puxley pressed the starter and after a couple of misfires the engine caught and he throttled back yelling at Gibbon to take the wheel, telling him to just keep the nose pointing out to sea. He then got down on his knees, turned Suzie over and pressed the neck of a hip flask to her lips. She swallowed, gasped, then swallowed again, felt sick, dry swallowed and felt the brandy spread fire down her throat into her stomach.

Branwell Puxley was still smiling, infuriatingly, as he staggered to his feet again, took over the wheel from Gibbon and gave the engine more power, leaning on the wheel to bring the bows on course, then opening the throttle so that the launch gave a roar, lifted her bows, the stern settling back into the water and the craft rattling across the waves, hitting the larger waves, raising to around fifteen feet in height, the vessel rolling and slapping against the seas.

An hour later they were keeping up the same fast rate as they swung across the sea, the bows still lifting, the hull rolling as the seas ran up to twenty feet high. Each time the bows came down the launch hit the water with a heavy crash and judder, then it would bounce back on the stern, and it rolled to and fro, banging and bumping as it went. Suzie was black and blue – "like riding in what my mum called a bone-shaker," she said out loud, wondering where the little whelpish cries were coming from, then realising they came from her.

She twisted her head, looking out through the windshield, from the cockpit, only the sea was visible, the sea and the hard grey cloud mingling with the horizon: nothing else. Suzie thought, *the lonely sea and the sky*. She didn't want a tall ship, nor a star to steer her by.

They slewed and leaped over the waves, steadily for another half-hour, then suddenly there was activity from the two men in the cockpit, a looking back and shouting, a sudden unexpected surge of power, a little extra bit of speed, an increased banging and rolling, and a look of fear in Gibbon's eyes, as he shouted at Puxley, who kept making quick excited glances behind him.

Out of the shriek of the winds, the roar of the engine and the clamour of the boat on the waves, came another noise, a great hooting, like a train signalling, a wild low and persistent whistle, calling for attention. Then a garbled voice shouting faintly in English, distorted across the water.

She couldn't understand what was being said but she thought she could distinguish the words "Make way," yet didn't know what it meant. Gibbon was pointing at her, shouting at Puxley who simply shook his head violently, again and again. Then Gibbon made a swooping dive towards her and Suzie, still unable to move, cringed away as he put his arms around her feet and began dragging her towards the upper decking.

Puxley continued to shout and Gibbon was yelling something about getting the weight off. Suzie, terrified, attempted to kick with her bound feet, and Monkey Gibbon spun around and began to drag her by the shoulders, pulling her towards the edge of the deck, attempting to manhandle her to the side of the launch, the business made more dangerous by the way the craft was tossing and bucking in the sea.

One minute Suzie found herself looking out to sea, the next she saw Puxley, screaming and shouting at the obviously frightened Gibbon, who hauled at her shoulders even harder bringing her almost to the edge of the deck.

She had a glimpse of another ship, some sixty or seventy feet astern – sleek with the figures 217 and RAF roundels on the bows and two things that looked like gun turrets from an aircraft on the superstructure. The guns appeared to be pointing towards Puxley's launch. The next thing she knew was Puxley, turning away from the wheel in the cockpit, bracing himself against one of the stanchions, his arm raised and his mouth moving as he levelled a pistol at Gibbon.

Suzie closed her eyes, terrified, feeling the spray soaking her as the launch bucked and rolled, almost carrying her over the side.

Far away she heard the shot, like hands clapping, whisked away by the wind, then another and above the other noises, the elements and the ship, Gibbon screaming. She saw him fall, felt him grab hold of her and knew she would be dragged overboard with him.

She had a fleeting glimpse of Puxley turning back to the wheel, and Gibbon's face pleading, his eyes wide with terror, his hand on her shoulder and the scream that was her as she was dragged over the side and into the pounding sea.

Chapter Twenty-One

SHE REMEMBERED SISTER Veronica Mary who taught them English literature at St Helen's quoting a poem in some long forgotten summer classroom. She could hear the nun's voice now: they used to call her voice "The Silver Bell" because Sister Veronica Mary obviously thought she had a voice that would rival the great voice of the trumpet as foretold in the Revelations of St John the Divine.

Sister Veronica Mary was quoting from some sixteenth century poet, saying:

> *The waters were his winding sheet, the sea was made his tomb,*
> *Yet for his fame the ocean sea was not sufficient room.*

Suzie knew the waters were fast becoming *her* winding sheet, bound as she was hand and foot, swallowing water, choking, rolling, unable to stay on the surface in the strong, roiling filthy sea. Until, miraculously that same sea spat her out. On the sharp incline of a building wave, there she was lying on her back, stable as a woman in a swimming pool. And it was then that the Royal Air Force air-sea rescue launch, all 63 feet of her with the two turrets and the Vickers K machine guns, bubbled alongside and Leading Airman J Hawkins leaped into the sea to save her.

"It's a wonder she's not dead with cold, 'cos it's bloody freezing in here," he reported to his captain, who was a Flying Officer with a lot of experience in the Pagham Yacht Club.

Suzie remembered very little of this. She in fact recalled only four things clearly: first, being turned over on the deck to have water pumped out of her and seeing for a moment, moving towards the horizon, Branwell Puxley's launch. "We'll never catch the bugger now," somebody said.

"Wonder what he was playing at?" said another.

Secondly, she had a clear memory of complaining bitterly

as one of the lads fished inside her blouse for the dog tags, finding the solid little brick-red labels and shouting, "She's with the bloody Met, Skipper. WDS Susannah Mountford. Met Police." And she responded by saying, "That should read DI. I got promoted. DI Mountford attached to War Office Intelligence Liaison."

Thirdly, before they took her down to the cabin, stripped her and somehow got the handcuffs off – they had untied the rope on the deck – rubbed her down with thick towels and poured brandy into her, she saw the sun come out and illuminate a rainbow in a patch of oily sea.

Fourth, one of the crew said, "That's a lovely coat, she was wearing," and the Flying Officer replied, "Yes, my mum's got one just like it. Bought it before clothes rationing at Fenwicks." And she felt bloody old.

As they were undressing her, she was later told that she muttered, "Red hat, no knickers," and the sergeant had replied, "So they say, Ma'am, but in my experience that just isn't true."

They poured coffee into her as well as the brandy while they made all speed to Folkstone where she went into a deep coma for five days. When she came round a sexy-looking nursing sister told her they'd all been very worried about her. She said there was no need and promptly lapsed back into the coma for a further two days.

This time when she came to she stayed awake, couldn't sleep for three nights, but there was an intriguing vase of flowers on her locker. "Very posh bloke brought them," the sexy sister told her. "Drove down with a big bloke. Big bloke with a little black tash. Wouldn't leave any messages."

"Didn't call you 'heart' by any chance?"

"No, but the big bloke with the tash called him Chief."

Big bloke with a little black tash fitted Brian to a tee.

After two weeks they moved her to a hospital nearer London, where Elsie Partridge came to see her and stayed a while. She had started to sleep a little by then, but was troubled by vivid and horrible dreams.

She kept seeing Branwell Bomber Puxley, drowning under a green-grey sea. He would turn towards her with a pleading look, still alive, then he returned and this time his face was dead, nibbled at by sea creatures, pieces of flesh flapping free: his cheeks like wings.

TWO GERMAN E-BOATS picked up Puxley's launch about two miles off Ostend and they escorted him into the harbour, thinking themselves no end of a pair of dogs for capturing a British spy. But Bomber argued and told them to get hold of Nicholaus Ritter in Hamburg. He arrived in Ostend two days later, and immediately played merry hell with the people there who'd been keeping him in their local jail under a close armed guard.

Now Puxley began to live high on the hog, in a suite of rooms in a local hotel that was being used for senior officers. Ritter talked to him for a long time and he answered the questions effusively, handing over his report which he turned into a detailed *en clair* statement which Ritter took away by hand and had typed by three different high security typists and ready to be sent on to the most important intelligence analysts in the western region.

"You'll be the most highly thought of agent of the Third Reich," he told Puxley. "They will write of you in military history books as an agent *nonpararreil*. This is the key to the invasion plans."

"I know it," Puxley said sipping his champagne and knowing that his success would embrace Ritter as well.

SUZIE'S MOTHER, HELEN, had one vulgar expression which she still used quite often, and which, to be honest, rather shocked her second husband, Major Ross Gordon

Lowe (or Gordon-Lowe as he preferred it). When examining government forms she would express herself graphically by saying that these people wanted to know the far end of a fart.

Now, after Elsie Partridge first visited her Suzie said, loudly, "Bloody hell, Elsie wants to know the far end of a fart." Shocking the sexy nursing sister who wasn't over fond of ladies speaking plainly.

This was true. Elsie asked about every detail of the journey with Puxley and Gibbon, plus a large number of things Suzie really couldn't tell him: technical things about Puxley's launch, the car, and exactly what Monkey Gibbon was wearing. Regarding this latter Elsie told her, "A body's been washed up, d'you see? Not much of it left, but oddly some of the clothing is intact."

Naturally, Suzie didn't want to think about it. She told him all she could, said she really wanted to get her special thanks to the commander and crew of air-sea rescue launch 217 and Elsie said he'd do that for her. He also told her Curry Shepherd sent his best wishes. "Bit busy at the moment," Elsie said. "They're talking about wedding bells."

"Who're talking about wedding bells?"

"Curry and that popsie Ruth who mans the phones, does the typing and all that in the Ivor Place office."

"Ah," said Suzie.

"Personally I don't think it's going to happen, but I think they've been having a bit of the old romantic entanglement for some time. I rather feel she's pushing but Curry's not all that keen. Personal observation of course."

"I don't think Curry'll ever be tied down by one woman," Suzie observed. "Personal observation, of course."

Elsie said they had people assessing how far *Overlord* had been compromised. He told her that in due course she would have to appear in front of a tribunal looking into the whole business of Puxley and the *Overlord* plans.

"Of course. Be glad to," Suzie told him.

"Oh no you won't," Elsie grinned. "You'll only tell 'em what I say you can tell 'em," and he laid his right forefinger along the side of his nose conspiratorially.

"Anything come about that flaxen-haired Squadron Leader?" she asked. "One with a flourish of a moustache?"

"Couldn't prove a thing. He was one of our Whitley pilots, towing the gliders. Been put where he can't hurt anyone."

"And that woman?"

Elsie gave her his inscrutable look. "Got her salted away," he grinned smoothing his bald pate with the flat of his right hand. "She's being put to the question."

For some unaccountable reason this made Suzie shudder.

WHEN COLONEL BARON Alexis von Roenne arrived at Field Marshal Erwin Rommel's headquarters in the chateau at La Roche Guyon, he came heralded by many warnings, for the Colonel Baron was head of the FHW the western Intelligence arm of the Supreme Command, OKW.

Rommel greeted von Roenne and took him into his private quarters for lunch which was a pleasant meal – a brace of pheasants and a chestnut soufflé during which they spoke of Rommel's many plans and changes for the reinforcing of Fortress Europe, in particular the Channel coast.

When the two men were finally left alone, von Roenne asked if Rommel had read the latest intelligence reports. "I mean this stuff that's come from our source Sattler?"

"Of course. I've been wanting to talk to you about it."

Roenne laughed, "Does it deserve any detailed discussion?"

"Why don't you tell me? After all, you're the expert."

The Colonel shook his head. "I've been looking at this Sattler's *bona fides*." He paused. "And also the *bona fides* of the man who recruited him, and the others who appear to have so much faith in him."

"And?"

"Field-Marshal, I'm not going to insult your intelligence. We already know that the Allies will make their assault in the Pas de Calais. To do otherwise would be folly. Madness. This is obviously an attempt to make us look in another direction."

"You mean it is a deception plan?"

"Of course. There is one already – a fake army up in Scotland trying to make us believe that they are coming in via Norway." Another laugh and a dismissive gesture of his right hand.

"And they want us to believe they'll also come in through Normandy and Brittany?"

"Of course. You've seen the traffic signals we've been receiving from their huge First US Army Group, Patton's army. You've seen the reports from our agents in England. Could you doubt their strength?"

"No. I'm inclined to believe they'll come through the Pas de Calais. If I were in Eisenhower's place that's what I'd do, and I'd be at the Rhine within weeks. The country inland in Normandy and Brittany is just not suitable for tank warfare."

"Then the only thing left for us to discover is who this Sattler thinks he is? Is he a dupe, a man who has swallowed the story whole, deception and all? Or is he something more sinister? A double perhaps?"

"That's for you to discover, my dear Baron."

The Colonel shook his head, "No, Field-Marshal, I think our friends in the RSHA should have a little talk with him." The RSHA was the Reich Security Administration. The Party Intelligence Service. Basically the Gestapo. Twenty-four hours later two officers called upon Puxley and asked him to come with them to Berlin to clear up one or two points. "Nothing serious," they said. "Just a few technical points."

He was never heard of again.

* * *

SUZIE MOUNTFORD WAS discharged from hospital on the first Wednesday in February, 1944, on the understanding that she would go on leave for a month.

She was given a jeep and driver to take her back to Upper St Martin's Lane where she arrived at a little after two in the afternoon. She had been given her lunch in the hospital but was undoubtedly feeling a little weak and oddly, she thought, unhappy.

There was a pile of mail inside the door. So much that it almost jammed the door and she was forced to push it open with her shoulder. She gathered up the mail and plonked it on the little hall table, piles of it, all her Christmas cards and bills, and lord knew what else.

She went straight into the kitchen, put the kettle on then walked around, peeping into every room, something she did automatically when the flat had been empty for a while, coming back into the kitchen. Making tea, realising she had no milk and deciding to drink it without.

She planned to ring her mother and go down to Newbury, to Larksbrook, the family home, later. Perhaps the 'Galloping Major' could drive up and take her down, if he had the petrol. She poured her tea then went into the hall again to fetch the mail.

She began to sort it on the kitchen table, separate piles, cards, bills, letters...

She stopped, recognising the handwriting, ripping it open and looking at the sheet of heavy crested notepaper. Tommy had written to her from the estate, from his father's, the Earl of Kingscote's estate. He had written over Christmas. They used to have a joke about it, she always talked about him going down to flog the peasants at Christmas. Last year she had gone with him, the Honourable Tommy Livermore.

She began to read –

Suzie, My Darling Heart,

    This is to apologise, though I know that a mere apology is not enough. What I did to you about the possible GM, and all the other ways I treated you – all of them – are unforgivable so I have no right to ask for your forgiveness. But my dear heart, I love you more than I can ever express, and miss you with all my heart and mind. I miss you with such pain, a pain that causes me anguish with each breath I take.

    I miss you and long for you. I see you and hear you everywhere. O God I miss you so much and in every way. I miss you now. I miss your touch and the feel of you. I miss seeing and hearing you. In the night, I miss your dark triangle and the Elysian Fields that lie beyond.

    Please. Please. My love ever,

    Tommy

Dandy Tom, she thought reaching for the telephone.

There is absolutely no evidence to suggest there was a particular spy sent to search out the plans for *Overlord*. However, all the agents sent into Britain by the German Intelligence services were put in the bag, and all but two of them were turned, sending back a large amount of intelligence to back up Operation *Fortitude*.

Also, Colonel Baron Alexis von Roenne was the head of German Intelligence in the West – as opposed to the brilliant Reinhard Gehlen in the East. At the end of World War II, Gehlen set up his own Intelligence Service on behalf of the Allies.

Alexis von Roenne took the bait of *Fortitude* and, while he rejected the possibility of an invasion through Norway, was completely hooked on the Pas de Calais deception and was one of the many reasons for the German indecision in the first week of the Normandy landings.

[1] American senior officers had little faith in Fortitude, mainly because they remained ignorant of the amount of disinformation being played back by the XX Committee from captured German secret agents.

[2] In present day money this translates into just under £95.

[3] The Chief of the Imperial General Staff, Sir Alan Brooke wrote, as late as June 1944, 'It may well be the most ghastly disaster of the whole war.'

[4] L C Partridge should have known better: Anthony Eden, the Foreign Secretary, was in Cairo with the Prime Minister.